TALES FROM THE
ZOMBIE ROAD

THE LONG HAUL ANTHOLOGY

DAVID A SIMPSON   PHEOBE JACKSON
RICH RESTUCCI   TONY URBAN   RICKY FLEET
ROMA GRAY   CHRISTOPHER ARTINIAN
ANN RILEY   DAVINA PURNELL
LORI SAFRANEK   T.D. RICKETTS
VALERIE LIOUDRIS   GREG BENNETT
GRIVANTE   W.J. WATT   EMILY STIVER
R.L. CHAMBERS   CODY MANN
MICHAEL PIERCE   ALINA IONESCU
WESLEY R. NORRIS

CONTENTS

Tales from the Zombie Road   v
Introduction   vii

1. Alone Together   1
2. A Family Matter   6
3. All in a Day's Work   16
4. Brokedown   29
5. Carnival of Carnage   42
6. Catch-A-Zombie   80
7. Condemned   83
8. Dead Land   98
9. Deadly Silence   108
10. Freaked Out Zombies   110
11. Hunted in the Hills   127
12. John the Bastard   141
13. Mother's Day Behind the Quarantine Fence   143
14. My Cup of Tea   161
15. Sgt Joan   167
16. "Sparky"   176
17. The Glass City Escape   189
18. The Highlander   199
19. The Midland Crew   228
20. The Prison   238
21. The Vegan   251
22. Truckers Dilemma   261
23. Battle for Warehouse 3   264
24. Trucking in Pink   276
25. Scarecrows   287
26. Flash Fiction   305
27. More Flash Fiction   313

Afterword   317

TALES FROM THE ZOMBIE ROAD

THE LONG HAUL ANTHOLOGY

Two-Fisted Tales
from the
Zombie Road World

Tales from the Zombie Road
The Long Haul Anthology

Copyright 2017 Wise Pug Publications
Individual stories copyright of their respective authors.
ISBN-13:978-1979713764
ISBN-10:1979713766

All rights reserved. No part of this book may be reproduced or transmitted in any form or by any means without written permission of the authors (this means you, torrent pirates) except for review purposes.
All characters contained herein are fictional and all similarities to actual persons, living or dead, are purely coincidental.
Cover Art by Dean Samed
Editing by Tamra Crow
Book Design by David A. Simpson

INTRODUCTION

Hey y'all. Simpson here. What you are about to dive into is a fine collection of short stories, poetry and art that was inspired by the world created in the Zombie Road series of books. The books have a dedicated fan base who are active in the David Simpson Fan Club on Facebook and some of the best contests held there are flash fiction stories. Many of them were very good, all of them entertaining. Some were expanded into real stories and are included in this book.

It was suggested we slap together a fan fiction collection. A kind of "Thank You" to all the people who helped the Zombie Road books become a success. Unpublished people with flair and skill could join us other indie authors and get published, hold a book in their hands with their work in print. What started out as a fun little project soon ballooned nearly out of control when it was announced that ALL proceeds, not just the *profit* after publishing expenses, would go to the Wounded Warriors Project.

Why them?

Because I'm a vet, my books are filled with vets, most of my family have served and most of my friends have proudly and selflessly wrote a blank check, payable to the American People, for an amount of "up to, and including my life."

Because the Wounded Warriors Project gave 213 million dollars to our vets last year (2016), their admin costs are less than 7% of what they raise and they don't take any government funding. It all comes from people like us. Like the people who donated their stories which they could have sold and people like you who forked over your hard-earned cash to buy this book.

Which brings me to the stories included. There are a few first-timers in here but if you don't read the bios on them, I'd bet you would have a hard time picking them out from some of the #1 best-selling authors who have donated their tales. There are some heavy hitters awaiting you, some well-established indie writers with their own massive followings. People from all over the world have submitted their visions of the zombie uprising so keep that in mind when you see certain words spelled in the old English (or Scottish) way.

Some of the fan art sent in is an added bonus although sadly a lot of it couldn't be included because of limitations of uploading pictures and the quality of images in 'pulp' paperback books. We've included a sprinkling throughout, though.

It's been a hoot working with so many different people and I want to thank them again for donating their time, their stories, their art and their patience with me as I stumbled through the whole process of trying to take an idea and turn it into a quality product.

I hope you find them entertaining, leave us a review and remember, 100% of everything this book earns goes to our damaged boys and girls who wrote that check and paid that bill.

Introduction | ix

x | *Introduction*

Gunny

Trapped in a Truck Stop outside of Reno thousands of miles from home, Gunny just wants to armor his truck and get started back across the Country to his family.

1

ALONE TOGETHER

DAVID A. SIMPSON

Her breathing was ragged as she sat down beside me on the steps outside the back door of the makeshift club in the warehouse. I could smell her sweat, she was fresh from the mosh pit.

I didn't look over, I wasn't interested, I had problems of my own.

I'd been outside the barricades, I'd seen my whole unit wiped out, my friends torn to shreds. I'd seen the innumerable hordes of the undead screaming after us as we fled to the end of the island. They were unstoppable, unrelenting, uncountable. They flowed like a river over every obstacle they came across, leaving everyone and everything dead in their wake.

I stared into my mug of beer.

I don't know how long we sat apart, yet together. It was late September on Long Island and the night air was chilly.

Time passed.

Her sweat cooled and a hazy steam rose off of her. She said nothing and slowly her panting breaths returned to normal, winding down from the violent thrash dancing she had been doing. Trying to not remember, pretending to not know, dancing in violence and anger and rage and pain.

Even out here the band drowned out the sound of the generators and they were so loud that normal conversation was impossible. They played hard and raw. Angry and desperate.

A half mile away at Saint Mary's, the orchestra played sad and slow and older couples waltzed with their finest clothes and jewelry.

I had hoped coming here would pull me up out of my despair for a few hours but it hadn't worked. I couldn't forget and I couldn't get drunk enough to not remember, it wasn't possible. I had been with my National Guard unit on our weekend of live fire training, living off of MRE's, beef jerky and candy bars. We got to pretend we were real soldiers every fall, when we would camp out at the local gun range and do our annual weapons qualifications.

The silence between us was nice. It wasn't strained or uncomfortable like some silences are. She knew the truth. I knew the truth. Hell, the whole town knew the truth. There was no place left to go. We were on the edge of the ocean and the last of the boats, overloaded and sitting low in the water, were gone. The walls we threw up with semi-trucks and sandbags were fourteen feet tall. The horde stumbling towards us was a million strong, drawn East like lemmings marching towards the sea, always searching for fresh meat. The barricade was strong, it would hold but the horde would simply swarm over the top. There were too many coming out of New York.

The beer cupped in my hands was warming, the bubbles I had been watching rise to the top were slowing, now only coming up occasionally.

I pulled out a cigarette.

She pulled out a straight razor.

I still hadn't looked over at her and I had a feeling she hadn't looked at me since she'd sat down. She saw from my haircut and dirty uniform as she came out that I was a soldier. One of the very few that were left. One of the very few who had retreated back to this quiet little town at the very tip of Long Island, surrounded by the ocean. I was one of the very few that managed to out-run the horde as they lost interest in the Hum-V. They would rather chase a person fleeing on foot than the metal box.

When I arrived, I had no more ammo and no extra guns. I only had tales of an incalculable number of the undead slowly making their way East. They would be here by morning. Once the first wandering zombie found its way to the barricade and sensed we were here, it would start up with that ungodly keening scream they do. It would call the others and they would come on the run.

Earlier that evening, the whole town had sat around and listened to the radio as an Army Sergeant told them the new government was rebuilding in Oklahoma. He asked everyone to get there if they could. It was too late for the people at the very tip of the island. The only road out was impassable, clogged by hundreds of thousands of the undead and anything that would float had long since been put to sea.

Her tangled mass of black hair obscured her face completely as she mimicked my casual slope-shouldered stoop, elbows on knees, hands forward.

Only mine held a beer.

Hers held a razor.

I put the lighter to my cigarette and she still didn't move, just stared at the surgical steel in her hands. She turned her wrist towards me and I saw the scars of prior attempts. Horizontal and vertical, but not deep enough. Scars of one who had lost her nerve. Scars of one not quite fully committed.

The blade glinted in the harsh sodium lights and the pounding bass was relentless as the band played like it was the last time they ever would. The people in this nothing club, in this nowhere town, were counting down the minutes and living each one to its fullest.

She moved the blade slightly towards me, holding it in her open palm, her head still hung.

An offering.

I took a drag off of my cigarette, the surreal orange glow brightening the scene that burned itself into my mind. This last concert, in this last town. Dancing while the Titanic sank. I sat down my beer and reached for the razor, staring deep into her eyes as she finally faced me. I saw a bleakness, an understanding and a raw terror barely held in check.

I saw my own eyes mirrored.

I took the blade and before I could lose my nerve, I slashed deep and long into my own wrist, all the way to my elbow. It stung, but not much.

My eyes never left hers.

I smiled, silently thanked her for showing me a way.

Her dark eyes were begging me to take her, too.

The blade flashed again under the lights and we sat side by side, leaning into each other, fingers intertwined, our lives flowing warm down the stairs.

Alone.

Together.

David A. Simpson

Simpson has been a burger flipper, a log cabin builder, a soldier, a repo man, a rancher, did a short stint as a bounty hunter and was a starving artist. He got tired of being hungry so started driving a truck. It suits his wanderlust and he's pretty good at it. He hasn't actually encountered any real zombies but he thinks he'd be pretty good at killing them, too.

His books are available at Amazon.

Find him on Facebook in the David Simpson Fan club.

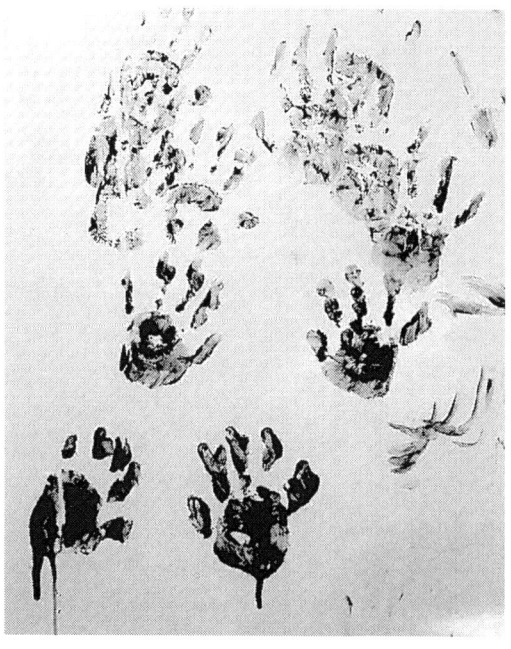

Dirty Windows
By Evelyn (age 3)

2

A FAMILY MATTER

PHOEBE JACKSON

"Mom...Mom! Will you please go see why Liz is crying before she brings the horde down on us? I am up to my elbows in soapy water," Jewels says.

Shaking off the dark disturbing thoughts I am wallowing in, I push my chair back from the table to go check on Liz. A few minutes later I return to the lukewarm coffee I had been nursing since lunch. I tell Jewels, "She just needed a clean butt and her pacifier."

Looking around the dim room, I wonder how much more time we have left together and if it wouldn't be better to end it all than to keep living every day feeling as though we are playing Russian Roulette.

It's not that I don't love my family, it is that I love Jewels and the kids so very much. I have watched Jewels get more haggard looking by the day. I see how she struggles and worries about the little ones. We both know with the undead increasing in numbers in our area more every day, it is just a matter of time before they find out that we are here in this little clapboard farm house. It is not an easy task keeping babies and small children quiet when their very lives depend on it. This new and dangerous world is not meant for children. Ben, at age 4, can't understand why he can't go out and play on the swing set or in the sandbox like he used to.

It is summer time in the Midwest and we have the windows boarded up, with strategically placed peep holes so we can see out. With just a few fans to move around the hot stale air, it is downright miserable inside and hot children are cranky, whiny children. Sure, we try to keep them happy, cool and entertained but you can't impress upon such small children just how dangerous this world has become. How laughing just a little too loud or making car noises while playing is putting us all in peril.

"Mom, what is on your mind? You look like you are miles away from this place. I was thinking if you are up to it, once the kids are down for their nap we could go out to the garden and bring in what is ready to be picked. I know the green beans should be just about ready for canning, as well as the tomatoes, plus the strawberries for jam. That is, if there are only a few of those undead things out there. In the early afternoon they don't seem to be that agitated. What do you think?" Jewels asks..

"Jewels, I think you need to stay in the house with the little ones. I will go out and get the veggies. You can watch from the balcony off the master bedroom and give a bird call if danger is approaching. Are you still a pretty good shot with a bow and arrow? Have you been able to raise that husband of yours on the CB lately? When was the last time you talked to him and where was he? Did he say when he thought him and the boys would be here?" I ask.

"Mom, that is too much work for one person and we can

get more in less time if we both go out there to harvest the crops. I heard from Dale three days ago, he thought he would be here by now. Last I heard he was coming from the east and the roads were rough. Abandoned cars are blocking the road and in some of the small towns they have set up heavily armed road blocks and are not letting anyone in or out. I have faith he will find a way to get home to us," Jewels tells me.

"Listen girly, you will stay in with the kids! They need their mom and if something happens out there, I will feel better knowing you are in here with them. I will pick what I can and if I need to make a few trips, so be it. I won't hear another word on the subject," I tell my daughter.

Armed with my hatchet, a few bottles of water, a big floppy hat, the baskets and what I will need to collect the crops, I head out to the garden that is the farthest from the house first. I'm thinking it will make it easier to get fresh food as things get hairier in the days to come. I look over my shoulder and see Jewels on the balcony with her bow and binoculars. I get to work, thinking I will leave the baskets at the ends of the rows and pick them up with the golf cart when I am finished. It is quieter than the tractor and wagon. It isn't long before I start getting overheated, wearing jeans and a long-sleeved shirt in summer is not ideal for picking. But I wanted as much protection as I could get should I encounter the dead. There is, of course, the stray lone shuffling dead I have to dispatch to the great beyond while I work but nothing I can't handle.

After about two hours of harvesting, I hear Jewels' Cardinal call, I look up to where she is keeping watch to find out from which direction the larger group is coming from. She flashed her open hands three times indicating there are about 30 coming up on my right. I would be lying if I said panic wasn't creeping in, threatening to take over. As I look around, trying to come up with a plan on the fly, I glance back at Jewels, who then flashes her open hands once indicating there is a second herd coming in from directly in front of me. She then put her open hands out to the sides and brought them together and laced her fingers together, indicating it looks like the two groups are going to merge. My thought is to run to the left where there is a stand of trees and try to climb up as far as I can and make myself small. No one knows much about these creatures except that they are cannibals and that even a scratch from one of them is a death sentence. I don't think they will look up should they pass my way, but who can say for sure?

My hands are wet from sweating and nerves, I try to control my breathing so as not to give my hiding spot away, hoping they won't catch my scent on the breeze and turn around and head in my direction. Most of them have passed but I can see from my vantage point a few stragglers from both groups of the dead slowly making their way to the now larger group. I had planned to stay put for a little longer, then I saw Ben come running out of the house and head right for the swing set. My heart stopped, I find myself saying, "No, no, no!" breathlessly, just barely audible to myself. The swing set is old and the chains clank and squeak when in use, not to mention Ben likes to add sound effects when playing, either air plane noises or fighter pilot sounds. Oh Lord please, please DO NOT LET the grisly horde turn around! I look up to where Jewels is watching the dead move along and start gesturing wildly toward the swing set. Jewels has not seen the small boy make his way out of the house and toward the swing set. Her jaw drops and she goes, running fast. By now I have jumped out of the tree and I'm running toward the house.

As I run as fast as my legs will carry me, I know Jewels will get to Ben first but I need to kill the stragglers that have heard the child playing and are now headed toward the house, before they can alert the others they've found food. The first straggler I encounter is a male, probably in his mid-twenties when he died, wearing long shorts and a torn shirt that proclaimed "Where's the beef?" He must have taken the shirt from his dad's or older sibling's closet is my first thought, then I shake my head at myself to get my head back in the game. He has several chunks missing out of the right side of his face and neck. I feel my meager lunch rise up from my stomach as I jump and bring the hatchet down on top of his head with all my might. His body slumped into a pile of putrefied black and green goo. Just then I lose the battle of trying to keep my lunch where it is. Running up to the next one I approach it from behind and deliver the death blow, this time the body does not slide away from my hatchet, it is stuck in the skull. As the body of the old woman falls I step on her back and pull the hatchet out. I do not see the third one as it is coming from my right until it has lunged toward me out of the rows of tall corn. It is a hefty man who was about 50 years old when he died. He has a death grip on my shoulder, clawing at me with his other hand, all the while trying to pull me in so he can take a bite out of my face.

I am afraid our struggle will bring more in, I hear Jewels yelling for me to duck so I do, THWAT, (the sound of an arrow leaving the bow and hitting it's mark.) the big man sways on his feet for what feels like forever before dragging me down with him as he falls face first, still clutching my shoulder. Thank goodness, he fell to the left of me and not on top of me. I pry his fingers loose and run to the house, shutting and locking the kitchen door behind me. Bounding up the steps two at a time I have to see with my own eyes if the undead group has changed direction. I only see two of the remaining stragglers heading toward the larger group of dead. I sink to the floor of the balcony trying to catch my breath and calm my nerves.

I stop by my room and the bathroom to get cleaned up before I return to the living room, where Jewels is giving Ben a stern talking to. Before I reach the living room I hear Liz crying so I go get her out of her crib. I sit in the old broken-down rocker and rock Liz while patting her back gently. As I survey the room, both Jewels and Ben are crying. Jewels looks up and asks if the dead are heading our way. I tell her no, that we have gotten lucky this time. She starts to apologize and I hold up my hand to stop the flow of emotions and words as I shake my head.

Months have passed and there hasn't been word one from Jewels' husband Dale. We fear the worst. Things have gotten worse around the farm and we are beginning to get weary of what the future will hold. I have scavenged the last of the diapers and formula I can find in the neighboring townships. Ben has gotten increasingly unruly as he can no longer play on the main floor due to the dead hanging around outside, he has to play in the cellar and he is not happy about it. Jewels has aged at least 20 years in appearance in the last few months, due to worry alone. I know what I have to do, yet I am struggling with the moral dilemma of the old world. Jewels has mentioned more and more her thoughts on whether the kids would be better off at peace than remaining in this inhospitable world. They are so unhappy and they cry for their daddy all the time now. She cannot bear the thought of them starving, being torn apart by those things outside or becoming one of them... will she be able to give them peace then when the need arises? No...It has to be me.

I have made up my mind and I know how I am going to do it. I can no longer stand to watch my loved ones die a little at a time from uncertainty, sadness and worry.

I inform Jewels I am going to go salvage this morning, after I help her with the kids for breakfast. I go into the basement and grab one of the backpacks and check my handy work on the furnace. When I return to the kitchen Jewels comments that she has a headache again today and is feeling a little sick to her stomach, and that she is feeling so tired. I tell her it is probably from worry and that she hasn't eaten much the past few days. I tell her to lay down and take a nap when she gets the kids down for their nap. I kiss her on the forehead and tell her how proud I am of her and give the kids some extra loving, too, before I leave.

I am halfway down the block when I start openly grieving for the ones I love, I am shaking so bad, knowing what is still left to be done upon my return to our lovely farm house. It holds so many wonderful memories and a few sad ones. The good outweigh the bad, we have truly been blessed.

I am remembering how tough we all use to talk in the Facebook zombie groups, how we were going to be real hard cases if the Z-poc ever happened, how we planned on doing anything for our family's survival. I wonder now how many would have been able to do this? My guess is... not very many of them. When I said I would do anything for my loved ones, Not once, did I entertain the thought that I would have to kill my loved ones before they turned into one of the undead. It never even made a blip on my radar. This is not easy by any stretch of the imagination, but it is better to know they will all be at peace soon. No more suffering or grieving for what has been lost.

I find what I expected upon my return, everyone is in a deep sleep. I go down to the basement and remove all traces of foul play. I return to the upstairs bedrooms, first Liz, then Ben and last my beautiful baby girl's room. I whisper in Jewels' ear, "Darling, no more worry, sadness or dread, the kids are at peace. I love you more than words can convey, you have been the source of so much joy, go be at peace." I plunge the ice pick into her ear, as well, as I bend over to kiss her forehead. I do not want them coming back as one of the monstrosities that are outside. I then go to my room and sit in the rocking chair by the window and pull the trigger of my Berretta that was a gift from my husband on our wedding day.

Dale felt deep in his bones something was really wrong. He was only a mile from home and he couldn't wait to see Jewels and the kids again. This trip over the road had been his last. Somewhere in Kentucky he had damaged the CB antenna, he missed hearing his wife's voice. She must be worried sick by now, fearing the worst. He knew she was strong and would carry on in his absence. Wouldn't her and the kids be so glad to see him, almost as glad as he would be to finally be home. Oh, how he had missed them all.

From the moment he pulled up in his Peterbilt, the house just seemed wrong somehow. His excitement and relief at being home started to turn to dread. As he walked up to the back door he could see it was alive with blowflies, his heart sank but still, he wouldn't let his deepest fear surface. He unlocked the door as fast as he could. Once the door opened he could smell the vile smell of death and decay. He ran through the house yelling Jewels' name, not waiting for an answer, he bounded up the stairs three at a time. Reaching the room he shared with his wife of fifteen years he opened the door, had it not been for the smell, the flies buzzing around and the sickly color of Jewels' arm that was above the covers, he could have made himself believe his wife was sleeping. He didn't want to go any closer but he had to, he had to try and make sense of what he was looking at. As he rounded the bed, this giant of a man crumbled to his knees and wept. The peaceful look on Jewels' face did little to ease the pain he was feeling. He found himself repeating over and over, "No, Baby, what happened here?" He was so consumed with grief, he was moving onward down the hall as if he were a sleep walker. He didn't want to see any more but he know somewhere deep in his mind he would never be able to go on without knowing what happened to his children. His mind was no longer able to process what his eyes were seeing.

Phoebe Mary Ann Petenstine Jackson

A retired Nurse, has been writing since she was in elementary school. She has penned short stories and articles for P.E.T.S. Magazine, Her Stories have appeared in various anthologies over the years. entered writing competitions, has written a book of family history, a book filled with funny family stories for family. She considers herself "a jack of all trades, but the master of none." When she is not writing she enjoys: repurposing old items into something new, crafting, deep woods camping & hiking, swimming, reading, gardening, music, playing with her five grandkids and spending time with family. She has a wicked sense of humor and loves all things darker or horror related. A Proud Supporter and advocate of Indie Authors.

∽

Most recent published short story "Skinned" under the pen name of Mary Petenstine Jackson May 4th 2015, in the book "Give: An Anthology of Anatomical Entries."

3

ALL IN A DAY'S WORK

RICH RESTUCCI

"How many of them are out there?"

"I don't know."

"Is it more than one?"

"No idea, but they're right outside the door."

"But, you don't know how many?"

"For fuck's sake, Chuckie, I don't know. Keep your voice down or you'll let them know what we're up to."

"Sorry, Tom," Chuckie whispered. They both stared at the office door, knowing what would happen if they burst out too soon or too late. Timing was crucial. There would be no taking it back if they screwed it up. Today of all days was not a day to make a mistake. Tom looked at the old-school clock on the wall: 8:49 AM. The day had just started and he was already anxious.

Chuckie looked down at the crude, hastily constructed implement he held with both hands. It would have to do. He was nervous as well.

Tom, his hand on the door handle, looked back over his shoulder, "Ready?"

Chuckie nodded, swallowing hard. Tom pushed the

All in a Day's Work | 17

door open and stared briefly at the backs of his coworkers. They were leaning over something, reaching down and touching it.

"Surprise!" Tom yelled and strode forward. Chuckie followed him out quickly. Their coworkers turned away from the client presentation on the table, indeed surprised.

"Happy birthday, Angelica," both Tom and Chuckie announced.

Smiles from the folks in front of them indicated their success had been achieved. Tom approached the Birthday girl with a card he and Chuckie had designed using the company software. Chuckie held a platter of breakfast food for everyone. His "platter" was a banker's box he had put the food in.

Chuckie doled out to his friends eight individually wrapped bacon, egg, and cheese sandwiches he had purchased from the coffee shop in the building lobby. He had miscounted, somehow, as there were nine people. Nobody noticed that the guy who had procured the snacks was the only one not to get one. Chuckie didn't mind. He had gotten the food for his friends, and after all, today was Angelica's birthday.

Nine office mates discussed the pros and cons of the new marketing software around a beautiful mahogany table in Meeting Room A. Chuckie, the newest hire at Simpson Marketing, regarded his crew: Four women and five men sat behind steaming cups of fresh coffee. The paper wrappings of the sandwiches Chuckie had brought littered the table next to coffee mugs and three ring binders. Sara, the intern, had left her sandwich at her desk, intending to enjoy it later. Chuckie looked around the room at all the vacant chairs, then through the glass wall toward the empty cubicles. Almost two dozen people had called in sick today, six of whom should have been in this meeting.

A red dot flickered across the large green portion of a pie graph on an easel. Chuckie smiled. Angelica never went anywhere without that laser pointer. She was indicating that sales were up with a particular client. She put the back of her hand to her forehead briefly, but pulled it back just as quickly. Phillip, one of the marketing guys, and a bit of a showoff, crumpled the paper from his breakfast sandwich and made an overhanded basketball shot into the wastebasket. He winked at Chuckie as he finished chewing, and wiped his mouth with a napkin.

"You ok, Angelica?" Phillip asked.

"Yes, thank you. Just a bit warm." She raised her eyebrows and asked the group, "Anybody else think it's hot in here?"

Affirmative nods went around the room. Chuckie felt great, and thought that the temperature was comfortable, but Angelica was standing and he was sitting, so maybe that was it. He furrowed his brow in thought. Maybe she was coming down with whatever had stricken his coworkers. Some of those out sick hadn't even called in.

Angelica sat down when she finished her portion of the presentation, pulling on her collar a bit. Her color was just a tad off as she put her face in her hands, rubbing. Tom and Lillian stood when it was their turn to present, but Lillian sat back down immediately.

Lillian took a deep breath, "Ooooh. I feel a bit woozy."

"Actually, I'm not feeling great either," Tom added. "I'm wondering if a few of us aren't coming down with whatever everybody called in with."

Carlton, one of the junior executives, suddenly stood,

retched a bit, and ran for the glass door. He was out and running for the restroom in short order. The rest of the group stared after him for a moment until both Tammy and Steve began to cough. Tammy held her stomach as she coughed harder, then stood up, a bit of panic on her face. She took in a deep ragged breath, her eyelids fluttered, and she face-planted on the table, her head snapping back before she hit the carpeted floor.

"Holy shit!" Steve exclaimed through coughs. He looked at his hand, pink phlegm dotted his thumb and forefinger where he had expectorated.

Phillip and Sara rushed to help Tammy. She had smashed her face hard on the table and blood flowed freely from her nose and lips. Chuckie looked on as they tried to administer first aid. Lying on her back on the floor, she sputtered a bit, then let a long breath out. "Jesus, this looks bad," Phillip choked. He put his ear to Tammy's chest for a moment then quickly withdrew it. "She's not breathing! You," he pointed at Chuckie, "get the defibrillator, it's on the wall right there!" Phillip pointed through the glass toward a blue bag set in an alcove in the wall outside Meeting Room A.

Chuckie sprinted from the room and across the short hall. He opened the small panel and grabbed the AED off the wall. He was back at the glass door in short order, everyone looking at him. Including Tammy. She had opened her eyes. Her gaze shifted to Phillip, who was leaning over her but focused on Chuckie's return. Chuckie noticed her eyes go wide and her lips curl into a snarl. She threw her arms around Phillip, gripping his hair and shirt. Her mouth opened as she pulled Phillip to her. She sank her teeth into his neck, biting down hard, arterial spray coating the new presentation on the easel. Sara screamed, and crab-crawled backwards away from the scene on all fours. Phillip's horrible scream of pain and terror bubbled through the blood that filled his throat from the wound.

Everyone in the room decided that now was the time to be somewhere else and they attempted to flee. Angelica looked up from the palms of her hands, shrieked, and leapt across the table, scrabbling for purchase. Chuckie saw her fingernail snap off as it dug into the polished wood. Angelica threw herself at Tom, slashing at him, her hands curled into claws. He tried to fight her off, but Tammy picked that moment to turn on him as well, both women ripping into him before anyone could do anything. Sara had reached the door, and both she and Chuckie exited the meeting room to stare at the carnage through the glass.

Steve made for the door as well, but he was tackled from the side by blood-soaked Phillip. Steve screamed as a chunk of his arm was bitten off by his coworker.

Tammy, Tom, and Angelica stood, covered in gore, their eyes searching. Tom and Tammy sprinted at Lillian, who had remained frozen in her chair, her eyes transfixed on the multiple attacks occurring in front of her. She screamed when she saw what was coming, but it was way too late. Angelica launched herself toward Sara and Chuckie, her face impacting the glass wall with a nauseating crunch. Stunned, Chuckie and Sara watched as vile fluids dribbled down the glass from where their colleague had hit it. Angelica reared her head back and glared with black malice and iniquitous intent at the two people on the other side of the barrier. Her face had been destroyed by the impact against the hardened glass. Nose broken and twisted, her bottom lip hanging by threads of flesh, and shards of her fractured right cheekbone jutting through her skin at odd angles, she threw herself at the partition again.

Sara latched onto Chuckie's wrist and screamed, "Let's get out of here!" They ran for the elevator. It was nineteen floors to the lobby. Through the cube farm they sprinted, carnage and death a short distance behind them beating on the glass.

"What the hell was that?" demanded Sara. She dared a hasty glance down the hall to the meeting room. Six of her colleagues, some of whom she had called friends, were scratching and smashing themselves against the glass wall trying to get to her. Dark smears and handprints coated the transparent meeting room wall. She gave an involuntary shudder.

Chuckie shook his head, "I've never seen anything like it. One minute we were all talking and then..." He let the statement hang. He could barely hear the wails of sirens outside in the street. On the nineteenth floor, they usually didn't hear too many city noises, but there seemed to be so many that the sound carried. Sara let go of Chuckie's wrist and furiously pushed the down button on the elevator panel.

Chuckie glanced at the floor indicator above the stainless-steel door panels. The number 28 was illuminated and had been for a few dozen seconds. "I know it's a long way down, but maybe we should just take the stairs?" Not waiting for an answer, he pushed open the heavy steel fire door to the stairwell. There was a scuffle occurring somewhere above him, but on the landing, not ten feet from him, a man and a woman were heading down the stairs at high speed. "Hey," he shouted, "do you know what's..." Both people rounded on him. They were covered in blood and horrible wounds adorned their bodies. They both screeched, fighting each other to sprint back up the short flight of stairs toward Chuckie, who pulled the door closed. The two things on the other side began to furiously pound the steel, and soon there were more than just four fists.

Chuckie and Sara backed away from the door slowly. Sara glanced at Chuckie's face, for the first time realizing that he was as terrified as she. "Do you think the sirens—" Her question was interrupted by a streak of brown that slammed into her friend and took him to the ground, howling. The thing slashed and screamed as it tried to tear into him. Chuckie had both of its wrists and was trying to keep its face away from his. The thing's elbow snapped and it got a better angle, reaching its jaws down to gnaw at the spot just under her friend's left pectoral muscle.

"Ahhh!" he yelled, "AHHHH! Get it off!"

She took a step back, completely unsure of what she should do. She looked around, searching for a weapon, but the only thing she could come up with was a bowling trophy from Phillip's desk. She brought the marble base of the trophy down on the back of the thing's skull, shaving a piece of its scalp away. The thing whipped its head around and stared at her. It was Carlton. He had run for the bathroom earlier. Carlton decided that the prey he had was a better meal and returned to it. Sara smashed the trophy into the thing's head again and stunned, it let go of Chuckie and fell away. Sara charged and leapt on Carlton screaming. She brought the weapon down on the thing's face again and again until it stopped moving.

Heaving, she got off the dead body and helped her friend up. He held his hand to his chest. Blood seeped through his blue shirt, staining it crimson. "This is a new shirt," he grunted through clenched teeth. He looked at the body of the thing that had been Carlton, then shifted his gaze to Sara. "You really kicked his ass."

She smiled back, "Did not know who he was screwing

with. Let's get you sitting down." She helped him move to a wheeled office chair in Phillip's cubicle. There were photos of Phillip doing various sports mounted all over the place. She picked up a nine iron that was propped up next to his desk. "Yeah, now I find it." She rolled her eyes. Setting the golf club to the side, she got down on one knee to take a look at Chuckie's wound.

"It hurts," he told her.

"Well, somebody bit you."

"No, I mean it hurts all over."

The wound wasn't terribly bad, but because the skin was so thin over his ribs, there was a considerable amount of blood. She stood. "There's a first aid kit in the other hallway. Hang on I'll be right back."

He smiled at her again, "Be careful. Take this." He handed her the nine-iron.

She peered down the long hall toward the meeting room. Most of the creatures had moved away from the glass wall and were meandering around the room touching things. Angelica was still clawing at the glass, but the action was half-hearted. Sara moved through the cubicles as stealthily as possible, not wanting to be seen by her former coworkers. She peeked out from behind a corner and noticed that the coast was clear. She grabbed the red first aid kit and made her way quietly back to Chuckie. He sat hunched over in the cubicle, holding his chest with his right hand.

"I got it!" Sara announced triumphantly.

He whipped his head up and looked Sara in the eyes. No trace of Chuckie remained. What sat in front of her was a *thing* whose sole intent was to kill her.

Need... Neeeeeed! The thing felt. Thoughts were beyond it now as pure instinct had taken over. Memories, compassion, mercy, and remorse had fled with the part of Chuckie that had made him who he had been. The monster didn't know or care whether the soul that used to inhabit this body had left of his own accord, or had been forced out when he died. Only the thing remained, and that thing was malevolent.

A frenzied necessity for it to rend and eat anything not like itself consumed the creature and when it saw the meat in front of it, it leapt, screaming.

Sara swung the golf club in a sideways arc smashing the thing that had been her friend but a moment before in the left eye socket. The impact knocked the creature back, stumbling. Sara dropped the first aid bag, and sprinted through the cubes, taking a quick right and ducking into one. She dove under a desk, skinning her knee on the carpet and pulled the chair in after her. Fat tears rolled down her cheeks, but she knew she had to be silent.

The meat had been right there. Right in front of it. The creature *had* to rip into the meat. Feel the thick warm life of its prey pour down it's throat. Taste the flesh and sinew. The desire was more than need, it was a primal essential. The creature would hunt its quarry until it tore it to pieces. Until there was nothing left of it. Another feeling came to the creature and it shrieked, long and loud. Muffled screams and thumps answered its call and it bounded over the waist-high partitions, lacking the mental capacity to take the path of least resistance. Forgotten office supplies were crushed and scattered under its feet as it screeched again, seeing more meat moving in front of it.

At full sprint, it impacted the glass door of Meeting

Room A, smashing through the glass and nearly tearing the heavy door off its hinges. It had shredded itself on the shards, but it took no notice. It immediately turned in a crouch, ready to spring at the meat it had seen through the glass. But this wasn't meat. These things weren't meat. There was no meat here, just more like itself. Where was the meat? It stared into the eyes of the other things in the room. One of them pushed past him and out into the office, looking frantically in every direction. It took off, sprinting down the carpet between the cubes.

Not seeing any meat, the rest of the creatures, including the thing that had been Chuckie, meandered out of the meeting room, searching. The singular compulsion they felt drove them all. They would search until they found the meat, then they would shred and eat it.

Sara ceased her crying. All that would do was get her killed. Whatever this was, it was damn fast. It had to be the bites. In only a few minutes, sometimes seconds of being bitten, her friends had turned savage and had torn each other apart. But what started it. Maybe…

Her thoughts were interrupted by ragged sounds. One of the things was standing not three feet from her. The skirted legs, covered in gore, were in plain view just outside her hiding place. Sara followed the skirt up to a pair of hands. They were flexing and unflexing into claws while the thing heaved. It was Angelica, or what was left of Angelica. The thing began to turn toward Sara when a noise came from near the elevator lobby, and someone yelled, "Hey, is anybody in here?"

The response was instantaneous, the group of former humans screamed as one and sprinted for the sound, fighting each other to be first. When the Angelica-thing bounded off, something dropped from her pocket onto the carpet. Sara didn't know why, but after a moment she reached out and grabbed the item. She cradled the laser pointer in her hands like it was a life-saving weapon.

The Chuckie-thing howled in unbridled frustration. It had seen two of the things it wanted to rend and eat come in through an opening but quickly duck back out.

All the infected screamed and caterwauled, smashing themselves against the door the living humans had just peeked in They pounded until their fingers and wrists were broken, bones poking through the dead flesh. The Phillip-thing was shoved against the push bar and the steel door, dripping with infected fluids, opened from the office side. The Simpson's Marketing infected poured into the stairwell. Not knowing which way to go, some sprinted up, while others ran down. The door closed slowly behind them.

Sometime later, after not hearing anything for a while, Sara pushed the wheeled chair gently away and crept out from under the desk. She slowly raised her head until she could peek over the partition walls. She saw nothing. Slowly, ever so slowly, she crawled across the hall into a different cubicle. From this vantage, she could survey the area a bit better.

She was not alone. The Angelica-thing stood, looking the other way, leaning one shoulder against a blood-spattered wall. The creature was forty feet down the corridor. Sara glanced at the pieces of broken glass from the meeting room door. The shards gave her an idea.

Sara took the laser pointer and focused the beam on the floor-to-ceiling exterior glass window inside Meeting Room A. The angle was such that the window both refracted and reflected the red beam. She moved the pointer around a bit, the beam point moving as well.

All in a Day's Work | 27

"Hey, bitch!" she screamed, "I never liked you!" She continued to focus the beam on the window.

The Angelica thing screeched that horrible, keening wail. *Meat! Need! Need meat!* It sprinted toward the red light, gaining speed due to the length of the corridor. It threw its arms out in front of it just before it impacted the glass. The entire window burst outward, as did the creature who had hit it, both plummeted almost two hundred feet to the busy street below. The street was full of more infected, searching for meat.

The phones didn't work. She had tried for hours. She couldn't get in touch with anyone. She had peered through the broken window into the city below her. It was chaos. Fires raged and those things were everywhere. Sara had heard things in the stairwell and realized that using them was not an option. Just after dark, she pried the doors to the elevator open. The car was stuck several floors above her.

She moved back to her cube, sat in her chair, and cried. She didn't know what to do. She needed food and water. She smiled through the tears just then, remembering her friend Chuckie. Picking up an object, she thanked him even though he had tried to kill her. It would be cold, but still delicious. Sara smiled once more and settled in for a bacon sandwich.

∽

∽

∽

Rich Restucci

Rich Restucci is a practicing chemist living in Pembroke Massachusetts. He resides with his lovely wife, three children, and a permanent hangover. He enjoys drinking beer, stocking up on weapons and supplies, playing with explosives and reading/writing anything zombie related. An up and coming writer, Rich is currently working on two series set in the same undead world: The Run Series, and the Theories Series.. Rich's work can be found on the fiction section of Homepage of the dead.com, or you could check out his blog on Zombie Fiend.com. Rich's novels can be found wherever books are sold.

4

BROKEDOWN

TONY URBAN

"Jason pinched me!"

The voice was shrill and full of whiny, spoiled-rotten bitchiness and Peggy Benoit knew who it belonged to without even looking in the wide mirror that hung above the bus's windshield.

"Jason, up front," Peggy said in her firm, husky voice. She did glance into the mirror now, and saw eight-year-old Jason Thomas shuffling toward her. The boy was chubby with a brown mop of hair that dangled to his shoulders. When he reached her, he kept his chin pressed against his chest and stole short glances at the bus driver.

"Did you pinch Ellie?"

He chewed his bottom lip like it was a piece of saltwater taffy.

"Answer me."

The boy looked up and Peggy saw his eyes were wet. She lessened some of the pressure on the gas pedal and let the bus's speed fall from forty to twenty-five. She gave a wan smile and waved him closer.

"It's okay. She probably needs a good pinch every now and again."

Jason took a long look at her and then he smiled too. "Really?"

"That's just between you and me though." Peggy pressed her finger to her lips and Jason's smile morphed into a full-on grin. "Now sit behind me and don't cause no more ruckus."

She watched as the boy waddled to the seat and plopped down in it. Across from him sat Teddy Stader, the oldest of her afternoon riders. Teddy was of driving age but, from what Peggy could gather, was far too poor to afford a car so he was relegated to riding the bus to and from school each day, mostly with kids half to three fourths his age. He had a spiky, green mohawk and multiple piercings in his face but she couldn't see them at the moment because his head was turned downward, toward a sketchbook, as he scribbled away.

Peggy steered the bus through a series of sharp curves and it was two minutes before she reached the next straightaway. It was about that time that someone at the rear of the bus screamed.

Unlike Ellie's fake, attention seeking squall, this sounded genuinely important.

Peggy glanced in the mirror and saw most of the students huddled around a seat two thirds of the way back.

"What's going on back there?"

No one answered. She slowed the bus further. Twenty miles per hour now.

"Someone tell me what's going on?"

Finally, Clea Direnzo, a twelve-year-old with bright red pigtails, looked her way.

"Doug fell off his seat, Miss Peggy. And he's not breathing."

Not breathing? Peggy strained to see what was happening back there. She squinted into the mirror and saw the bottom halves of legs prone on the metal floor. She sucked in a mouthful of air.

"Peggy!"

This voice was closer. Alarmed. What else could be wrong? She searched in the mirror for the voice and found Teddy Stader pointing past her, toward the road.

"Peggy, look!"

She did but it was too late. The front passenger side of the bus careened over a tree branch the size of a car's bumper. It rocked up and smashed down and the sound of an exploding tire was a sound Peggy knew almost as well as Ellie's shrill voice.

Peggy smashed down the brake pedal and the remaining tires squealed as the bus slowed, then stopped.

"Damnit," she muttered to herself. There wasn't any time to worry about the flat though. She unbuckled her seatbelt, grabbing her trustworthy metal flashlight as she pulled her round, squat frame out of the seat and moved toward the bus's passenger section.

Aside from Teddy Stader and Jason Thomas, all her other regular riders were huddled in the back. As she passed the boys, she glanced at Teddy.

"Can you work the radio?"

Teddy nodded. "I'm not an imbecile."

"Call in and tell them we're brokedown. We'll need a mechanic. And maybe an ambulance."

When she passed by, Teddy left his seat and went to the front of the bus.

Peggy continued but couldn't see anything through the

throng of looky-loos. "Let me through." She wasn't scared, after all, would a girl that probably hadn't even had her period yet really be able to tell if someone was breathing? But she could feel her heart beating a bit quicker nonetheless.

"Come on, kids. Move."

The students parted retreating sideways into the green vinyl seats that lined both sides of her. When the scene was finally clear, she saw the boy on the floor. Doug Atherton was seven or eight years old and barely bigger than a rag doll. She'd often wondered if he had some sort of disease that kept him so small, but had never asked. It wasn't any of her business, after all, she was just the bus driver. She shined the flashlight down onto him.

Now, Doug wasn't just undersized, he was gray and motionless.

Her first instinct was that he'd choked. Clea had said he'd fallen off the seat. Maybe he'd been eating a cookie or an apple or a fruit roll up when he took a tumble and the afternoon snack was lodged in his windpipe.

Peggy pulled the boy from the footwell and into the aisle between the seats. Then she knelt over him and leaned in close to his face. She couldn't feel any hot air coming out of him so she reached down and opened his mouth.

The skin inside looked strangely desaturated, like a TV with the tube going wonky and everything wasn't quite black and white but had lost 80 percent of its color. She could see his tongue, the dangly bit at the back of his throat, but no obstructions whatsoever.

"Hey there, Dougie. What's the matter? What happened?"

Doug laid motionless, unanswering, unresponsive. Peggy felt his throat, trying to find a pulse. She wasn't entirely sure she had the right spot but she couldn't feel anything anywhere and her building anxiety rocketed.

She worked her way back to her feet and turned toward the front of the bus where Teddy held the radio to his lips.

"Teddy! Tell them we need that ambulance. Right now!"

Teddy turned his attention toward her. "No one's answering!" He shouted back.

Damnit, she thought, annoyed with the boy who'd promised her he could use the radio, that he was not an imbecile, but was proving to be just that. She glanced at the other children. A few were crying. All looked to be suffering various degrees of shock.

"You let Doug be while I get help. He's sick."

"He ain't sick! He's dead!" Ellie protested.

Whiny little bitch, Peggy thought, but didn't say out loud. "He is not!" Peggy said, but she suspected otherwise. "Now everyone stay calm." She said that as much for her own benefit as that of the children.

She trudged up the aisle which suddenly seemed longer and narrower. She felt her breaths come faster. She thought she might be on the verge of a panic attack. She'd never had one before but supposed now wouldn't be a bad time to start. Calm yourself, big gal. These kids need you to keep your head on straight.

When she reached Teddy he pushed the radio toward her. "Like I said, no one's answering."

She still thought he was wrong. That he'd twisted the dial instead of turned it or something simple like that. But when she looked, all the settings were correct. She tried anyway.

"Dispatch. Come on. This is bus 253. We have an emergency - a couple emergencies really - on Huckleberry Highway."

She waited. Nothing. "Dispatch, come on."

Nothing.

She reluctantly looked to Teddy who raised a pierced eyebrow at her in a 'told you so' gesture.

Peggy unclipped her cell phone from the visor and flipped it open. She punched in 9-1-1. Waited.

From the back of the bus came another scream. She turned to look but the phone clicked in her ear.

"All circuits are currently busy. Please try again."

What the hell? She redialed. 9-1--

Another scream.

Peggy stared into the back of the bus and thought she might have lost her marbles.

Doug, the boy who less than a minute ago she assumed dead, was now on his feet. On his feet and chewing on the arm of Clea Direnzo. He ripped his head back and forth sending blood flying through the air like raindrops on a windy day.

Peggy dropped the phone. It clattered against the floor but she didn't notice.

Scott Downy, a stocky boy in the seventh grade, grabbed on to Doug's shoulders and pulled him off Clea who was doing some strange amalgamation of screaming, crying, and yelling.

Doug spun around, losing interest in the girl and turning his attention to the older boy. Doug caught Scott's hand and went to bite, but the bigger, stronger boy pulled free. Then he used that hand to punch Doug square in the nose. Peggy heard the crunch from twenty feet away.

Doug paid no attention to his smashed nose. He dove forward, landed against Scott's broad chest and started snapping his jaws like a piranha. He got a mouthful of

Scott's chest, biting right through the shirt and into the soft flesh beneath.

Scott yelled, a sound Peggy found surprisingly high pitched for such a bulky boy and shoved Doug backward. A ragged, masticated hole seeped blood but Peggy's attention quickly left the wound and turned to Clea who had jumped onto the back of a seat and grabbed hold of Ellie's blonde locks.

Ellie screamed - real terror this time, not fake - and thrashed with her arms trying to escape. Another girl, Daphne, also tried to push Clea away but the girl, despite her injuries, refused to let go. She pulled Ellie up and back, the blonde child's head getting closer and closer to her gaping mouth.

"Clea! You stop that right now!" Peggy's voice exploded out of her mouth, so loud that she surprised herself and wasn't sure it was actually hers. When all heads turned in her direction, she realized it was.

Clea stared at her and growled. No, that can't be, Peggy thought. She's a girl, not an animal. Then she snarled, leaned into Ellie and bit down on the girl's ear.

Ellie screamed again but Peggy could barely focus because Doug was now chewing on Fiona Shaw, a chubby, raven-haired girl who had only moved to the area a month earlier. While Doug gnawed away at her flesh, Scott tackled Frederick Brocker a boy who always made Peggy feel bad because he had a hare lip that had been poorly operated on. That didn't matter much because Scott was eating Frederick's face.

Peggy thought this must be a nightmare. Maybe she'd conked her head when she hit the tree branch and got the flat. Or maybe she was still in bed and the alarm hadn't gone off and none of this day had actually happened. Heck, maybe she was locked up in a loony bin tied up in one of those white jackets that kept you from moving your arms. Any of those scenarios was better than this being real.

Someone grabbed her shoulder from behind. If this was a dream or a delusion it was a darn realistic one. She forced herself to turn and look, scared as to who or what she might find, and saw Teddy Stader looming over her.

"Peggy, we got to get off the bus, They're zombies!"

Zombies? That's not a real thing. She always thought Teddy was a bit of an oddball, but even he had to know truth from fantasy.

Then Frederick jump to his feet. The boy's face was gone from the nose down. All his tiny teeth were visible in his lipless jaws. His cheeks were mostly missing, just ragged holes with bits of tissue and sinew holding all the pieces in shape like a macabre connect the dots. The tip of his tongue was missing and the remaining muscle writhed inside his all too visible mouth like a headless snake.

Maybe zombies were real.

Teddy grabbed hold of her beefy forearm and pulled her backward, toward the front of the bus. She allowed herself to be dragged away but knew it was wrong. These children were her wards. Her responsibility. It was her job - her duty - to protect them.

But as she looked upon the carnage unfolding on bus 253 she realized that was impossible. Every child in the rear third of the bus was either eating someone or being eaten. It was a gruesome, violent mashup of children fighting and flailing and biting and screaming and dying. It was too late to help them.

"Okay," Peggy said, as much to herself as Teddy. "We'll go."

They reached the front of the bus where Jason Thomas

sobbed. Thick rivulets of tears streamed down his chubby cheeks which were flame red in fear.

Peggy grabbed the lever and threw open the door. She pushed Jason toward it and he almost fell down the two big steps that led the way to freedom.

"Go!"

He did, half running, half stumbling into the light outside. He hit the road and skidded to his knees.

"Now you," she said to Teddy. He didn't waste any time and when he was outside he looked up at her.

"Peggy! Hurry!"

Peggy wanted to go but she had to take one more look into the mirror. She'd been driving this bus for over 30 years and never had a child experience anything worse than a bloody nose. Now... she'd lost them all. She felt sick. She felt like a failure.

The distorted view in the mirror revealed that, in the last minute, the situation had changed. There were no longer children dying. They were all dead. Dead and coming for her. They crowded the narrow aisle, squeezing through, trying to get ahead of one another. Others had given up on the aisle and crawled over seats like some kind of demented, clumsy monkeys, falling into the footwells and bouncing up again unharmed and undeterred.

The closest of them were within four rows from her. Peggy knew the proper thing to do would be to close the door and trap them inside where they couldn't hurt anyone else. She wasn't a sea captain, but this was her bus. It wasn't a glamorous job or a well-paying one, but she'd always taken pride in it nonetheless. And if her ship was going down, wasn't she supposed to go down with it? She started to close the door. The hinges writhed with a pained screech.

"Peggy!"

Teddy's voice snapped her out of her daze. She looked into the bright afternoon light where he held onto Jason's hand. She realized there were two live children out there that needed her. To the others, she was nothing more than a hot meal.

Peggy let go of the lever and fled the bus. Once outside, she grabbed the folding door and slammed it shut. She knew it couldn't be opened again without someone working the lever and she hoped - prayed - that these monsters that used to be children couldn't figure that out.

The first of them, Scott, hit the door from the inside. He pressed against it, smearing blood and flattening his features against the dirty glass. More fell down the steps, into the exit behind him. She could see them packing in tight, filling the small space in a way that made her think of clowns in a car. But Peggy wasn't laughing.

The escapees were so caught up in watching them that they didn't see Caryn Hess, the smallest girl on the bus, squirm through an open window headfirst. She barely cleared and when the frame birthed her, she fell ten feet to the ground, landing hard on the pavement. Her arms took the brunt of the impact and broke in the fall. One was twisted around like she was some sort of contortionist. The other was worse. Bones poked through the skin like ivory chopsticks and her hand dangled uselessly with only the skin still keeping it part of her body. Caryn worked her way back to her feet. It took only a moment before she'd shaken off the fall and ran toward the trio.

Peggy heard the footsteps first, but it was already too late. She turned as Caryn dove onto Jason. The two hit the ground in a thud and Caryn came out on top. Teddy grabbed her arm and tried to pull the little girl away but he got the bad arm and her hand ripped free from the rest of her limb. Teddy stared at it like he'd just been on the receiving end of a gory magic act.

Caryn was not deterred and she chomped down on Jason's cheek, tearing away a wad of skin so large white bone gleamed from within the wound. The boy screamed and grabbed at his disfigurement. With his hand in range, Caryn decided to dine on phalanges a la Jason and bit the pinky and ring fingers of his left hand clean off. She chewed on the severed digits like she had a mouthful of beef jerky.

Peggy didn't realize that Teddy had cast aside Caryn's arm until she saw him stride up behind the girl and swing his book bag. It connected with the back of Caryn's head and she toppled over sideways like a bowling pin. The girl skidded along the pavement, coming to a stop on her side.

Teddy didn't waste any time. He rushed to her and bashed her again with the book bag, then again, and a third time. What remained of the girl's skull was in bits and chunks on the faded, gray asphalt.

"What the hell do you have in there?" Peggy asked.

Teddy held up his bag, which was soaked and dripping blood. "Physics textbook." He managed a grin that showed off his crooked teeth.

"Well thank God for math," she said.

Peggy forgot about the textbook when she saw Jason jump to his feet. The boy gave no care to his wounds. His crazed eyes were all too familiar and Peggy knew he'd come for them any second. Part of her wanted to let Teddy handle it. He'd taken out little Caryn easy enough, after all. But she knew it wasn't fair to make the boy do all the dirty work. She was the grown up, after all.

Jason took one wobbly step, then another. With the third he had his feet under him and picked up the pace.

Peggy pulled the flashlight out of her belt. The black

metal felt so cold in her hand even though it had turned into quite the hot afternoon. She choked down on the long handle and made sure she had a strong grip.

Jason was coming for her but she was ready. When the boy got within reach, Peggy swung the flashlight and it connected with his forehead, just above his right eye. There was an audible crack that reminded Peggy of breaking eggs to make cookies. Then she heard the boy emit something between a grunt and a sigh.

He hit the ground and stayed down.

"It's science, actually."

The voice behind her made her jump, or jiggle anyway. She turned and found Teddy still grinning, even more so now.

"What?"

"Physics. That's science. Not math."

"Oh."

Peggy tried to smile back but above him she saw dozens of tiny hands clawing and pounding at the bus's windows. Half a head and one arm were wedged into the opening where Caryn had emerged and whoever they belonged to writhed furiously from behind the glass as it tried to escape.

"We need to go," Peggy said and Teddy nodded.

"Where to?"

Peggy didn't know. The hospital? The police station? They were miles from both. "Anywhere away from here."

"I like that plan," Teddy said.

They trudged away from the bus, down the road, not knowing where they'd end up or what would be waiting for them.

∾

Tony Urban

A #1 Best Selling horror author on Amazon, wannabe cryptozoologist/monster hunter, and fan of general weirdness (both real and imagined), Tony Urban has traveled over one hundred thousand miles seeking out everything from haunted asylums to UFO crash sites to creatures like Bigfoot and the Mothman. In a previous life, he worked as a hack in the independent movie industry, but he finds his current career much more exciting.

His first books were offbeat travelogues, but recently his zombie apocalypse series, "Life of the Dead", has been a bestseller online and has grossed out readers all over the globe. He's currently finishing that series and writing way... too... slow... Next up is probably a horror novel about a monster in the woods of Pennsylvania. He's basing it on real life incidents. Not really.

Tony is a Jeeper who always tries to wave, a huge fan of dogs, loves road trips, obsesses over Maine, enjoys a good conspiracy theory, and watches way too many horror movies. His ultimate goal in life is to be killed by a monster thought by most to be imaginary. Sasquatch, werewolves, chupacabras...he's not picky. If that fails, he'd enjoy a long and prosperous career as a full-time writer. Which of those two scenarios is more likely is up to the readers to decide.

Read his "Life of the Dead" series available on Amazon.

5

CARNIVAL OF CARNAGE

RICKY FLEET

Steven watched the taillights glow, the red hue matching the hellish temperature and humidity of the afternoon. Each stifled breath felt like it was drawn through a hot, moist towel. Sweat beaded on his forehead before running in rivulets towards his eyes. The stinging sensation was an aggravation which did nothing to help his souring mood. Rubbing at the moisture with his forearm, he carelessly placed the exposed skin onto the black rubber window seal. Hissing in pain, he cursed the inopportune death of the air conditioning system of his old rust bucket. The silent vents mocked him from the dashboard. If they hadn't been closed, the only air expelled by the thin slits was just as hot as that outside. The sweltering torment was inescapable.

A deep, overly dramatic sigh came from the passenger seat. The icy wave of disapproval washed over him but did nothing to lessen the blazing shroud that came from their immobility under the sun's searing rays. Another pouting exhalation was followed by a discontented tut.

"There was space, why didn't you pull into the other lane?"

"We're bumper to bumper. I'd have hit the car in front!"

Folding her arms, Jackie huffed and fell silent. Obviously, the honeymoon period of their relationship was over and the immature outbursts were increasing in frequency. Being eighteen, she was six years his junior. What had begun with flirty glances in the weekend queue for coffee at the local cafe had quickly developed into dates and dinner with the parents. Whirlwind romance was an understatement.

"There! Go!" she barked.

A tiny gap had opened between his beater and the shiny new BMW in front, so he quickly pulled right, much to the ire of the car which had been forced to swerve to avoid a prang. A few expletives and hand gestures were forthcoming, but if he ever wanted to get her back in the sack he needed to take a few risks.

"Be careful, you could've crashed!"

"Fuck me, Jackie. You were the one telling me to get over!"

"Yeah, but I want to get there in one piece."

Think of the sex. Think of the sex. Think of the sex. Steven repeated the silent mantra, trying to remain calm. He knew that if he could pull this off, she would be insatiable when they finally got home. Her favorite film crush was waiting half a mile away at the Carnival of Carnage horror convention. Mason Force was a legend in the teen slasher genre. His iconic role of a murdered outcast seeking revenge in Death Party 1, 2, and 3 ensured he was a draw to any event. Steven thought it was a ridiculous, contrived name. He looked like a Brad, or Kyle; a typical jock straight from football to movies. Bronzed, sculpted chest, oiled six pack, and a chiseled jaw that was perfect for the big screen. Just watching one of his films was an aphrodisiac for Jackie, though. Seeing him in the flesh would undoubtedly result in debauchery and salacious acts the likes of which he could only imagine in his wettest dreams.

"Look out!" she shrieked.

The tire rubber screamed its reply as Steven narrowly prevented a rear end collision with his untimely daydreaming. Heart pounding, he meekly avoided the rear view and the renewed gestures from the irate motorist behind.

"Sorry," he muttered.

The brief flash of fear was quickly replaced by anger when she caught sight of the time displayed on the radio. "Why did you have to go to work anyway? You knew how important this is for me."

"I know it is. We're nearly there," he replied, trying to stroke her leg.

Pushing it away forcibly, she ignored his efforts to placate her and turned away.

"You know why I had to work. Eddie called me in and if I'd said no he'd have fired me. How am I supposed to get a nice car if I'm unemployed? I already paid out nearly four hundred bucks for your photo op."

"Yeah, thanks," she sighed. "It won't mean much if we don't make it in time, though. Will it?"

Maybe we took it too quickly? he wondered. *You're kidding yourself, you know exactly what the problem is.* Admitting their differing ages was the issue would only go to prove his friends correct. He could still remember the teasing about picking her up from high school and hoping the cops didn't find out. They weren't quite so dismissive after seeing her in a bikini at Josh's pool party two weeks ago. Her long, blonde hair clinging to her tanned body as she climbed the steps. The tiny patches of red cloth held together by thin straps which barely concealed her modesty. The way all eyes would follow her every move. Her knowing, sultry smiles at the reactions to her exhibitionism. He knew it was love, as in *love*. The big one. Time would iron out the kinks, he was certain.

"Thank God. It's finally moving."

Ahead, the sea of red light slowly blinked out as each row pulled away.

"There might've been an accident."

"Who cares? We're going to make it!"

Taking the off ramp, her mood improved with each passing mile.

∼

Pulling into the Pine View Hotel, Steven could see their chances of finding a parking space were close to zero. Every square inch of available tarmac was covered with vehicles, some even going to the extreme of mounting the curb to park on grass verges and, in one case, a flower bed.

"You've got to be kidding me," Jackie groaned.

"I'll try around the back. They've got to have an overflow parking lot."

"There's not enough time, just pull over and drop me here. You can meet me inside if you find somewhere."

"Gee, thanks," Steven replied, swinging to the curb.

"Don't sulk, silly. I'll see you in a few minutes," she said, grabbing her purse.

After giving him a quick kiss, she jumped from the car and hurried towards the entrance. Her uplift in disposition was contagious and he found himself smiling as she walked away. It was times like this that he forgot about the irritating childishness. The tight jeans accentuated her firm rump as she strutted away, hips swinging. Looking over her shoulder, she gave him a wink before disappearing into the reception. His own figure had suffered of late and his six pack had become more like a keg. He needed to spend less time smoking weed and more time back in the gym.

"I'll go Monday," he vowed.

Maneuvering around hastily abandoned cars, he cursed their owner's stupidity. The sight of a tow truck loading one of the more blatant offenders caused him to chuckle. Passing the man, Steven nodded. The heavyset enforcer doffed an imaginary cap in return and continued with his task. *Poor guy looks like he's melting.* The navy-blue overalls had growing patches of sweat under the arms, back, and chest. Even the crack of his ass hadn't escaped the trapped perspiration. *At least I'm in a tee shirt and shorts.*

Passing the furthest corner of the hotel, Steven was met by a fleet of emergency vehicles waiting outside the service entrance. He counted at least four ambulances and three police cars.

"What the hell?" he whispered.

Something was happening and Steven felt a twinge of fear for Jackie. Navigating the packed rows, he quickly gave up any notion of parking legally. Picking the opposite end of the lot, he came to a stop on double yellow lines and turned off the engine. With any luck, his friend in the moist overalls would be too busy with the cars at the front to worry about his clapped-out heap in the back. Twisting the window handle far too quickly, it snapped off in his hands.

Looking at the black plastic, he flipped his car the bird. "If you get stolen and burned out, don't come crying to me."

Tossing the cracked lever into the bush, Steven jogged towards the flashing lights of the first responders. No one could be seen, not even a member of hotel staff. Looking in the rear doors of an ambulance, he recoiled and nearly tripped over the curb. A body bag lay on the stretcher and another sat in the empty space on the floor.

"Holy shit!"

Morbid curiosity took over and he slowly approached the zipped corpses. What was happening? If there had been fatalities, why was the event still going on? Where were all the panicking, screaming guests? Then it hit him.

"It's all part of the show, you idiot!" he chastised himself for being so foolish.

Movement stirred within the bag on the gurney, confirming his suspicions. Leaning inside the open door, he whispered, "Your secret's safe with me. Jackie will be blown away."

Feeling a whole lot better Steven left the writhing actor to practice. The shadows of the building provided some small relief to his discomfort, but the shade ended at the corner. Walking around the building, the full force of the sun bore down on him. *I know how a vampire feels now.* It was easy to imagine the only thing preventing spontaneous combustion was the running sweat which soaked his body.

"I hope you've parked sensibly, young man!" called a voice.

"Er... of course, sir," replied Steven sheepishly.

"Sir? Well you've got manners, I'll give you that, son. You're not causing an obstruction, are you?"

"No, sir. I've parked as far out as possible and I'm not blocking anyone. I can move it and park a few streets over if you'd like?"

"I think we can let it slide. You have a fine day now."

"You too, sir," Steven replied cheerfully.

The man tipped his imaginary hat again and retrieved a handkerchief from his breast pocket. Dabbing at his brow, the cloth drizzled with accumulated sweat. Instead of helping, it seemed to be adding moisture to his creased forehead.

"Pardon me, sir? Would you like a drink of water? I can pop in and get you one."

"That's very kind, son, but I've got a bottle in the cab. I've always been a bit prone to overheating, that's all," he replied, wafting at his red face.

"Sounds like my car," Steven said and the repo man chuckled. "You have a good day."

A huge billboard with dripping red font welcomed the patrons. Alongside 'CARNIVAL *of* CARNAGE' were smiling pictures of the more famous guests in the venue. Mason's face stared out from beneath the bloody C. The arrogance was evident from his cold eyes which even his disarming smile couldn't hide. Moving underneath the canopy, Steven's sun strained eyes struggled to adjust to the shadows. Stepping aside to let others past, he leaned against the bare concrete. The cool render was bliss.

"Are you ok, sir?"

The sweet voice shocked him and he laughed nervously. "Yeah, sorry. I was just enjoying the cold wall."

The woman smiled. She was dressed up as a zombie, her close cropped brown hair matted with fake blood and dirt. The tattered clothing revealed amazingly realistic bite wounds on her torso.

"The AC is on inside. It's like the North Pole."

"That sounds great."

"Are you here alone?" she asked, showing him inside.

"I'm looking for my girlfriend. She has a photo with Mason Force in ten minutes," he replied, following her through the two sets of automatic doors.

"Poor thing."

"What do you mean?"

Glancing around to make sure none of the other organizers were listening, she leaned close. "He's a dick. He tried to grab my ass earlier."

"Are you ok?"

"Yeah, I threatened to kick him in the nuts if he tried it again. I got taken off duty in the celebrity room and put out on meet and greet. Can't be upsetting the big names, can we?"

"That's awful. Thanks for the warning, though."

"You're welcome. The queue starts at the end of the foyer, on the right."

With his worst fears confirmed, Steven hurried off in search of Jackie. A banner hung from the ceiling above the reception desk, showing the walking dead and an advertisement for the afternoon 'Zombie Walk'. *I was right after all.* Squeezing past people in a variety of scary outfits, he noticed activity through the doors of the dining room. Paramedics and cops were dealing with people either laid on the floor or slumped at the tables. Figuring it was part of the upcoming show, he ignored the concerned faces.

"Steven!"

Jackie was waving excitedly from the front of the long line.

"See, I told you we'd make it in time," he said, ducking under the barrier.

"Hey! You can't cut in line!" shrieked Elvira, or at least a lady who was dressed as the eighties vamp.

"He's not cutting in line," Jackie shouted back. "We've got a scheduled photo."

As the raven-haired beauty fell quiet, the usher approached and checked the ticket against his clipboard. Jackie was buzzing and pulled on his arm like an over exuberant toddler.

"Here you go," said the man, handing the ticket back. "Mr. Force will be ready in about two minutes."

"Thank you so much!" gushed Jackie.

"Calm down, he's just an average guy."

She looked at him incredulously. "Mason Force is *not* just an average guy. He's a legend. His performance in Death Party 2 should've earned him an Oscar."

The temptation to make a cutting remark about the guy's unconvincing, wooden acting was nearly overwhelming. Deciding that discretion was the better part of valor, Steven shut his mouth and took in the fantastic sights. The organizers had gone to great lengths to create a spooky atmosphere. Every square inch of bare wall was covered with cobwebs and other horror paraphernalia. Glass display cases filled with movie props had been wheeled in. Most notable was the original machete from *Friday the 13th* infamy. Mounted above it was a stained hockey mask, no less scary for lacking the dead eyed gaze of Jason Voorhees. The vendors hawked their wares from elaborately decorated tables, yet glancing about, it became clear that over half the tables were unattended. Confused faces looked around for someone to take their hard-earned money.

"I wonder where all the authors and retailers are?" Steven said.

Jackie shrugged disinterestedly. The usher caught the question and explained. "We think the breakfast bacon was off. It tasted fine, but everyone who's eaten it has gone down with a bad stomach."

"That sucks. I'm sorry to hear that."

"It's only since the hotel switched its supplier to the Salaam Meat Company a few days ago. Anything to save a few bucks," he replied, shaking his head in frustration.

"Hold on a minute." Steven caught the sleeve of the

assistant. "You mean the emergency services are here legitimately?"

"I'm afraid so. There're a lot of people with food poisoning."

"But I saw body bags in the back of the ambulances. That's got to be for the zombie walk, right? I mean, no one's died from the food, have they?"

"I doubt it. There was a lot of vomiting, but that's all I know."

At that, another vendor stumbled away towards the bathroom, clutching his abdomen and groaning. The pale face was sweating profusely despite the chilled interior of the building.

"God damnit!" muttered the man with the clipboard. Speaking into his radio, he asked for help before moving towards the stricken victim.

"Wait! What about us?"

Steven rolled his eyes at Jackie's selfish attitude.

"You can both go in now. I'll be right back."

"Oh my God, it's happening!" Jackie shouted, throwing the velvet curtain aside.

Steven hesitated for a few seconds before pushing through the heavy drape. This was going to be a long day.

∽

"Hi, I'm Anne, Mason's personal assistant. There are a few rules you need to abide by for the picture. You may only talk to him about the movies, no politics or personal questions. The picture will involve you placing an arm around his midsection while he places an arm across each of your shoulders. Do you understand?"

"Don't bother telling me," Steven scoffed. "I'm not here for a picture with him."

"Oh, I see," Anne replied.

"Steven, don't be rude! Is there anything else? I really don't want to annoy Mason."

"It's best to avoid eye contact. Especially you." Anne pointed at Steven.

"You're shitting me?"

"No, I'm deadly serious. If he feels you're being disrespectful he'll just cancel the picture."

"I'd better get a fucking refund if he does."

"That's not our policy. You've been forewarned," she snapped at him. Turning to Jackie, the professional smile came back and they linked arms like old friends.

"What a crock," Steven muttered under his breath.

"Don't you dare ruin this for me!" Jackie hissed over her shoulder.

They emerged into the room and Mason was relaxing in his chair wearing sunglasses while reading a magazine. He ignored them for a while until Anne coughed politely and he tossed it down with evident displeasure. *What a fucking douchebag*, thought Steven. Even the photographer was growing sick of the man judging by the slight shake of her head. The haughty disdain disappeared in an instant at the sight of Jackie. Even the sunglasses were removed to get a better view of her.

"Well, isn't this interesting? Hi, I'm Mason," he gushed, favoring her with the million-dollar smile.

"I'm Jackie and this is Steven," she said, giggling.

He came around the table, never taking his eyes off her. The way he looked her up and down made Steven's skin crawl. It hadn't escaped his attention that Jackie had refused to acknowledge him as her significant other, so Steven took it upon himself. "I'm her boyfriend," he said, holding out a hand to shake.

Ignoring the proffered palm, Mason pushed him to one side and shook Jackie's instead. "It's a pleasure to meet you, Jackie. How're you today?"

"I'm amazing, thank you. It's such an honor to meet you. I've seen all your films a million times. Your acting in Death Party 2 was outstanding," she babbled, refusing to let him go.

The contact continued until Mason raised the shaking hand to his lips. Instead of a peck, his kiss lingered for a second while he stared deeply into her eyes. *Smooth move, asshole. I wonder how many airheads that's worked on.*

"It was nothing," he purred. "Without people like you, I'd be just another gorgeous guy working out seven days a week. The fans are what keep me going."

"Even if you weren't in movies, I'm sure you'd be modeling. You have such an amazing bone structure. Not to mention your body."

"Well, I do model on the side. I'm not sure if you knew that. I'm part of a campaign that's travelling to Milan next month."

"Really? That's incredible. I've always wanted to go to Italy and see the sights."

"You'd fit right in. Someone as gorgeous as you should be walking the catwalk alongside me."

Steven laughed derisively; the false flattery was vomit-inducing. "It's funny. You've never mentioned that to me before."

"Perhaps it's because she knew you wouldn't be able to afford it," Mason goaded. He didn't even have the courtesy to break eye contact from Jackie who giggled in agreement.

Anne could see the growing tension and the way Steven

narrowed his eyes while clenching his fist. Whether it was a reaction to her client's lewd behavior or to keep her meal ticket as pretty as possible, she stepped in. "Let's get that photograph taken, shall we? We've still got over a hundred people waiting."

"Let them wait," Mason snapped. "I want to get to know this aspiring supermodel a bit better."

"Give me a fucking break!"

"Now you see, there's the problem." Mason sneered, turning to face Steven. "How's she ever supposed to succeed in fashion when her boyfriend can't even accept how beautiful she is?"

"I know how good looking she is, that's why she's *my* girlfriend."

Jackie scowled at him. "You've never once supported my dream to be a model."

"That's because you've *never once* mentioned it!" he argued.

"A good boyfriend would be in sync with his girlfriend's inner desires. Their chakras would be in tune and he'd just *know*."

"Spare me your pick up lines, you talentless prick. I've seen oak trees with more acting ability."

"Fuck off, Steven!" Jackie shrieked. "You're ruining the best day of my life."

"Security!"

Anne's shout had summoned two burly guards from their concealment in a back room.

"What's the problem?"

The barn door of a man with a military high and tight, moved to protect the movie star. One hand curled under his shirt to the concealed carry weapon hidden within.

"Get rid of these two, please."

Mason glared at Anne. "Jackie's been an angel. It's Shaun that's been the asshole."

"My name's Steven. Asshole."

"Who cares? Just get rid of him," Mason said to the ex-military behemoth. "I'm going to get to know Jackie a whole lot better."

"What about the fans waiting outside? We're already three minutes behind schedule," complained Anne, looking at her clipboard.

"Let them wait. It's not as if they're going to leave, is it?"

"But it looks unprofessional."

"The opportunity to see me is the one small pleasure in their otherwise pointless existence. They'll be patient or be removed like this loser here. Get him out of my sight."

"Sir, please come with us," said the second bodyguard. He was smaller than his friend but bore the same distinctive haircut and confident poise.

Steven had never felt so tiny. Mason smirked while curling a protective arm around Jackie who glared poison at him. Anne looked furious, but he couldn't tell whether it was aimed at him or the star. The security were watching him closely, ready to react at the first sign of any aggression.

"Enjoy walking home later!" Steven mocked, despising the childish tone in his own voice.

Mason laughed. "Don't worry, I'll get her a taxi… tomorrow morning."

Pre-empting the inevitable attack, the guards each took an arm and frog marched him through the curtains. Expecting to be thrown through the main doors with them still closed, Steven was taken aback when they gently released him and simply positioned themselves in front of the curtain to prevent his re-entry.

"I'm sorry about that," said barn door.

"Me too," said slightly smaller barn door. "He's a prize son of a bitch."

"Then why do you guys protect him?" Steven demanded.

"Bills, buddy. They never end."

Sighing, Steven rubbed at his face. "Look, I understand. Can you do me a favor, though?"

"If we can, sure."

"Can you keep an eye on Jackie for me? I guess we're through, but I still don't want to see her treated like a cheap whore."

"You have our word."

"Thank you."

"Are you going to hang around? In case he loses... interest?" asked barn door, trying to be diplomatic.

"I'm not really enjoying it much to be honest, so I'm just going to head home. I think she has a few bucks on her, but can you give her this just in case he lets her down on the taxi?" he said, handing over a fifty-dollar bill to the embarrassed guard.

"You're a good kid. I'm sure she'll see sense."

"How can I compete with that?" Steven asked weakly, pointing at Mason's beaming portrait.

Walking away, he ignored the hushed titters of the lined up guests. It pained Steven to admit the depth of feeling he had towards the shallow teenager. Before he'd taken ten paces, the dull ache in his heart became intolerable and the first tears started to flow. Ducking into a small side room, Steven placed his back to the wall and tried to compose himself. Rows of books showing various horrific scenes on the covers adorned the metal racks. The cash purse had been abandoned on the table, with small and large denominations hanging from the pouch. The trader was nowhere to be seen. *That's weird.* At least he couldn't be judged for the pathetic sobbing. It was going to be embarrassing enough trying to make it past the other attendees with red rimmed eyes.

From the overhead speaker system came the announcement of the impending zombie walk. Everyone taking part was to gather in the lobby.

"Thank you," he whispered, grateful for the distraction it would cause.

Keeping his head down, Steven pushed through the gathering crowd towards the front doors. Entering the vestibule, the chilled interior air markedly increased in temperature. As the second set sighed open, a blanket of heat enveloped him. Freed from the watchful gaze of the attendees, the tears flowed freely again. The feeling of betrayal was a crushing weight, making each step away from his lover a monumental struggle.

"You ok, son?"

The voice of the friendly tow truck man couldn't pull Steven out of the dark pit of grief and he walked on by without acknowledging the question. Reaching the back of the hotel, the flashing lights of the emergency vehicles strobed across his face, it was the sight of the ambulance that finally pulled him back from the brink. The body bags had been ripped to pieces and lay empty. A lone figure caught sight of him from across the expansive parking lot. Screaming like a banshee, it took off at a full sprint. Making a beeline straight for Steven, the man bounded cleanly over any car in the way.

"Holy shit!"

The power required to leap that height was utterly inhuman and Steven found himself backing away. The chatter of clacking teeth carried over the rapidly shortening distance and for the first time he could see the bloody stains covering its chest. Whirling on his heels, Steven bolted towards the entrance, skidding on the loose gravel as he rounded the corner. By a miracle or blind luck, he managed to maintain his balance and started yelling at his sweaty friend to get clear. Out of nowhere it felt like he'd been hit by a truck. Sliding agonizingly across the concrete, the tee shirt was torn from his body. The squirming sensation grinding him into the ground could only be coming from the enraged psychopath.

"Get off him!" came a shout, and the weight was removed with a dull thunk of steel on flesh.

Rolling over, Steven saw that the repo man was wielding a long metal bar. Offering a hand, he pulled Steven from the ground. Rubbing grit from his chest, the hand came away bloody. Looking down, the myriad scratches from the unforgiving surface looked like he'd been attacked with a cheese grater.

"Stay down, asshole!"

The crazed man's arm was broken just below the shoulder. Trying to push itself up, the jagged bone of its humerus ripped through the fleshy meat of his bicep and it fell on its side.

"What the hell is that thing?"

"I have no fucking idea, but we need to get away from it!"

Snarling, it displayed an extraordinary litheness and sprung from the ground effortlessly. Like a crouching lion, it pounced, flying through the air with unbelievable speed and agility. Repo man went down hard in a tangle of frenzied biting and clawing before he could swing the bar which went clattering away. Grabbing it by the hair, Steven tried to pull it from his friend. Even with repo man pushing with his thick, hairy arms from below, and his own efforts to wrestle it clear, the creature clung on. The protruding bone slashed deeply into repo's forearms as he tried desperately to defend his neck from the bloody, snapping maw. Releasing the hair, Steven kicked at the midsection. Ribs cracked under the blows but did nothing to slow down the attacker. Exhaustion finally won the day and teeth sank deeply into exposed flesh. Blood arced across the dusty, grey concrete.

"Go!" gurgled Repo.

Looking around frantically for the steel bar, he came up empty. Calling for help, no one answered. Feeling helpless, Steven watched as the monster fed on his friend, cramming handfuls of meat into its mouth. The blue eyes looked skyward, glazed and dead.

"I'm so sorry," Steven whispered, backing away.

Jackie! If the other bodies were inside the hotel walls she was in just as much danger. In his adrenaline fuelled fight for survival, he had completely forgotten about the earlier ugliness. Leaving the spreading pool of gore, Steven raced for the front entrance. Barging through the startled onlookers, shouts of anger and confusion followed.

"Jesus, are you ok?" asked the pretty elfin girl, stopping him in the foyer.

"I need to get to Jackie. There's a psycho outside eating people and there may be more inside!"

"Is this part of the events?" she replied. Her concern had turned to annoyance at being kept in the dark of the changes to the schedule.

"No, I'm serious. Get security to raise the alarm and then get more cops. A lot more, these things aren't human."

"They're going all out this year," said an older man, clapping excitedly as Steven pushed past.

Screaming came from the direction of the dining area. Unaware of the peril, some in the hall commented how well acted it was, with real fear captured in the tone. Peeking through the doorway, the crowd was trying to catch sight of the display. Cracks of gunfire rang out, bringing rapturous applause.

If only you knew.

Those gathered by the doors cheered at each new twist to the amazing show. Event security were already moving towards the disturbance, ordering people to vacate the area. Military or law enforcement training was kicking in as the nature of the ruckus became clear. Between the throng, Steven caught glimpses of the dining room. It resembled nothing less than a charnel house. Tables and chairs had been destroyed or tossed aside in the melee. Blood covered every surface, even trickling from the ceiling from arterial spray. Six assailants were hunched over, tearing into uniformed bodies. One of the police officers was backed into a corner, firing point blank into the chest of a seventh attacker. The shots staggered the woman, puffs of misty blood bursting from her back. The trigger clicked empty and the woman roared triumphantly. Springing forward, she drove the cop back into the wall with enough force to crash straight through the drywall.

"That's so realistic!" applauded a young Goth girl as white dust swirled.

"It is real! For God's sake get away from there!" Steven yelled as he passed.

One of the security team called after him. "How can that be? He shot her at least eight times centre mass and she didn't go down!"

Steven ignored the guard's question and fought against the tide of attendees which were trying to reach the incredible show. He had to reach Jackie and get her to safety!

"Whoa, slow down, son!" warned barn door. Pistol in

hand, he was aiming at the ground. Men of his kind were not prone to panic under any circumstances.

"Please, I have to get Jackie and get the fuck out of here! There are people being eaten alive back there!"

"Yeah, good one, kid."

"I know you're upset, but a little fake blood isn't going to make us risk our jobs."

Steven wiped at his torn chest and stomach, holding the dripping hand out to the men. "Does this look fake to you?"

"I've seen at least a dozen tables selling bottled makeup blood. You're going to have to do better than that," said smaller barn door.

"You've got to let me pass!"

Trying to dodge between the men proved as successful as trying to ice skate uphill. Solid arms turned him around and gently pushed him away. They knew love could do crazy things to people and didn't want to hurt the spurned youth unless absolutely necessary.

"Holy shit! Are those footprints?" gasped barn door, reaching out.

Steven tried to look over his shoulder at the damage. *You're not an owl, dumbass.* Twisting his arm behind his back instead, he winced at the tender spots of damaged muscle.

"That's not makeup," said smaller barn door. "Over here, kid."

Pulling him to the side, they showed him to a floor to ceiling mirror. The twin purple patches of heavy bruising were unmistakably foot shaped.

"That's where the guy jumped on me. Do you believe me now?"

Barn door ran a fingertip across Steven's chest wound and sniffed at the scarlet liquid. With a single look, the smaller man withdrew his own pistol and scanned down the hallway for threats. Keeping the guns at high ready to prevent undue danger to the guests, they both moved towards the velvet curtains. Rapid gunfire of varying calibers barked from the entrance to the dining area. The security guards were unloading everything they had into the room. Surging through the doors, the cannibals shrieked and gibbered, tearing at anyone in range. Finally, the crowd of onlookers could see the creatures. Up close, the flesh torn away by ravenous teeth was real. The blood spraying all over their costumes was real. The monsters were real! A single scream grew into a chorus of pandemonium as the crowd scattered in all directions. Men and women that were too slow were trampled underfoot in the chaotic retreat.

"We have to do something!" shouted Steven over the din.

The crippling fear for Jackie's welfare was still at the forefront of his mind, but the innocent blood being spilled couldn't be ignored. Dozens were dying in front of their very eyes; men, women, old, young, all fell to the ferocity of the psychopaths.

"Kid, what's your name?" asked barn door, ushering people towards the emergency exit.

"Steven."

"I'm TJ and that's Shawn. We'll hold them here while you get Jackie. You can leave Mason for all I care."

"Do you have a spare gun?"

"No, sorry. Get moving!"

Three older guests had pulled their own concealed carry firearms and were shooting into the swarming mass. Bullets hammered into the bodies but did nothing to stop the feeding frenzy.

"How the fuck is that possible?" gasped Shawn.

A stray shot hit one of the women in the temple, snapping her head sideways as the bullet exited the skull. Her lifeless body collapsed amongst the deadly brawl.

The passageway had emptied and injured people tried to crawl away or lay unconscious on the marble floor. Finally, they could see the horrifically shredded bodies of the first responders who were also eating the fallen. That they were dead was undeniable. No one could live without a throat. A female paramedic crammed chunks of dripping flesh into her mouth, chewed, and then swallowed, only to have it fall from the gaping trachea. The brave guests were trying to reload, but never got the chance. Losing interest in the dead security at their feet, they swarmed over the new targets. The screams of pain were short and shrill.

Using the distraction, Steven ran to the display cabinet housing the infamous machete. A small lock required a key that wasn't in his possession.

"Move!" yelled TJ before firing a single shot, destroying the glass.

Reaching inside, Steven took the weapon and looked it over. The blade was razor sharp, which surprised him considering it was a movie prop. *It could be just an imitation*, he considered, *and was sharpened to look the part for any public appearance*. Regardless, he was glad for the scant protection it offered. A heavy hand closed over his shoulder, pulling him backwards.

"We need to get clear," whispered Shawn.

"The rear parking lot was empty except for the guy that attacked me."

"That's good enough for me. Go!"

Backtracking through the curtains while the monsters fed, they found the others without a care in the world. Mason was laughing at some inane comment by Jackie. Anne was trying to make small talk with the photographer while shooting withering glances at the floozie who'd messed up her schedule. Seeing Steven, she went berserk.

"What the hell are you doing?" Anne demanded, marching over.

"I'm trying to save your lives!"

She glanced over his bloodied torso, making the same mistake as the guards. "Why the hell have you taken your shirt off and poured fake blood over yourself?"

"Shhhh!" TJ hissed, holding a finger to his lips.

"What do you mean, shhhh? I told you I wanted him gone and you've brought him back. And with a fucking weapon!"

"There's a situation. I need you to be quiet and follow me."

"There's some kind of outbreak," Shawn whispered. "People are killing each other and we have to get out of here."

"Don't be ridiculous, it's a horror convention. There'll be people cos-playing and putting on a show. Besides, isn't it time for the zombie walk?"

"This isn't a fucking zombie walk! People are killing each other!" Steven argued.

Moving around the table, he tried to take Jackie by the hand. She pulled away with a look of disgust and moved closer to Mason who laughed scornfully.

"You look even more of a loser than you did before. That's impressive."

"I'm not going home with you, so just get lost! I wish I'd never met you!"

Steven could feel his heart tearing in two. Eyes that had once favored him with desire now scowled with malice. The photo had been a chance to show his affection and it had cost him everything. Feeling the comforting weight of the handle, he found himself circling the table towards the man who would happily fuck his girlfriend. The glint of the blade caught Mason's attention and for the first time his contemptuous façade slipped. A look of fear passed over his face until Anne intervened.

"Get away from him, you lunatic," she yelled, pushing him in the chest with the clipboard. "How dare you threaten Mason Force?"

TJ pulled him away and Shawn placed a restraining hand over Anne's mouth. Speaking directly into her ear, he said, "We don't want to draw attention to ourselves. Those things have killed the floor security and I want to get you all out through the back doors while we still can."

"This better not be a joke. If I find out you've come up with this to help him, I'll have your asses," Mason sneered.

Tiring of the obnoxious actor, TJ let Steven go and Mason blanched as he moved towards him again. Even in imminent danger, the two military men exchanged a look of amusement. Raising the chopper, Steven pointed it directly at Mason's exquisite face while he approached, step by menacing step.

"I've been attacked by a man who could leap over cars without breaking his stride. I've seen a friend have his throat torn out trying to help me. I've seen people ripped apart and eaten while they're still alive."

"Steven, this isn't funny."

"He's not joking. There have been massive casualties and we need to go. *Now!*" TJ ordered in a voice that brooked no argument.

"I'll check the way's clear."

Shawn listened at the rear access door until he was satisfied no threat lurked beyond. Leading with the Glock, he swept left and right before nodding. A slight flutter caught his eye on the inner curtains. Something had moved into the small passage separating the two sets of drapes and a muffled growl confirmed the source wasn't human.

"Hurry!" TJ hissed quietly enough to be barely audible. The frantically waving hand ushering them through was enough to get the civilians moving like their asses were on fire. He tried to yank the door most of the way closed before silently latching it, but the obstinate slow closure mechanism above fought him every inch of the way. Before the door fully met the frame, a bloodied, incomplete face pushed past the curtain. Locking eyes through the slowly shrinking gap, it screamed in fury and raced across the short distance. Driven by inhuman needs, it lacked the cognition to simply reach through the crack and peel the door open. Slamming into the wood like a battering ram, the remaining sliver snapped shut with a deafening crack. Shawn had been poised to open fire, but instead reached up and slipped the thick metal bolts home.

"It's a fire door, it'll hold for a while. Let's go!"

The creature's cries had summoned more of its companions who all started to throw themselves against the barricade. Hollow thuds echoed down the service corridor as TJ pushed the survivors onward. Coming to a complete stop, he slowly turned his head in disbelief. The thuds were accompanied by the sound of splintering; the pop and crack of straining wood as it was pushed past its limit. With a thunderous roar, the whole frame burst from its housing. Scrabbling bodies spilled into the passageway, clawing and biting each other.

"Get out of here!" yelled Shawn over the shrieking din.

"We'll hold them for as long as we can!" TJ barked, taking a shooter's stance.

Steven took up position next to the two men, machete clasped tightly over his shoulder ready to swing.

"Get the fuck out of here! You need to get Jackie and the others to safety!"

"I can help!"

Shawn smiled at the brave youth. "We can't win this, buddy. You need to take over and get them clear, do you understand?"

It was a statement that said; *goodbye*. Their last stand would buy the others a small window of opportunity to escape. Steven had no words. Giving them a tearful nod, he sprinted after the others.

"Well if this don't beat all, brother," TJ muttered.

"What a complete clusterfuck," Shawn sighed as the first creatures escaped the pile of scuffling monsters.

The Glock bucked in his hands, the slug hitting a female cop in the shoulder which sent her pirouetting back into the crush. A young girl dressed like Samara from *The Ring* took two in the heart. The force of the impacts knocked her to the ground, but in a split second she was back on her feet.

"Remember the old folks outside, a headshot was the only thing that stops them!" shouted TJ.

Aiming the sight directly at its forehead, he squeezed the trigger. The lank, black hair jumped as the bullet punched cleanly through her head. Crumpling to the floor, she didn't move. Muscle memory kicked in and they took careful aim as each new target presented itself. Lacking any sense of self preservation, the monsters came straight on into the hot lead. Round after round spat from the barrels, killing indiscriminately. Drawn by the sharp cracks, the numbers were unceasing. The piled corpses at the shattered door were acting as a temporary blockage to the newcomers who gathered in the photo room.

As the last shot rang out and the slide stop locked in place, Shawn looked across at TJ and showed him the empty gun. "I'm out."

"Three left," he replied, holding up his fingers.

"Let's get while the getting's good!" he shouted, unable to make out the words through the ringing in his ears.

TJ nodded. "Let's go!"

Spinning on their heels, the spent casings and empty magazines went flying across the carpet. Elation at the chance of survival died at the sight before them. Obscured by the loss of hearing, a swarm of the cannibals were flowing their way. Pushing, tearing, or leaping over each other in the haste to feed, the tide washed over the pair before they could even cry out.

∼

Steven led the way, preparing for an attack from any doorway or alcove. The sounds of gunfire followed them as they fled down the serpentine hallways. Catching the scent of cooking, he followed the smells to the massive hotel kitchen. Stainless steel as far as the eye could see waited beyond the swing doors. Unattended pots seethed and bubbled on the ranges. Smoke was starting to issue from the vents of an oven in the far corner.

"Where is everyone?" asked Anne.

"They probably got the hell out of here which is what we should be doing!" Mason blurted.

"I'm working on it."

Mason rounded on his PA. "Then work harder! I'm far too important to be caught up in this shit."

"Calm down or they'll hear you," Steven grumbled, peeking through a small glass window. "Shit!" He quickly ducked out of sight. It was the entrance to the dining room for the wait staff to use. A dozen of the things were skulking around, sniffing at the scattered meat and spilled blood.

"What is it?" whispered the photographer.

"They're in there. Come on, let's try the other doors. Stay low."

Mason scurried towards him on hands and knees, closely followed by Jackie, his new shadow. "Give me the machete!"

"Fuck off."

"Give it to me, now. You haven't got any experience of this kind of thing."

Steven shook his head in disbelief before moving towards another exit. "And you have?"

"Yes. If you'd bothered to watch my films I've fought all kinds of monsters."

"You've got to be kidding me? You think acting the tough guy makes you one?"

"More than a fucking loser like you, yeah," he sneered.

"Shut up and keep down, asshole."

Hearing a clatter, Steven turned to see the star wielding a carving knife. "I'll take that chopper. *Now.*"

"Are you nuts? They're going to hear you!"

Jackie crawled forward, glaring at him. "Just give it to him, Steven. He's a lot stronger than you and I want him to protect me."

"This really isn't the time for an argument," warned Anne.

A sudden, shrill wail caused them all to jump in fright. The smoke alarm on the ceiling had been triggered by the scorched entrée in the oven. Covering their ears to try and block out some of the noise, they scurried towards the other exit.

"Oh my God!" screamed the photographer who'd chanced a look over the countertop. A face was pressed to the circular glass, missing its nose and lips. Blood poured from what was left of its mouth as it shrieked. The door swung open, crashing against the wall. Taking two steps, it launched itself across the steel work table, landing on the poor woman. Its trailing leg caught a saucepan, dragging the bubbling contents from the burning ring. The tomato sauce splashed everywhere, coating the two thrashing bodies. The screams of pain rose to a crescendo of agony as her skin blistered and the dead man bit down on her scalded arm. Mixed with the warning siren were the cries of the other dining room dwellers. One by one they slammed through the door until the hinges gave up completely and it went clattering across the tiled floor. Drawn to the uneven struggle of the dying woman, they tore her apart in seconds. Anne vomited at the sounds of rending flesh which carried over the piercing alarm.

"I can't die here!" muttered Mason, staring at the machete.

Steven was desperately trying to think of a way out without being seen. The route to the closest door would leave them visible to the feasting creatures and the other exits were too far away. With the speed of their adversary, they would have no chance of getting close. Searing pain traced its way up Steven's right arm and his unresponsive fingers released the machete. A gaping wound stretched across the pale skin, showing severed tendons and spurting veins.

"Mason, what the hell are you doing?"

Tossing the blood streaked knife aside, he claimed the machete with a smile of grim satisfaction. Turning to his shocked PA, he replied, "I'm surviving."

Dragging Jackie behind him, they barged through the door and were gone. By some miracle the creatures had been intent on their meal and missed the rapid escape.

Anne was too scared to move. Steven was quickly weakening and slumped to the floor in a growing pool of crimson. He stared at her with a mixture of sadness and fear.

"I'm so sorry," she sobbed as the shadows moved in their direction.

∾

"Why'd you have to do that?" Jackie whined.

"Because he's a nobody and I'm a living legend. Just be grateful I'm saving you and not leaving you behind as well."

"But he could be really hurt!"

"Fine! Go back and help him, but I'm out of here, you ungrateful bitch!"

"I'm sorry, Mason, I didn't mean to upset you. I want to get out of here and go home just as much as you do."

"Then keep your mouth shut and follow me," he snapped.

Hanging from the ceiling was a sign with a glowing green *EXIT* illuminated. Placing both hands on the panic bar, Mason waited for a few seconds. Unable to hear anything of the outside world over the squalling cacophony, he ground his teeth in frustration. Anything could be waiting on the other side of the door.

"Fuck!"

"What's wrong?" Jackie asked fearfully.

"Your fucking questions! Shut up and let me think!"

Their best chance was to make it below to the underground garage where his limousine and driver were waiting.

There was no way to make it back through the lobby and down the elevator without being devoured. If they could make it to the ramp without being seen, there was only a flimsy barrier standing in the way. This route was the only option, regardless of what may be lurking beyond.

"Come on."

Pressing down on the cold steel, he gently eased the door open. Daylight poured in, and with it the sounds of chaos which had been held at bay. Taking cover behind a well-tended rose bush, they watched the carnage unfold. Uninjured guests were careening around the parking lot, crashing into cars and creatures alike until they crippled their vehicles. Squad cars raced up the main street which ran alongside the hotel grounds. Gunshots chattered from the other side of the complex where people, including the arriving police officers, were doing battle with the dead. Glass shattered, preceding screams of abject terror as the occupants of the stricken vehicles were overwhelmed.

"Quickly, we can get away while they're eating!"

Jackie winced inwardly at his brutal narcissism. The cries of the victims pursued them as they moved from bush to bush, hiding in the shadows. Scores of the infected ran towards any stimuli, be it living flesh or noise.

"We're nearly there," whispered Mason, pointing to a gradual decline in the road that angled away to the right.

"How do we know they aren't waiting down there for us?"

"They don't lay traps, you idiot. They chase you and murder you."

"I didn't mean it like that," she whimpered. "I meant how do we know there aren't any down there just searching for people. Your driver is by the car, so he could've been attacked."

"He'd better be sat behind the wheel with the engine running if he knows what's good for him!"

"What if they've smashed the windows and killed him?"

"Impossible. My limo is top of the line, like the ones they use for politicians and stuff. Not even bullets can break the windows, so a few psychos wouldn't stand a chance."

A small group charged past, intent on the diminishing cracks of pistols and shotguns. Those surrounding the vehicles were rapt upon their feast.

"Now's our chance."

Darting from the foliage, he didn't even check to see if she was following. The patter of her footsteps crunching over the sun-baked earth confirmed her continued obedience and he allowed himself a sly grin. The celebrities always made it out alive, and his luck so far proved it beyond all doubt. Moving into the shadows of the subterranean garage, the barrier had already been broken. Blood trickled down the glass of the attendant booth and ran out to pool in the road. Tire tracks ran directly through the crimson puddle, tracing a line back into the light.

"They've been here!" Jackie whispered, pulling on his shirt.

"They've been everywhere. Just shut the fuck up while I take a look."

Staying close to the wall, Mason scouted ahead. The structure was eerily quiet after the bedlam of the hotel and grounds. Trying to listen for any sign of movement, all that presented itself was the cessation of the armed resistance above. *Pussies! But at least you made a good distraction for me.* Nothing appeared to be moving between the cars, so he quickly scurried to the first row. Expensive models far in excess of anything the schmucks who paid to see him could afford lined the garage. His Cadillac limousine was given its own space closer to the elevators about fifty yards away. Only VIPs could use the cordoned off area and they didn't come much more important than Mason Force. Dropping to the ground, he peered beneath the empty vehicles. More than a few bodies lay unmoving. Brains and skull were visible as was the glint of empty brass casings.

"There's been trouble down here."

"Are we safe?"

"I can't see anything else moving. I think they were drawn to the cops."

"Then we're going to make it?" she asked hopefully.

Ignoring her, Mason carried on crawling, careful to keep the machete from clanging on the concrete. His thousand-dollar designer jeans were ruined and the grime under the immaculately manicured fingernails set his teeth on edge. If there was one thing he hated, it was dirt. It took every ounce of willpower to ignore the wing mirrors. A cursory inspection right now would likely reveal blood and filth that would bring him out in hives. Jackie could wash him down when they made it safely back to his adequate, five-star hotel. It was the least he would expect to repay the debt of saving her life.

"Is it much further?" Jackie whispered.

"About five cars away," he replied. "Hold still a minute."

Peering beneath the undercarriages again, he glimpsed a pair of polished black shoes and immaculately pressed trousers. The disembodied legs walked away, disappearing behind a concrete column. The uniform that had been visible bore no bloodstains or signs of struggle like the freaks outside. This close to safety, Mason gave up the stealth routine and rose to his feet. The driver emerged from the wide, grey stanchion and the back of his suit jacket was similarly unscathed. He'd been having a crafty cigarette!

After all the warnings of the stench carrying into the rear of the limo, the insubordinate prick had still chosen to ignore him. When they were safely away from this place, the unemployment line beckoned.

"Bob, what the fuck are you doing? I've told you about smoking on the job!"

"Mason, I don't like this," whined Jackie.

"Bob! I'm talking to you, asshole! Get the fucking car open and get me out of here!"

It didn't immediately register that the chauffeur was twitching uncontrollably as he stumbled along. His whole body shook from the spasms which pulsed through his body. Head cocking to the left, he slowly turned. Mason whimpered in horror and started to back away. A mixture of vomit tinged with blood poured from Bob's gaping mouth, soaking the front of his jacket. Vacant eyes stared from the leaden grey face.

"Oh God, no!" Jackie shrieked.

Catching sight of the terrified duo, Bob howled in reply and launched himself into the air. Reacting instinctively, Mason swung the machete into the descending creature with every ounce of terror aided strength he could summon. The blade buried itself deeply in Bob's flank with a wet thud, cutting through ribs and organs. Unfazed by the wound, the momentum of the jump carried him forward. Slamming into the ground, Mason could only gasp as the air was crushed from his lungs. *How can this be happening to me? The star always wins,* he thought as the snarling mouth descended towards his beautiful face.

"Get off him!" screamed Jackie, catching Bob's ponytail before the snapping teeth could find purchase.

Rounding on the teenager, he snarled and pounced. Driven back into the limo by his attack, she felt a sickening crunch in her upper spine. Suddenly, her legs felt like jelly and she collapsed under the driver's weight.

"Help me!"

Mason pulled himself to his feet and hesitated, clutching at his aching chest. Facing an opponent driven by insatiable hunger and rage, her futile attempts to hold Bob away failed. As his teeth bit down, a white-hot agony seemed to explode from the side of Jackie's face. Pulling away, he chewed eagerly on the flesh. Inured by the shock, Jackie probed at the wound with her tongue. It met no resistance where the cheek used to be, just a ragged flap at the gum lines.

"Sorry," Mason mouthed.

As Bob dove in for another bite, he glanced around in panic. Footsteps hammered on the ramp from the monsters who had been summoned by the screams. Ten, twenty, then more came streaming down towards him. *You've got to do this yourself, buddy. You're the hero, after all.* Flinging the door open, he jumped into the driver's seat and pulled it closed. Pressing the lock button, he could hear the satisfying sound of reinforced bolts sliding into place. Outside, Jackie was still struggling feebly. Her face was completely gone; only a skinless, ravaged skull remaining, topped by blonde hair.

"Better you than me," Mason sighed. Lips curling into a smile, he started to laugh hysterically. An unhealthy, crazed tone mingled with the elation and he fell silent. *Can't be losing it. Not this close to safety.*

Like a tsunami, the other creatures flooded over the car to get at the tender meat. Their madly flailing forms completely obscured the final moments of his young fan's life.

"Time to get out of here, Mason. Your adoring public needs the next installment of Death Party."

Reaching for the key, the ignition was empty.

"No! No! No! They have to be here!"

Pulling the sun visor down yielded nothing. Glove box? Nothing. Footwells? Nothing. Under the seats? Nothing. In the ashtray? Nothing.

"Did you get in the back and relax? Try and feel what it's like to be important for a few hours? I bet you did!"

Climbing through the privacy window, he checked in every nook and cranny. Nothing, except for a half-eaten bacon sandwich sequestered in the small refrigerator.

"Fuck!"

Fists started to hammer on the reinforced windows. Dead faces glared in at him, biting at the glass. Every inch of the luxury vehicle was surrounded. As the minutes passed, more of the freaks joined the fray. Mason was frantically thinking of any hiding spot that he could have overlooked when a glint of fluorescent light caught something metallic laid on the ground outside. The set of keys had been in plain sight next to Jackie's body the whole time.

"Why didn't you check? You should've seen them, you idiot!"

Taking long, deep breaths to calm his racing heart, he considered the situation. All he had to do was wait for the National Guard to regain control and they would save him.

"No need to panic."

The monsters couldn't get to him, and he couldn't get out, which was fine. It was just a matter of time. From the red stained concrete, the smiling face of Bob's wife stared at him from a key ring. Her pretty face had taken on an ominous, mocking quality and Mason had to look away.

~

Hours passed, and the underground garage filled with countless numbers of the frenzied cannibals. As the sun faded in the world above, the undead pestilence spread like wildfire, consuming every living thing.

"It won't be long now," Mason muttered, feeling the twinges of hunger pangs. *I can always eat that sandwich if I get too hungry,* he thought, staring at the fridge.

∼

Ricky Fleet

Ricky Fleet has been a lifelong horror fan. One dark night, many years ago, he 'borrowed' a copy of Salem's Lot from his mum's bedside table. Sneaking it into his room, the terrifying visage of Barlow gazed out from the cover. Doomed townsfolk stretched into the distance, and in bold, silver font was a name - Stephen King. The story contained within those pages spawned an appetite for horror that has yet to be sated. Masterton, Lumley, Koontz, Laws, Herbert, Hutson, Laymon, Barker, and many more have influenced both his life and his writing.

After spending years working in the plumbing and gas trade, he then decided to start teaching, passing on his knowledge to the next generation of engineers.

Born and raised in the UK, cups of tea are a non-negotiable staple of the English life and serve as brain fuel for his first love - writing.

With the Hellspawn series being enjoyed across the world, the growing saga has a dark edge that begins to explore the true horror of a world without rules. A nod to the master, George A. Romero. the only thing running on his zombies are the fluids of decay. What they lack in velocity, they more than make up for with utter remorselessness and insatiable hunger.

Infernal – Emergence is the first in his new demon series. A tale of conspiracy, untapped powers and the vast armies of Hell who yearn to tear our world apart. Only one man stands in their way; he just doesn't know it yet.

Today he shares his time between his real-life students, and the students of the zombie apocalypse in Hellspawn. At least the fictional students do as they're told. Most of the time, anyway.

Ricky's books are on Amazon and you can find him clowning around on Facebook.

6

CATCH-A-ZOMBIE

GREG BENNETT

"So what the fuck are we supposed to do?"

"I don't know, man. I don't know."

Joe was getting pissed and rightly so. The summer heat just added to his frustration.

We were part of a tech group at the Sanderson Research Center. After the initial zombie outbreak was somewhat contained, scientists and medical experts focused on trying to understand how the zombies' bodies functioned. To understand what enabled them to move so quickly. Initially, inactive zombies were okay for research, but gradually the experts needed moving subjects.

That's where we came in. Our job was to go out, find some active zombies and bring one back, mostly in one piece. They wanted a larger specimen with the muscles and tendons intact, if possible. Oh, and by the way, to do it without getting bitten. The problem is, nobody really told us how to do it. "Just go get one," the tech manager ordered.

So, here we were, roasting our asses in one of the maintenance trucks trying to figure out what to do.

"Those fuckers are faaaaast," Joe said. "They can hit

almost 20 miles an hour; we'll have to use the truck to stay ahead of 'em."

"I know," I replied. "And that'll be the easy part. It's gonna be tough getting one into the back of the truck and secured."

Joe got his patented 'idea with no thought' look on his face. "What if we take one of the maintenance safety harnesses, strap me standing up in the truck bed and use a rope to lasso one of 'em?"

"When did you become Roy Fuckin' Rodgers, you dipshit? You're lucky to tie your boots, much less lasso a zombie outta a bunch chasing us," I replied. "We're gonna need to somehow grab one and get it in the truck."

"Or grab one and hang on to it," said Joe, slowly pointing at the rear of the maintenance building.

It was the old International logging truck. They'd used it while clearing out the land for the Research Center years ago. It had one of those long-reaching arms with some big-ass jaws that picked up logs and stacked them on the truck.

"Look," said Joe. "We get the maintenance guys to help get it started and build a cage around the control seat. I'll operate the arm from the cage and you drive. We go out, find some zombie stragglers and back up toward them honking the horn to get their attention. When they start chasing, you'll drive away just fast enough to keep us from being caught and I'll snatch one with the jaws. It'll be just like picking toys at that fuckin' carnival game."

"Which you suck at," I replied.

"We could play Sling the Zombie. Could be some fuckin' fun, man," Joe said.

I had to admit, it was a pretty good plan, especially from Joe.

"Shit, I've always wanted to be a Zombie Picker," I said. "Let's go have some fun."

Greg Bennett

Greg Bennett writes badly…and that's okay. He knows he's not a real author; but that doesn't stop him from having a little fun pretending to be one.

His day work involves developing and testing product for a major manufacturing company in the Midwest. When he's not blowing things up in the Lab, he spends his free time working on home projects, playing golf or getting leg cramps on his bicycle.

He enjoys classic rock music, occasional reading and B-movies of the horror and science fiction genres. His relationship with his cat, Jango, can be best described as "mutual toleration". He and his wife live in Kearney, Missouri, just a stone's throw from Kansas City.

7

CONDEMNED

CHRISTOPHER ARTINIAN

"We're down to fifty gallons of diesel for the two emergency generators. Food supplies... we've got ten days if we're steady, but if we bring anyone else in, that goes down. The water is okay, it's been pissing it down for the last week, but there's a bigger problem." The young man paused. He stood there in his black jeans and t-shirt, waiting for the grizzled figure behind the desk to stop massaging his temples. The pause went on too long.

"I'm waiting. You've got my fucking attention, don't worry," said Frank as he finally looked up at the messenger.

"Rats." Another pause. "Rats are becoming a real problem, Frank. We should have dealt with them when we found them on the ground floor, but they're getting more confident... more aggressive."

"Anything else?"

"Erm... no," replied the young man.

"Right, all duly noted. I'll get on it," said Frank.

The young man turned and left, shutting the door behind him. The drizzly sky bled through the dirty windows of the small room on the first floor that Frank had made his office. He reached into the bottom drawer of his desk and pulled out a half empty bottle of vodka and a glass. He poured himself a shot. A double. A triple. Then he took a swig. He winced as the liquid burnt his throat, and he sat back in the creaky office chair.

"Fuck!" he said, feeling his age, feeling the responsibility of the two hundred plus inhabitants of Shipley Tower weighing heavily on his shoulders. He took another drink, this time wincing less, and followed it with a deep shuddery breath. Cold mist shot from his lips like white smoke. On top of everything else, he knew the cold would finish off a few of the older folks, and before winter even got into its full throes.

"Fuck!" he coughed, pulling a pack of cigarettes from his shirt pocket. He brought one up to his mouth, and lit it with the all-weather lighter he had found on their last supply run. He took a long drag and blew out a plume of rich blue smoke. He drained his glass too quickly and spluttered into a coughing fit.

"Fuck!" he said again, this time bringing his hand up to his mouth and wiping away a thin line of blood. He took another long drag on his cigarette and got up from his chair. It coasted over the carpet to the window, and he went to retrieve it, pausing long enough to look out at the grey morning. It looked like any other dull English morning, no different than before the... outbreak. The grass was a little more overgrown, and the pavement had wine coloured stains that no rain could wash away, but for the most part, little had changed. Frank looked over at one of the sister buildings. They had been abandoned at the same time. A few months before everything had gone to hell. Their ground floor windows and doors covered by stainless steel shutters making them almost impregnable to outside forces, living or dead.

Frank had been the caretaker of this complex for over twenty years. When the blocks were finally condemned, the council had kept him on for a while to help with the closing down, the shuttering up. Everyone had called them deathtraps. Who knew they would now be the salvation of the desperate. He poured himself another shot, smoking his cigarette while he finished off the vodka and then headed for the door. The corridor was dark, but he knew this place better than anywhere. There were still some flats not taken on this first floor, and the doors were left open allowing a little light to seep in. People thought the higher up they were, the safer they were. Just in case they got in... the risen. Frank walked into one of the flats. He took a final drag on his cigarette and coughed as he stubbed it out on the base of his shoe and flung it to the floor.

Charlie, the young guy who had just reported to him, hadn't been kidding. The place stank and there were even rat droppings on the kitchen work surfaces. He would have to get some poison on the next trip out. It wouldn't be a problem. When the world ends, the last thing people think about is pest control. How had he let things get so bad? He was the caretaker; he was responsible for everything that went on here, responsible for all these people. Frank heard a sound and turned around quickly.

"It's just me, Frank."

"Bloody 'ell, Liza. What're you trying to do to me, love?"

"Sorry," she said, and they both laughed. "I was speaking to Charlie. Sounds like we need to go out on another run."

"Yep," he said, surveying the flat once again.

Liza flicked her long brown hair back and pulled a rubber band from her pocket. She looped it round and made a pony tail. Her eyes met Frank's, and they both smiled. She sniffed the air. "You been smoking again, old man?" she asked, breaking the moment.

He rubbed his sandpaper chin. "Found one in my jacket. It was a shame to let it go to waste."

She walked across to him and put her hand out. "Give them to me, Frank."

He reached into his shirt pocket and handed her the packet. "Fuck's sake."

"If you think I'm gonna smooch with someone who smells like an ashtray at the Christmas party, you're very much mistaken," she said with a cheeky smile. "How's the cough anyway?" she asked, her smile hiding the concern that resonated through her words.

"Fine. Colder weather doesn't help. It's probably an allergy or something. Maybe there's some toxic mould under my bed," he said with a half-smile.

"Yeah," she replied, "toxic mould my arse. So, you don't wanna talk about it. Fair enough. How about telling me when the next run is," she said, the warmth leaving her face.

"It's just a cough Liza, don't get het up. And the run… we could do with that ASAP," he said.

"Ok," she said, "I'll arrange it." She turned to leave. "I'll get a list together."

"Make sure you put rat poison and traps on there will you, sweetheart?"

"No problem. I'll put cough medicine and allergy pills on there, too, shall I, Frank?" She left before he could reply.

∽

It was even colder the following day. Frank knew he didn't need to chase Liza to make the arrangements. When he said as soon as possible, they both knew that meant the next day at dawn. He knew she'd have a list of all the urgent stuff, and he knew she'd have a decent crew together for going out. He was already standing by the front door when the torches approached.

"Jesus, fuck!" said Liza, stifling a half scream. "You trying to kill me, Frank?" she said, lowering the torch from his face. "Why the hell do you scuttle around in the dark? You ever heard of a lantern?"

"It's barely six o'clock and already you're nagging. Did I miss something? Did we exchange vows?" asked Frank. The five men and three women with Liza all chuckled.

"Yeah," replied Liza, "we exchanged vows... in your fucking dreams, old man."

"Nightmares more like," he said underneath his breath. "Besides... now you know how it feels when you come creeping up on me." He smiled and winked. "Right. Who's the designated survivor?" He grinned, knowing full well that the term irritated Liza.

"Prick," she replied.

"That's me," said a boy, no more than fifteen.

"Okay son. It's Steven, isn't it?" said Frank. The boy nodded. "Y'know the drill. You stay on guard until we're back. You don't leave this position no matter what. You need to take a piss, you use a bucket. You need to do anything, you do it here. You do not leave this position." Frank paused. "Now, what did I say?"

"I don't leave this position," Steven replied.

"Good lad. Now let's go."

Frank picked up a cordless screwdriver and removed

eight screws from four brackets, and with the help of another man, pulled the stainless-steel shutter to one side. He then did the same with the outer shutter. Before moving it, he pulled a slide across revealing a peep hole. He looked out into the dark morning. There was no movement. He nodded to his companion, and the pair each took hold of a handle before removing the shutter. They let the rest of the crew out, then taking hold of handles on the other side, pushed the shutter back into position. They heard the sound of the cordless screwdriver whir into action, and after a minute, the cover of the peephole slid across. Frank put his thumb up.

"Right," whispered Liza, "everybody knows the drill."

With those words, the entire crew pulled out a variety of weapons ranging from kitchen knives and hatchets to a baseball bat and an ornamental, yet functional, sword. Liza and Frank walked side by side. He carried a 45 cm splitting axe in one hand and a long handled flathead screwdriver in the other, while Liza carried the baseball bat.

The group moved along in silence, always wary of their surroundings, always scouring the landscape. They had only been into town twice, each time they had lost people. Most of their supplies had been scavenged from houses and local shops, but the wants lists were getting bigger and bigger, and something as specialised as rat poison, well… that was going to require a well-stocked hardware store at the very least.

"Frank!" It was a shout that ripped through the grey morning like a rapier through brittle linen. Nine heads turned back to the entrance of Shipley tower. The young lad, Steven, stood in the drizzle, with a look of panic on his face. Eighteen feet pounded back to the entrance of the tower block.

"There's a fire," Steven said as they reached him. "Third floor."

As they ran through the foyer, they could already hear desperate screams from above. The thump of escaping feet resonated throughout the dark corridor as the stairwell door burst open, revealing the first of the escapees.

The rest of the group stayed in the darkness, afraid to climb the staircase, but Frank and Liza clattered up the steps, passing fleeing dwellers as they attempted to reach the source of the furor. As they burst through the third-floor fire escape, they saw the flames lashing out of the apartment doors and licking the ceiling with fiery tongues. The smoke stormed down the hallway as barely legal insulation combusted in the walls and made toxic vapours plume. Frank immediately began to splutter, and Liza grabbed him by the scruff of his collar and pulled him back through the door.

"That'll be through this place in no time," he managed to cough. "We need to get everybody downstairs. I'll head up to tell the others."

"No, Frank. I'll go, I'll be quicker."

He tried to argue but Liza was vaulting three steps at a time before he could even catch a breath. Happy the third floor was already evacuated, he headed back down to the lobby. Flickering lights greeted him; Steven had thought ahead and lit a few of the lanterns. Frank breathed a small sigh of relief that at least someone was showing common sense.

Frank heard more running feet behind him as fleeing residents rushed out of the stairwell into the reception area. Screams went up as windows exploded a few floors above. The sound was followed by the crashing of shattered glass on the pavement outside the shuttered door.

Frank scratched his whiskered cheek as he thought. The group who had been ready to go on the scavenging mission walked up to him.

Charlie said, "People are panicking, what do we do?"

"We can't fight the fire; we don't have the resources. We're going to have to head to one of the other blocks and hope to Christ the flames don't jump. How the fuck did it start anyway?" He looked around at the faces. They knew, but they didn't say. They didn't want to point fingers. "Not that it matters now." He shook his head. "Okay, Charlie, I want two people on the door. The rest of you head across to Bingley Tower. Take the screwdriver, get the shutters off and get inside. I'll wait here for Liza, and when we're sure we've got everyone, we'll head across." He paused to make sure they were all listening. "Grab what supplies you can from the store room before you head out, but everybody here knows what the priority is, yes?" He looked around and they all nodded.

He watched as more residents came flooding from the staircase. Panic and agitation were ingrained on their faces. He turned his head as he heard the screwdriver begin to unscrew the shutters. The metal clunked against the wall as it was placed to one side, and bodies surged out into the grey light. The smell of acrid smoke flooded the air, and Frank looked back to the staircase eager to see Liza re-emerge.

When a scream from outside echoed through the foyer, he thought someone had been hit by a piece of falling glass. He turned toward the open doorway letting in pallid light and everything powered down to slow motion. He watched as a woman stopped running and froze on the spot. The scream seemed to echo in the wind as a hideous creature dived through the air toward her. Its shriek sending a chilling alarm to all in earshot. It was followed by a chorus of shrieks as other creatures erupted into the song of the dead.

The woman, too terrified to do anything, just stood there. Frank let out a low mutter of sadness as he saw a dark patch form in the crotch of the woman's jeans. He didn't know a lot of the people who lived in the tower. Maybe only a handful of the original inhabitants were still alive, but he knew this woman. Because she was everyone. She was everyone who felt love and hate and fear and despair. Now, in that split second when she not only knew she was going to die, but she had lost her very dignity too. Frank wanted to weep for her... and himself. When the zombie finally hit her, it was with a howling, bloody explosion of violence. She collapsed to the ground, her face toward Frank, he couldn't see from this distance but he felt her tears of sadness wash over him as the beast ripped into her neck like it was nothing more than grilled meat on a drumstick. Her mouth opened to scream a final scream, but she was even robbed of that as her final breath left her.

Frank dropped his head. "Dear God have mercy," he said as he looked back up to see a fleeing family attacked.

He took a despairing last glance toward the stairwell. There was no sign of Liza. The biggest part of him wanted to head to the staircase to find her, but he knew he had to fight. He had to try and stave off the attack of the zombies, otherwise none of them would make it.

Frank began to run toward the door as he noticed a sudden backdraft of residents heading in, wondering whether the prospect of asphyxiation was preferable to being eviscerated at the hands of zombies. He barged past a few stutterers and out into the drizzle. He pulled the hatchet from his belt and took a quick survey of his surroundings.

Half a dozen of the scavenging group were in a pitched battle with a small flock of undead attackers. About ten men, women and children were on the ground, dead or dying. It wouldn't be long before they had to be dealt with, too.

Always methodical, Frank marched up to the woman he had seen die, she was already transforming. Her attacker was long gone, but the signs of her reanimation were clear as her dead eyes suddenly fluttered. He refused to look at those hellish portals to a forgotten soul as he whipped the blade down into her forehead, cracking through the bone like it was an eggshell. A fountain of blood raced the hatchet back out of her skull, but Frank just headed to the next victim. Lying on the ground in the midst of change, or hurtling toward you screeching and baring teeth, they were all threats, they all had to be dealt with.

Another window exploded in the tower, showering all of them with broken glass. A sharp stabbing pain shot through Frank's right shoulder. He moved his left hand up to touch it and felt a large shard embedded there. The agony intensified as he jerked it out, slicing more muscle and tissue. He growled with pain before erupting into another coughing fit.

"Frank!" a voice yelled.

Frank's teary eyes shot toward the doorway of the burning building. "Liza! Oh, thank God."

Liza ran out into the open. The scavenger group had things under control now. They were tidying up the last of the fallen - ending them before they began. She flung her arms around Frank and he winced, but embraced her tightly with his left arm. She pulled away and saw blood all over her sleeve.

"Oh my God, Frank. What's happened?"

"Just some glass. I'll get it patched up in a bit," he replied.

Liza grabbed hold of his arm. "We'll get it patched up right now."

She began to lead him toward the door of their new residence when a sound like a volcano erupting tore through the morning. They both turned toward Shipley Tower. The flames were lashing up the outside of the building.

"Dear God," said Liza as the heat hit her.

There was another muffled boom from inside just as three zombies appeared at the other end of the square.

"Go," said Frank. "Me and the squad will take care of this lot," he said, nodding toward the scavenger team. "You get everybody across and inside the other building.

"No way," she replied, "I'm..."

Frank took a tight hold of her upper arm. "Do as I say, Liza. People follow you. People trust you. Get them safe. I'll take care of the... things."

This time, she didn't argue. Instead, she started leading people across and inside. The steel shutter had been taken off by Charlie. Inside, it smelt damp, it looked dismal. There were none of the luxuries they had enjoyed, like a generator or a food cupboard, but at least it was shelter and it gave them a chance.

She delivered the first group, then sprinted back across the court as she saw Frank and a few others start to hack away at the attacking zombies. She should be grateful it was three and not fifty-three, but she still worried. Many of the people who had gone running back into Shipley Tower were now exiting again, deciding they would prefer to take their chances in the open with the zombies than in the inferno.

"Come on!" she shouted, and began waving her arms as people started running across, seeing that the majority of the undead attackers had been taken care of and a small band of heroes were battling the remainder. "Hurry!" she shouted, mumbling, "you fucking cowards" under her breath. Men, women and children ran across, fearful for their lives, happy for others to take all the risks.

When there was no-one left outside but her and the ones battling the zombies, she ran across to the burning tower, throwing wary glances upward to avoid falling masonry and timber. She sprinted through the entrance. There was no smoke here yet, but she could hear the fire roaring above.

"Hello?!" When she was sure there was no-one left inside, she dashed back out into the open and headed toward Frank and the others, just as the final zombie collapsed. "C'mon," she shouted over the grinding sound of metal girders giving way.

The group began to follow her as they beat a path toward their new home. Then a chorus of shrieks exploded through the smoke-stenched air. A small army of zombies darted into the square and started heading straight for them. Frank quickly realized the creatures would be on them before they had time to re-barricade the door. He stopped.

Sensing it rather than seeing it, Liza turned to see what he was doing. She stopped, too. "Frank. Come on!"

"We both know this isn't an allergy I've got sweetheart. Keep them safe. Keep them all safe. I know you'll make me proud." He turned and began to jog toward the group of zombies before sharply changing direction and heading toward the burning building. The creatures followed him.

"No! Frank!"

Seeing what was going on, two of the other group members grabbed Liza by her arms and forced her to run. She struggled and burst out crying, but relented. She had been happy to live in denial. She knew Frank did not have an allergy. She had seen her mother go the same way. There was no chemo or radiotherapy now. He didn't have long left. Deep down she knew it. That's what made it all the more sad. She had been saying goodbye to him for months, and now she had been deprived of that final farewell.

They were just about to head through the entrance to their new home when she managed to break free. She turned and saw Frank as the clutch of zombies were gaining on him. Another window exploded in the burning tower as he disappeared through the dark doorway. The zombies followed. A chilling song of shrieks echoed over the roaring sound of the inferno, and the chiming of falling glass. Liza's head fell. Her tears streamed onto her chest and an arm reached around her shoulder and gently guided her toward the door.

Another window shattered in the tower, but the sound was a little different than before. There was no thunderous whoosh following it, just a muffled clatter. Liza turned to see it was on the ground floor and a high backed office chair was coming to rest on the ground outside, as Frank climbed and stumbled through the gap it had created.

Liza gasped as Frank began to run towards her. She couldn't hear his coughing and spluttering over the throng of noise, but she could see he was struggling. Suddenly two figures flanked her and began sprinting toward Frank. They were members of the scavenger team from earlier. They reached him, and he gratefully put an arm around each of their shoulders as the three of them headed toward the door. Frank's feet occasionally stumbled, but the two younger men supported him.

"We're fine. Get in!" shouted one of the men as they approached.

The small group disappeared through the opening and the two men, who were now carrying Frank between them as he coughed and struggled for breath, followed a moment later.

They laid Frank down in the dim foyer as the shutter was bolted back into place. Liza knelt down on the floor and cradled Frank while he got his coughing and breathing under control.

"They're fast, but not very bright those things," he muttered between a series of coughs. "I realized, I couldn't go before I taught you the job. Being a caretaker is a bit different now than what it used to be."

"I'm not letting you go anywhere for a while, old man," replied Liza kissing his forehead. "I love you, Frank."

"Yeah, well… you're only human kid." They both smiled.

She shoved him playfully. "I mean it, you funny bastard."

"I know. I love you too, Liza. I always will."

∼

Christopher Artinian

Christopher Artinian was born and raised in Leeds, West Yorkshire. Wanting to escape life in a big city and concentrate more on working to live than living to work, he moved to the Outer Hebrides in the north-west of Scotland in 2004, and has lived there ever since with his wife and dogs.

He released his debut novel, Safe Haven: Rise of the Rams in February 2017. This was the first installment of a post-apocalyptic zombie trilogy. Book two, Safe Haven: Realm of the Raiders continues the fast moving and often terrifying story and book three is expected to be released later in the year.

For fans of the Safe Haven books, a stand-alone short story was released as part of Undead Worlds anthology and another of Christopher's zombie tales was published in the charity anthology, Treasured Chests.

For more information on his past, present and future work find him on the web and Facebook.

8

DEAD LAND

ANN RILEY

A Southern Zombies Tale

"Tell me again why we stopped at this store. It looks creepy," Diane says as we exit the truck.

"We need gas and a few supplies. If you have a better idea, now is the time to let it be known," I tell her.

"I just have a bad feeling about this place."

"How many places have we been to since the zombies came that projected any good feelings?"

I wait for her to roll her eyes at me. Instead she shoots me a glare that says, "Tracie, stop being a smart ass." Her being my older sister always entitles her to reprimand me. Or so she thinks.

"Let's just be quiet, gas up, then if the area is still zombie free, we will go inside and grab a few things. This is a big convenience store in rural Alabama, with no major highways running to and from it, so it couldn't have been ransacked this soon. Could it?" I ask her.

"I hope not. But look around," Diane replies.

"Yeah. It looks like a dead land."

The Texaco convenience store lot looks to have been the scene of a previous battle. Zombie parts are scattered across the parking lot, a couple of burned out cars grace the entrance to the lot, and the brand sign showing the store name has fallen onto the awning above the pumps.

Taking one last look around, I step onto the back bumper and climb into the bed of the truck. Easing myself over to the toolbox, I reach underneath and pull out the hand pump so we can get some gas.

Diane keeps a watch while I take care of the fill up.

"Oh, what I wouldn't give to be able to pump gas normally again," I say with a smile.

Diane snorts.

As I fill our tank, I continue to look around.

Diane's head snaps to her right, and she holds her hand up to me.

"What?"

"I heard something."

"Something?"

"An engine running. Sounds like it's getting closer."

"Well hell."

I took the pump and threw it into the back of the truck.

Before we can decide what to do, I see a horde of about thirty zombies. These aren't your regular shambling, stumbling zombies. These look like they were track stars in their previous life and continued their sport in their undead life.

"What the hell are those?" Diane yells.

"Racers, track stars? Take your pick. Let's go," I tell her.

When I turn to yank the truck door open a tattered green hand, with missing fingernails and fungus sprouting from the empty nail beds, grabs my wrist. I scream and jerk my arm, trying to loosen the grip it has on me. Gary the Grabber seems to be a very tenacious flesh eater as his hold on me tightens and he tries to pull my arm up to his mouth.

"Not today fucker!" I hear Diane yell as her blade slams into Gary's temple.

He drops like a rock, pulling my arm down as he goes. I struggle to free myself from his death grip and am finally rewarded with his fingers breaking off and releasing me.

"That's just nasty," I say.

The truck will be surrounded before we can get in so I grab Diane's hand and start running toward the store.

As we run, I can hear the slapping of bare feet gaining on us and another shot of adrenaline kicks in, making us run faster.

We finally reach the doors but, unable to slow down, we barrel right through them. Saying a quick thank you to the heavens for the doors being unlocked and the kind that open inward, I spin around to shove them closed. I quickly engage the locks at the top and bottom of the double doors, backing away fast.

The zombies slam into the glass doors one by one as they attempt to get to their dinner. Sludge and gore from open wounds, missing skin and partially exposed brains smear across the glass.

"Holy shit! Will the glass break?" Diane asks.

"I don't know. The glass in these doors are fairly strong, or at least they were when I was a store manager, but I'm sure no one ever tested them against a horde of ravenous zombies."

I jump when I hear a gunshot. I look over at Diane, who has her rifle up to her shoulder and a dead zombie on the floor.

"We need to check this place out," I tell her.

"No shit."

The sun is shining high in the sky so the front part of the store is fairly well lit. The back part, however, is not. The sun can only shine so far through the windows that spread across the store front.

"This is not a defendable place. Not with all this glass," I tell Diane.

Slinging my rifle around and bringing it up to my shoulder, I walk to the left and Diane goes right. The banging on the windows continues as we inch our way around the store, looking behind shelving and down aisles as we go.

The back of the store has coolers lining the wall from one end to the other. The stench of soured milk and rotting food reaches our noses at about the same time the face of a zombie slams into what was once the Pepsi section of the cooler. The cooler door flies open, then slowly closes. The shelf inside the door that once held the delicious calorie packed goodness is the only thing holding the zombie inside.

Raising my rifle slightly higher, I drill a hole into the forehead of our stalker, shattering the glass in the door.

Zombie goo sprays across the remnants of the cooler door, adding the pleasant aroma of zombie stench to the curdled milk.

I walk over to the door that leads inside the coolers and look around for the small pin that can be inserted into the outside handle to keep it from being opened from the inside.

Sending another thank you to the heavens, I take the pin, which is hanging loosely by a keyring from a screw in the wall, and slide it into the opening in the handle.

Another shot rings out and I spin to see Diane dropping the cashier, who has sprinted from the back of the darkened store.

"Damn, how many are in here?" she asks.

I don't answer.

"Come help me move these shelves," I tell Diane.

"To where?"

"Well, there is a room back there and from my experience, those rooms are generally used for holding stock. I want to move some of these shelves in front of that door so we can at least slow down any flesh eaters that may be back there. I don't know if the door is shut properly or if any of our new friends have the dexterity to open doors. But I'm in no hurry to find out."

We start pulling shelves that still have a few bags of potato chips, beef jerky, snack cakes and other items on them over to the door.

Walking over to the checkout counter, I grab a plastic bag from the bag holder and go back to start filling it with the snacks and chips.

The zombies are still slamming into the windows, which are apparently stronger than I gave them credit for since they are still intact.

The vibration starts subtly. Sort of like an audio system in a car turned to full volume with a high-priced sub-woofer that is worth more than the whole car itself.

Diane and I look up at the same time.

"You hear that?" she asks.

I nod.

"Is that what you heard earlier?" I ask her.

"Yeah."

The sound of numerous engines approaching makes the windows vibrate and the floor rumble.

"What the hell is that?" I ask.

"I don't know, but there's a whole shitload of them heading this way," Diane says.

Looking back at our truck I can see it has been surrounded by the horde.

"This sure is a shitty set of options we've been presented with," I say.

"Yeah. Go out and be a meal or stay inside and face the threat of idiots who think they rule the world," Diane says.

"Yeah. It just gets better and better."

∾

I look back to the doors that are rattling and being slammed by zombies. The rumbling of engines is beginning to make the whole store vibrate. The zombies are paying no attention to the approaching noise as they have their ravenous sights set on us.

The press of their bodies against the glass is causing the doors to bulge inward.

"What should we do?" Diane asks.

I look around. There is nowhere to hide in this damn store. The only option is the storage room that we tried to barricade, but that door doesn't look too sturdy.

Before I can answer, the vehicle engines we heard are pulling into the parking lot.

"Just fucking great!" I yell.

Diane looks out the window and curses.

Eight pickup trucks, four-wheel drives to be exact, painted in camouflage paint, sporting makeshift gun turrets, smoke stacks and a shitload of rednecks in the back with a driver in each truck, roll slowly into the lot.

They start firing at the zombies who are still interested in their meal that seems to be just out of their reach.

"They will never be able to kill them all," Diane says.

"Probably not."

More ravenous speeding zombies run into the lot, surrounding the trucks.

"These zombies seem to be faster than any we've seen before," I say.

The rednecks continue to fire at the approaching horde, sending arms, legs and brains flying across the lot. It doesn't slow them down, however. They continue to run at the trucks, with a look of hunger on their face. The zombies we've been dealing with are of the slow, ambling, type that will slowly walk their prey down. Not these new ones, though. They have a look of determination that surpasses anything I've seen so far.

"I think we need to move the barricade from the storage room. These glass doors won't hold much longer," I say to Diane.

Before we can turn to do that, we hear a scream. A high-pitched scream normally reserved for women, but since the zombies came, I've learned a man can reach that pitch, too.

We look out and see a zombie has grabbed one of the rednecks in the back of a truck and is trying to pull him out. The man is fighting and trying to kick his attacker, but he's losing the battle. The zombie gives one hard yank, and the redneck topples over the side of the truck, landing dead center of the horde.

Redneck's screams are quickly silenced as the horde ravenously devours him, even gnawing through the bones.

"Holy shit! They are eating every last bit of him," Diane says.

I gag. Normally my stomach is not weak, but the horde rips and tears at his flesh, sending bits flying over their heads. One has latched onto his tongue and is pulling desperately to tear it free.

The rednecks start firing through the glass windows of

the store. The glass begins to shatter as the first rounds hit.

"Let's go. These bastards are going to let them in on us!" I yell.

As we turn to run, the gun shots are silenced and we can hear the approach of more engines.

"There's more of those fuckers coming," Diane says.

The rumbling and vibrations of the engines shake the shattered glass and it begins to fall from the frames. The noise attracts the attention of the zombies trying to get to us and they turn to see what new flesh is on the menu.

The rednecks begin firing again, though not at the store this time. They are firing toward the road.

We hear three round bursts being fired and the rednecks start dropping like flies.

"What is going on?" I scream.

As the rumbling gets louder, we can see a huge semi-truck rolling slowly into the lot. Then another behind it. Then another. Each truck has a man firing from the passenger side window.

The lead truck has a huge blade attached to the front, maybe a dozer blade, or one that fits a snow plow. The man driving plows through the horde with ease, pressing the zombies into the concrete, leaving a smear behind him. Blood, guts and body parts hang from the blade letting me know this man has been doing this for some time.

The semis continue to roll in, firing at the rednecks and the zombies.

"It's a fucking convoy!" I yell.

"Haven't seen one of those in years," Diane says.

"Fucking Convoy of Carnage!" I say with a fist pump.

The truckers continue to roll through, taking out zombies, rednecks and anything else in their way.

We stand at the window, looking on in awe at the

massive semis that have been modified for the sole purpose of zombie elimination.

The horde slowly thins until there are none left in the lot and the rednecks lie scattered in the remnants of zombie gore.

The lead truck stops in front of the store and the driver looks toward us.

I look around to see if the threat is completely gone and cautiously turn the lock to open the doors. I pull it open warily as Diane and I stand in the doorway.

I'm not really sure how, but our truck has gone untouched by all the rounds being fired. Sure, it's covered in zombie sludge, but Marc, my nephew, and the owner of the truck, will have to kiss my ass and get over it.

As we stand there, not knowing the intent of these truckers, the lead driver rolls down his window and gives us a wave.

We wave back and Diane yells out, "Thank you."

The man nods and smiles.

Each truck, in succession, pulls down on their horns giving us a loud blast as they roll on through the lot.

"Holy hell. We got lucky this time," Diane says.

"I don't know if it was luck or divine intervention," I say with a smile.

"Yeah. Maybe a bit of both. Let's get the hell out of here and be on our way. Bobby is going to think we aren't coming for him," she says.

I smile, thinking about my husband who got stuck in Virginia when this shit storm hit.

Diane and I head out of the store and walk cautiously to the truck, watching the truckers leave and saying a silent prayer of thanks for their intervention.

"I forgot our bag of goodies that I gathered," I tell Diane.

She gave me her usual eye roll and cuffed me on the back of my head.

"I love you, too," I tell her.

∼

Ann Riley

Ann Riley is a writer who currently makes her home in Tupelo, MS. with her husband Bobby and their dachshund Riley. She has a full-time job and writes when not working.

She is an avid reader of dark fantasy, horror, dystopian, and post-apocalyptic books. She tries to take the serious edge off a post-apocalyptic world by adding humor and sarcasm into her books.

She started her Southern Zombies series in November 2015 and later added the Fynn Young series to her writings.

Her books are available on Amazon.

9

DEADLY SILENCE

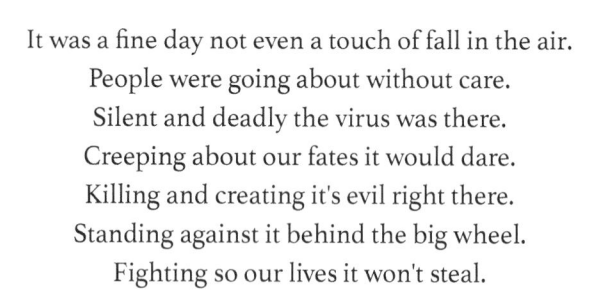

DAVINA PURNELL

It was a fine day not even a touch of fall in the air.
People were going about without care.
Silent and deadly the virus was there.
Creeping about our fates it would dare.
Killing and creating it's evil right there.
Standing against it behind the big wheel.
Fighting so our lives it won't steal.

Davina Purnell

Davina, was born in New Mexico. She has four sons, four grandchildren, a cat, two dogs, and a husband of 26 years. She writes poetry, fiction and romance. And loves to hear from her fans.

Davina's latest work, Simone and the Serpent's Sword, is available on Amazon.

10

FREAKED OUT ZOMBIES

LORI SAFRANEK

Wire Bender brought the message to Cobb right away.

"Just heard from Sara. She's made contact with a group from up north. It's five people, in an RV. They'd like to visit us, trade for some fuel, rest up," he said.

His boss stroked his chin. "How did they get this far? Hell, tell her to bring them in, they must be some tough bastards to get this far in an RV."

"She's waiting for an okay. They're about 10 miles away," Wire Bender said. Cobb nodded and Wire Bender hurried away.

He relayed the message, and about a half hour later Sara led the small group, plus another motorcycle, into the compound. The vehicles stopped just inside the walls. Sara got off her bike and strode toward Cobb.

"Hey, Cobb." She shook her hair out from the confines of her helmet. "These folks've been driving a while, they'd like to rest a couple days."

He nodded. Looking over their RV, it didn't look too

badly beat up, considering it had ridden through thousands of zombies.

"Tell them to come on out, but they'll have to be examined by the Sisters. Checked for bites and what not. All men?"

"No, two women, three men," she said. Pointing at the motorcycle parked near hers, she continued, "That lady there is named Gypsy. She took a chance and flagged me down first. She's their advance rider."

Cobb grunted and waited.

Sara went to the RV and pounded her fist on the door.

"Come on out. You gotta meet our boss first, then the nurses gotta check you out," she called. "But you're welcome here."

The door opened and a tall, thin man stepped out. Cobb took a long look at him, forcing his face to show no reaction to the sight of the man's scaly, dry skin. He had a brief flashback to a circus sideshow he had visited in his younger years, when he'd paid fifty cents to see Annie the Alligator Woman. She had had skin like that.

The bald alligator man stepped to the side and another man followed him out. This one was even taller and much broader and covered with tattoos. Truckers liked tattoos, so Cobb was used to them. Hell, he thought some were pure art. But this guy was covered with the things. Tattoo Man flashed a devilish grin and moved away from the exit.

A small, thin redheaded woman came out next, skipping down the steps and over to stand next to the tattooed man. She was a cute little thing, a bit too skinny, wearing shorts and a tank top, which showed off a nicely developed set of biceps.

The last person to walk out of the RV was a bit of a

surprise, even though he'd just seen a perky little woman traveling with an alligator skinned man and a completely tattooed man.

This guy, Cobb chuckled, oh boy. He'd have to lock up the single women. The man was slick. He wore a little goatee, which considering how hard it was to get a shave these days was testament to a real commitment to personal grooming. And he was dressed in tight leather pants and a silky red shirt with full sleeves. Not exactly practical clothing for the zombie apocalypse.

Slick stopped at the top of the stairs, smiling and searching the area to see who was looking at him. Cobb could tell what kind of man he was; he'd seen this type all his life. He hoped the guy wasn't going to be trouble.

He stepped forward to greet the newcomers.

"Hello," he said. "I'm the boss, my name is Cobb. This group has traveled a long way together and we've survived because we are organized and we are careful. So before anything else, our nurses will give you the once over, check you for bites. Then we'll see what we can do for you."

Stacey, the other half of the group's medical team, the Sisters, had joined Sara during his speech and the two started taking the visitors one by one back into the RV. They sent the girl back out with an all clear. The tattooed man went in and, after fifteen minutes, came out grinning.

Cobb frowned. "What's the problem?"

The tattooed man laughed. "No problem, they just had a hard time checking for bites with all these tattoos distracting them."

He winked at the girl and she glowered back at him. Okay, so that's how the wind blew.

"Next one, go in," Cobb said.

The slick guy trotted up the steps eagerly. Cobb shook his head. That guy was in for a rude

awakening. His nurses knew how to handle shenanigans and they'd sort this fella out in no time. As predicted, Slick was back out in record time, looking a bit crestfallen.

"You all clear?" Cobb asked. The fancy guy nodded without comment.

The alligator man went in and was out in a few minutes, accompanied by the nurses.

"They're all clear, Cobb. Kind of hard to tell with the unusual skin on him." She pointed to the alligator skinned man. "It's a case of severe itchyothis vulgaris, not contagious. And the beautiful tattoos on that one made our job a little harder. But they're clear.

Cobb thanked the Sisters and turned to the newcomers.

"Okay, you want to tell me who you are now? And what you want from us," he said.

The alligator man stepped forward with his hand extended. Cobb shook it.

"I'm Jason, I used to be the manager of a sideshow where all these folks performed. We were on break from traveling when the shit hit the fan," he said. "We've got a good set up back home, in Wisconsin. But these two, Smudge and Lily Dean, were caught down here in Oklahoma. We came to get them. We're on our way home now."

Cobb raised one eyebrow. "You just came to get them? How the hell did you do that? We've had one hell of trip here and we're some pretty tough folks. The two of you traveled all this way in an RV?"

"Actually, they had me, too," a feminine voice came from behind him. Cobb turned to see a pretty woman with a head full of curly hair and a motorcycle helmet under her arm. "I'm Gypsy, I'm the one came flying in here on a Harley."

Cobb shook her hand. "Sorry, Gypsy, I guess I forgot all about you. You rode that Harley all the way?"

She nodded and laughed.

"Just like me," Sara said.

Cobb snorted. "You got me there, Sara."

Jason said, "Gypsy has dodged more zombies than I did back when I used to play video games. That woman is a wonder and we owe our lives to her."

Cobb was confused still, but he let it slide. God forbid he underestimate anyone nowadays. He'd seen over and over how this nightmare had drawn more out of common people than they ever dreamed they had in them.

He pointed at the tattooed man.

"I didn't get your name."

"Hi, I'm Smudge and this lady is Lily Dean," the man said. He pointed to the slick dude.

"This fella is named Blade. He's not as worthless as he might appear."

Everyone snickered, including Blade, so Cobb figured it was an old and familiar joke. Blade extended his hand for a shake. "Nice to meet you, sir. We appreciate your welcoming us into your fortress. We'll be glad for the break."

Cobb shook his hand, rolling his eyes.

"Okay, then, we have you all checked out, let's head down to the café and get you something to eat," he said. "Then we'll need to talk to you about fueling up and what you might have to trade."

All five thanked him and Sara led them to the café where Martha and Cookie were serving meals. After weeks on the road, they were grateful for freshly cooked food made by someone else. They had scavenged canned goods and sometimes ate them straight out of the can. A real meal sounded like heaven.

The newcomers went to the front where food was set out buffet style. They filled their plates and gathered drinks. Sara left them alone to eat in peace. Once they were on second helpings, she took a seat at their table.

"So how are things in Wisconsin?" she asked, afraid of the answer but nowadays it was a habit to ask.

"Bad," Jason said, looking up from his mashed potatoes and gravy. "We're lucky. My wife has a paranoid streak and has been prepping for years. Our friends made it to our place, and we're secure."

The redhead piped up. "Me and Smudge went to Oklahoma for a gig, and got caught down here," Lily Ann said. She lowered her eyes. "It's really bad in Tulsa. I don't know how we got away."

She leaned against the tattooed man and he slipped an arm around her.

"It was touch and go, I admit, but luckily the fair we were working at was in a piss-ant small town and we saw the smoke from all the fires in Tulsa," he said. "The nearest town was small, but they had heard the news on their police radios. We were trapped there with some other people for a long time, living in an old bank, with bars on the window. Finally we stole a car and got the hell out of there."

He grinned devilishly at Sara. She laughed.

"Hey, man, we've all had to do some things," she said. "This apocalypse, no saints are surviving this thing."

"Luckily, before we left the small town, we were able to get ahold of Jason's house and let them know what a mess we were in," Smudge said. "These bad asses left the next day. Thank God."

Amens were muttered all around the table.

"What kind of gig were you two at?" she asked.

"I'm a snake charmer," Lily Dean said. Touching

Smudge on the chest, she said, "He's the Slide Show of the Sideshow."

Sara frowned. "What the hell?"

The group laughed.

"We're all sideshow freaks, honey," Gypsy said. "Haven't you figured that out? Jason's the Alligator Man, I'm a psychic, Blade here swallows swords, Lily Dean charms snakes and Smudge has tattoos that like to move around on his body."

"Well, I can say I've seen it all now," Sara said with a laugh. "I gotta ask, though. How'd you and Blade and Gypsy make it through to Oklahoma? We traveled a lot of that same route and we nearly didn't make it. These truckers are tough guys."

The group laughed and grinned at each other. Gypsy stood and took a bow.

Blade jumped up and grabbed her hand. "Ladies and gentleman, boys and girls," he sounded just like he did up on the stage at the sideshow. "May I introduce to you the amazing Gypsy! Want to know who your true love is? She already knows! Looking for a new job? She'll find you one! Want to talk to a dearly departed loved one? She'll get them on the line for you! She's a mind reader, a medium, and a psychic! Folks, she does it all!"

Everyone laughed, including Sara. Blade sat back down, pulling Gypsy into his lap.

"What can a psychic do?"

Gypsy nodded. "Oh, honey, I can tell where those zombie babies are going to be and we move on down the road, any road but where they are."

Sara's mouth dropped open.

Jason laughed. "Hard to believe, I know, but once we got

the hang of it, we believed her and she got us here! Before we quit being stubborn, I thought Blade and I were going to personally have to kill every zombie in the country."

"And we could have done it," Blade added. "It just would have taken longer."

Sara snorted and slapped her knee.

"Boy, you are full of shit," she said, shaking her head. "I'm not sure I believe you guys, but a few months ago, I didn't know zombies exist."

Cobb walked into the café and pulled a chair up to their table.

"You get plenty to eat?" he asked.

They nodded and thanked him wholeheartedly.

"So you want to do some trading," Cobb said. He didn't hold much hope of them having much to trade.

"Yeah, we've got something for you to look at, and I think you might be interested," Jason said. "What we want to swap for is some fuel and some food to keep us going on our way home."

Cobb nodded.

"That we can do. You might have noticed we have a couple fuel tankers here. We'll fill your little RV, no problem," he said, grinning. "What are you going to do for fuel the rest of the way?"

Jason explained that they had added an auxiliary gas tank to their vehicle, and they'd learned how to get gas from the many abandoned gas stations along the highways.

"Good. You folks seem to have things figured out," he said. Sara quickly filled him in on Gypsy's technique for avoiding zombies. "I hope your friend here stays tuned into her zombie vibe. Those things seem to change the longer they exist."

Gypsy looked him in the eye.

"I see them changing, Cobb. They are frightening. We have to keep up," she said in an uncharacteristically flat voice. "It will be worse soon. That's why we need to get home."

The group sat quietly for a few minutes. Cobb thought of Gunny, headed to find his family miles away. He had no idea if they were alive or if they were safe, but he had left the safety of the group to find them.

"Well, you folks want to show me what you have to trade now?" he asked, standing.

The others stood and Jason nodded.

"Yes, Cobb, we can do that now. Do you have a place Gypsy, Smudge and Lily Dean could maybe clean up a bit? Blade and I will show you what we have," he said.

"Oh, sure," Cobb said. "I forgot my manners. I'll send someone over here to show you a place to shower. If you need clean clothes, we can probably dig you up something. Just hang out here for a few minutes. I'll meet you two at your RV."

By the time Cobb arrived, the men had their merchandise opened up and spread around the interior of the RV. They invited him inside, saying they did not like displaying their goods for everyone to see.

He stepped inside the trailer home to the sight of shining metal everywhere. Blades, knives, swords, machetes, katanas – it was too much to take in at once.

"What the hell?" he said slowly. "Where did you get all this?"

Blade laughed loudly.

"I've got a little addiction," he said. "You didn't ask what I did in the freak show. I'm a sword swallower and a knife thrower. And these are my babies."

He swept his arm toward all the shining weapons.

"You think you might want to trade with us?" Jason asked, grinning.

Cobb whistled. "Oh, hell yes."

He paused. "But on one condition. You have to teach us to use these things. We've been patching together our up-close fighting weapons or using guns. We'd need some training with these beautiful, beautiful things."

Blade bowed his head. "At your service. For twenty-four hours."

Cobb nodded. "That'll do. We got a couple fast learners."

He looked over the weapons, desire burning in his gut. He'd sure like a nice katana. And that switchblade would be good to slip in his boot. God damn, look at that sword! He'd only seen replicas of swords that long. Then a machete caught his eye and he picked it up. Nice weight to it, he thought. He'd worked with a machete a time or two.

Finally he realized the two freak show performers were grinning at him.

"Like looking at a girlie magazine, ain't it?" Blade said. "You kinda want them all."

Cobb laughed. "Yeah, and just like those girlies, my wife'll kick my butt if I bring that big katana home, or that sword. Maybe she'll put up with a machete, if I bring her a switchblade of her own. This sounds kind of kinky, now that you put it in those terms."

Jason and Blade laughed. The three men settled down to serious selection, Blade advising Cobb on which blades were most useful in close-up zombie fighting, which should be avoided at all costs, though both men knew it happened too often for comfort. The long swords weren't a bad choice, either.

Jason preferred the katana himself, strapped to his back

for easy access before they realized Gypsy's powers. Stopping the RV for rest periods or fuel, they often engaged in hand-to-hand combat with the undead. Jason left Blade with both hands full of knives, and he kept the katana close. They had worked well together, despite a few close shaves.

"Gypsy carries about eight knives on her," Blade said, blandly. "She's got one in her boot, one in the waist of her jeans, one strapped to her handlebars. She can yank that one off in seconds. A few I don't know where."

"Yep, and she has a katana strapped to her back, too," Jason continued. "Shorter than mine, because she's always sitting on the bike, but she knows how to use it."

Blade frowned.

"Just between us guys, Gypsy is good but she's been surprised a couple times," Blade said, looking toward the RV door as if he was afraid she would pop in any minute. "She gets too tired or too hungry, she can lose her powers. Well, not lose them really; they just get a bit weaker. And I want her safe out there, so she is fully armed."

Cobb grunted, thinking what it would take to outfit Sara. She'd had her share of narrow escapes. They'd taken ten years off his life.

"I need a full set up for Sara," he said. "I'll show you two of my men who will be training with you. I'm going to indulge myself in a machete and a switchblade. Make that two switchblades. Add a big old pig-sticker. Cookie will be thrilled."

Jason and Blade began pulling the items Cobb requested, as well as a few weapons to train his men on. Blade also pulled out his knife sharpening materials and carried them outside the RV.

"I'll be here until dark," he told Cobb. "Spread the word,

I'll sharpen anything that can be sharpened, for free. But at dark, I stop. Then I want to put on a show, if it's okay with you."

Cobb grinned and nodded. This crew could sure use a little entertainment.

By sundown, Blade had sharpened dozens of pocketknives, kitchen knives, hobbled together bayonet blades and even a couple hoes. Someone had lit a nice fire near their RV and a crowd had gathered. Blade faced nearly every person in the compound, except those on guard duty and a few party poopers. He was in heaven. He hadn't had a good audience since the zompoc broke out.

Blade was dressed resplendently, silk from head to the top of his leather boots. Cobb marveled how the man maintained his clothes. All in black, he'd tied a red sash around his waist.

The sword-swallower picked up the first sword and raised it high. The crowd immediately settled down to watch. He moved the sword to his mouth and licked it from the handle to the point and back. Cobb could have sworn he heard a few women sigh.

Blade pointed the sword point down over his face, which was tilted skyward. He opened his mouth wide and began lowering the blade downward, down his throat, lower and lower. The audience gasped when he paused, took his hands off the hilt entirely and turned his upper body toward each side of the group.

Then he stood perfectly straight, grabbed the hilt and slid the sword the rest of the way down his esophagus. A few kids squealed and some women clapped. The men were shaking their heads in wonder. Blade let go of the hilt once more.

Once everyone had a good look, he grasped the hilt again and began pulling the sword out quickly. In no time, he brandished the shiny slice of silver above his head. The crowd cheered.

He did a few more sword-swallowing maneuvers, involving longer and shorter swords and ended by inserting six down his throat at once. It was a crowd-pleaser, Cobb would sure give him that. Finally, Blade bowed deep and thanked the crowd.

Applause and laughter followed everyone back to their trucks and homes, a rare night of community and fun in their new hometown.

The next morning, Blade and Jason worked with Lars and Stabby, two of Cobb's fiercest fighters, teaching them how to handle the new weapons. They learned the best way to plunge a long sword into a zombie's head. The undead wouldn't quit until you cut off their heads or destroyed their brains.

Blade showed Lars and Stabby how to swing a katana, practicing until both men were sweating and breathing hard.

"Damn, Blade, I think we got the idea," Lars gasped. "We'll be dead from exhaustion if you don't stop soon."

Blade grinned and wiped a silk handkerchief across his brow.

"You're tired? I feel fresh as a daisy," he said. "How about you, Jason?"

"I'm fit as a fiddle," the alligator man said with a sideways smile and a gleam in his eye. "I could teach them all afternoon."

Stabby fell flat on his back in the dust.

"Oh, hell, no!" he said. "Water . . . I need water. . ."

The men laughed and Blade stopped the katana class for the day.

"You guys are doing great," Jason said. "Just never get cocky. Always go for the head. Don't think it's good enough to stop them; you have to cut their damned heads off."

"Cocky? Us?" Lars said innocently. "Never!"

Cobb walked up just then.

"Is that right?" he growled. Lars twirled around with his eyes wide.

"Oh, hey there, Cobb. I was just going to get some water," he said, scooting past the leader of the group. Jason and Blade laughed their butts off watching Stabby jump to his feet to follow Lars on his desperate dash away from their boss.

"Well, how'd those jackasses do? Did you knock any sense into 'em?"

Jason smiled. "They've got good instincts, both of them. Blade worked them hard, and muscle memory is important. Just keep them practicing until it's second nature."

Cobb nodded. He asked the men to join him at the café for dinner, where the rest of their group was already eating. When everyone was seated, Cobb joined them, drinking a cup of coffee.

"I figure you want to leave tomorrow morning, so before sundown, let's get your RV fueled up," he said. "Are you all stocked up? Everyone got what you need?

The two girls nodded with big smiles on their faces. Both wore fresh jeans and t-shirts. Their hair was shiny clean and so were they. Smudge had also found new clothes and had stacked and tied down boxes of food on top of the RV, along with large jugs of water.

"I think we're all good to go, Cobb, and we appreciate

your hospitality," Jason said. "You all sure have a good set up here. Thank you again for letting us stop by."

Cobb shook his hand.

"Glad to have you," he said. "My men learned some great skills and we have new weapons. Plus, Blade's performance gave us a break from all the gloom and doom. Much obliged."

Blade nodded his head. The others smiled and murmured their thanks.

Cobb rose to leave and Smudge went with him to move the RV to the fueling area.

The others were just finishing their meals when Cobb's wife, Martha, came bustling out of the kitchen. They had only seen her once, the night before at Blade's show. She was usually in the kitchen with Cookie feeding the people three times a day.

She pointed her finger at Jason.

"You. Take this," she plopped a large jar in front of him. Jason picked it up and looked at it.

"Well, thank you," he said, a little flustered.

"Don't say thank you, when you don't know what it is," she said, clucking her tongue at him. "It's balm, for skin. Helps the alligator go away. Now, goodbye."

With that, she spun on her heel and headed back to the kitchen.

Lily Dean had her hand pressed firmly over her mouth, trying to suppress a case of the giggles. Jason motioned her to get outside. The rest followed.

She collapsed on the ground in a pile of laughter, pointing at Jason. "Makes alligator go away!" she mimicked Martha's voice.

He grinned at her.

"Wouldn't that be something? Come home and all my

alligator's gone. Marie would faint dead away," he said with a laugh.

"Oh, she sure would!" Gypsy said. "I think Miss Marie's got a thing for that old reptile skin of yours. Whatever trips your trigger, baby."

Blade snorted.

"Let's just get going, before our head freak ends up as normal as apple pie."

By morning, they were on the road to Wisconsin, Gypsy leading them down the highway as fast as a psychic hippie girl could. They didn't encounter a zombie until Missouri. Blade chopped its head off with his sword. It was a good day of traveling.

∼

Lori Safranek

Lori Safranek writes horror stories, sometimes set in her home state of Nebraska, a locale scary enough that most people choose to fly over without stopping. A former newspaper reporter, Lori took the leap into fiction writing five years ago and has enjoyed exploring the dark side of life and the afterlife.

Lori has a six-story collection, Freakshow: The Complete Freaked Out Series which features characters from a circus freak show. Each character has an experience with the supernatural. Her other stories have been published in anthologies such as Dark Harvest from Scarlet Galleon, Simple Things and Final Masquerade, both from Lycan Valley Publications; Slaughter House--The Serial

Killer Edition from Sirens Call Publications; Cellar Door II from James Ward Kirk Publications; and Fifty Shades of Decay--Zombie Erotica, from Angelic Knight Press.

She lives in Omaha, Nebraska, with her husband, Chuck, and their two dogs, Scout and Arthur.

Lori's work can be found on Amazon.

11

HUNTED IN THE HILLS

T.D. RICKETTS

I
It Begins

The bacon sizzled in the pans and on the grate. The coffee pots burbled their call of morning goodness. I stretched my hands and arms over my head and yawned. My hammock swayed in the breeze as I dropped my arm over the side. A wet tongue caressed the back of my hand. "Good morning, good looking." I leaned over and gave Leena a scratch between the ears. "You want some breakfast?" A half bowl of dog food was quickly inhaled by my partner in crime. I grabbed my sweater to fight the chill of the morning. Leena yawned and stood up stretching her furry body.

"Damn it, if you put the bacon on you watch it, don't count on me," Cookie's voice carried through the still calm air, "You burned it all." Matt countered, "I didn't burn it all, I saw you guys snagging it earlier. I didn't even get any."

The sounds of early morning in our camp never seemed to change, guys giving each other a hard time. The smell of coffee and bacon floated on the air to me. Leena was licking her chops and my stomach started gurgling. That stew last night was too good, I had two bowls for dinner and another before I went to bed. I might have to pass on the bacon this morning. It was day twelve of a two-week trip with the six of us. Bacon every morning was wreaking havoc on my stomach. Cookie shouted at the guys again, "Well it's all garbage now and you already ate half of it. It's that new brand, too."

My stomach rumbled and I knew it was time to make a run to my favorite tree. A short walk in the woods would do me a world of good. I pulled my pants and a sweater on, found my boots and headed over the hill a bit. I heard Cookie bitching as I walked away. Leena bounced along beside me. She wasn't about to miss a chance to sniff around and play in the woods. The leaves crunched under my feet and released the smell of fall, until I found my tree then the smell was...well, you get where I'm going with this.

After a bit, when we got back to camp, I grabbed my .22 rifle and headed to the fire. I was ready for some hunting. Randy was sitting by the fire cleaning a pistol. Lloyd, the youngster of the bunch, was playing with some new gear he had just bought. The kid had all the new toys. Could always count on him to let you know what worked and what didn't. They both were quiet and looked a little green around the gills. Randy looked up as I walked over, "I don't know about you guys but I think he poisoned us with that new bacon, I don't feel so good. Morning Jim, don't eat the bacon." I thought for a second, "I didn't plan on it. I'm paying for being a pig with the stew last night." Leena walked over to Randy sniffing the whole time. She was normally up for a good back scratch and an ear rub but she stood back and just looked at the guys. She turned and came back, standing tight to my side. She was acting funny. Lloyd was sitting sideways in his hammock and chimed in, "I'm going to just lay here for a bit."

Jeffy's voice came from his brush lean-to at the edge of the woods. "You jerks have killed me, I'm dying here." "Was it the whiskey last night?" I asked. "No, it's that Hajji bacon they burned. I'm just going to sleep it off or shit it out."

"Well, you guys just lounge around, I'm taking Leena for a walk and I might try and shoot dinner." They all grunted and I got a single finger salute from Matt. "Leena, Toc." I laughed at them and headed up the gully to walk the ridges up top.

Leena is a Corb Shepherd and her commands are in Romanian. I got her as a pup and wanted commands nobody else would use. Corbs are also called Romanian Raven Shepherds because of their jet-black fur.

After walking the woods for three hours I decided to head back to camp. When I got there Leena immediately ran to me and walked tight against my leg. I didn't know what was up with that. She stopped and sniffed the air, I smelled a funny tang in the air. Matt was sitting on the ridge above camp, in the bushes. "What are you doing Matt?" "Jim, you're back!" Matt said frantically, "They have gone nuts. Randy and Lloyd attacked Cookie, they killed him and ate his face off. Don't let them see you, I tried to stop them and they went after me. Lloyd bit my arm." A rumble from Leena made me look at her. Her eyes were locked onto our camp and the figures standing there. Cookie stood swaying beside the fire. His face torn and bone exposed, blood covered his shirt. Randy and Lloyd staggered around camp. "I thought you said that they killed Cookie? He is standing right there."

"He *was* dead. I'm telling you. I stabbed Randy after he attacked me and he didn't even flinch. This is some weird shit. It's like a bad movie but they move so fast it's scary. We have to get out of here."

"Okay, you have the keys to your truck? Or a cell phone? Mine are all back in camp and I can't get a signal for the phone anyway." I started taking a mental inventory. My small hunting pack carried coffee, a canteen cup, a couple power bars, paracord and a fire-steel. In my pockets I had a couple magazines for my .22, a folding knife, half a pack of smokes and a lighter. On my belt was my trusty Hemphill Custom, a semi-clip point Damascus blade Bowie knife. A work of art with a Moran style handle of desert ironwood. I saved a lot of pennies to buy it but he was a Michigan guy and I like to support local businesses. My neck knife was a Hemphill Puukko made from A2 tool steel. I could get by with what I had but I wanted my big pack and my water filters.

"Well we sure aren't going to have the dog go get them. Matt, my hammock is the furthest away from them and the fire. I'm going to sneak down and get my keys." I started moving down the hill. I went slowly and kept brush between me and the camp whenever I could.

A low moaning came from the creatures in the camp. They staggered aimlessly in circles. Their clothes were covered in blood, vomit and other bodily fluids. It just plain scared the stuffing out of me. My friends had become zombies.

I slowly worked my way down a small depression. My hammock was hung near the top edge of the depression. I snore like a buzz saw so I tried to stay away from the fire and other people's set ups when I hung my hammock. Moving slowly and as quietly as I could, I got to my gear without being seen by anything. I ducked under my rain tarp and quickly grabbed my pack. It was the fastest, easiest way to get almost everything I wanted. I grabbed a hold of my sleeping bag and stuffed it into my pack just as Leena started barking from the top of the hill. Ducking down to look at the fire, I saw a pair of legs (they tend to travel in pairs) were headed my way. Leena had distracted the creature by barking. She tended to go nuts if she thought I was in danger or that she needed to be with me. I had told her "Stau" our word for her to stay. She would stay until I told her otherwise.

I grabbed my holster that was hanging on a line and ran like hell was on my heels. Brush crashed behind me as something fell into the bushes. The thrashing in the bushes continued for a bit. Looking back, I saw Cookie was trying to get out of some bushes with thorns that had snagged him. Randy and Lloyd were just turning and heading in my direction. I dropped out of their sight at the bottom of the depression. I couldn't see them and kept running. My pack was banging against my side as I hugged it to me. No time to put it on properly. I was stuffing my holster into my waist band. Not a good fit for a shoulder rig, the straps were flapping everywhere as I ran.

What I didn't know is that Jeffy had been wandering around and he was sick, too. He sprinted down the side of the depression right at me. A scream tore from his mouth. I pulled my .45 and managed to fumble and get it caught in the straps of the holster. I turned to look at Jeffy as he charged. I drew my bowie and waited. Ten feet from me Jeffy tripped as Leena grabbed his leg. He hit the ground like a ton of bricks. I jumped forward and swung the knife into his temple. The blade sank into his brain and he stopped moving immediately. I turned and ran. It wasn't the last time Leena would save my ass.

I made it to the top of the hill and shouted to Matt, "Run,

they are after me. Leena, Vin!" I'd never been so scared in my life. Matt gave me the slide sign and I slid under a bush next to him. Leena laid down next to me. I peeked over the ridge and saw Randy and Lloyd stalking Cookie as he thrashed in the the tangle of thorns and kudzu.

"Matt, we have to get out of here." He looked at me with a tear in his eye. "I've been bit and I'm sick. I can barely walk. You need to get out of here and back to your place pronto, buddy. I've got a pistol and I'm saving the last round. Someone has to take care of Cookie and the boys. I can't leave my friends like that, you git outta here." Matt reached over and ruffled the fur on Leena's head and I heard him say very softly, "Leena you're a good girl, take care of your master."

I turned and ran while I could still see, tears for my lost friends flooded my eyes. I couldn't say anymore. Leena kept pace as I hit the trail at a steady jog.

II

On the Run

The trail ran down hill and I leaned back as gravity sought once again to prove that it was in charge. Curving around an outcropping of local stone I stopped dead still. Leena growled, backed up and leaned against my leg. What used to be a human was stumbling up the hill. The worn and dirty clothes were stained with blood. They were ripped and torn, not in someone's idea of a stylish fashion but from brush and thorns. A pack was still fastened to its back. When it saw me, a low moan came from it, followed by a screech. It took off toward me in a sprint, this thing was fast. I pulled my .45 from my shoulder holster and double tapped it center mass. The big 230 grain bullets knocking it to the ground. My knees were already shaking and when it hit the ground my knees started knocking. The post adrenaline rush left me feeling woozy so I sat down. Leaves crunched and sticks broke as it started to crawl toward me. What the hell? Nothing got hit in the chest, with its spine blown out, and lived. I quickly stood and walked over to it. The stench of a dead thing emanated from its torn and rotting flesh. I heaved everything in my stomach on the side of the trail. Still shaking, it took me two shots to hit it in the head.

I was running out of water by this time. Any food I had stashed was going quickly. I had two ways to go. I could move off the trail and bushwhack it or I could continue on the trail. Leena would need something to eat, too. I had shared everything with her. If I got a power bar, she got half. A couple miles down the trail there was a shelter, I wanted the spring that was near it. There was no way I was staying in that shelter. It seemed like a great way to get trapped by these things.

When my stomach settled down and my knees quit knocking it was time to move out. I glanced around for Leena and saw her sitting at the base of a large oak tree, perfectly still with her nose pointed up the tree. I shook my head. "What the hell was I thinking? Zoning out on the side of a trail with raging cannibalistic creatures running around in the woods."

Leena had a good idea. I pulled my .22 rifle off my back as a squirrel crawled down the side of the tree. One quick shot dropped our dinner. As soon as I shot a thought ran through my head, "That noise just told anyone or anything in the area I'm here." No sooner did I have that thought when the pound of feet sounded behind me on the trail. I turned and brought up the .22, not the best weapon but a damn sight better than being unarmed. Coming up the slope were two creatures. They were fast but seemed to trip on brush and rocks. Their bodies were battered and cut from falls onto the rocky soil. The first was a skinny teen with dreadlocks wearing a ripped and torn T-shirt. Behind him was what used to be a skinny girl with jeans and no shoes. Her feet were shredded and bone was sticking out. "Nobody can use feet like that, there is no way!" Her braided hair was sticking out in all directions and her shirt was shredded, revealing what at some point in time was probably pretty impressive. They moaned and screamed running up the trail. I had my rifle in my hand and pulled it to my shoulder. I knew I had 9 shots left as the scope settled onto the first one's head. The seven-power setting of the scope made it easy. I fired one shot that hit in the middle of its forehead. A .22 is not the most powerful firearm out there but in this case, it worked. The thing staggered and its momentum carried it into the brush on the edge of the trail. I switched my sights to the other thing and started pulling the trigger. That's a bad choice of words because you're never supposed to "pull" the trigger. A gentle squeeze so you're surprised when it goes off. This wasn't the range and I didn't have time to waste. This thing was running at me and wanted to eat my face off. I PULLED! The .22 rounds smashed into the head rocking it backwards. I fired several rounds until it dropped to the ground.

The hike to the shelter was quiet. Even the birds seemed to be hiding, there wasn't a peep out of them. The Adirondack shelter was basically a shed with one wall gone. Totally open on one side, I could see the small piles of packs and gear along the walls. There had to be more people than I had already encountered. All I was worried about was getting some water. Leena quickly sprinted to the spring. She stopped long enough to look around and sniff the air. The breeze blew straight into her face from the spring. "I guess it's good girl, you get your drink and I'll watch." Leena's nose plunged into the cold water and greedily gulped down mouthful after mouthful. While Leena was getting her drink, I pulled my filter out and every container I had in my packs. Leena backed off and looked at me as if to say I'm done it's your turn. Smart dog.

I filled everything I had and hoped it was enough to make it through the last of the trail. With everything loaded and the pack weighing a ton I figured it was a chance to find some food. With those packs in the shelter there had to be something to eat. The uphill walk to the shelter took only a minute but I succeeded in choking myself on a line between two trees. Good thing I did because it dawned on me that some rookies had hung a bear canister. A bear canister is meant to keep a bear from getting your food. Kind of funny because nobody had seen a bear on this part of the trail in at least fifteen years. Cutting it down and lashing it to my pack took all of five minutes and then we were off into the brush. No more trail for us, time to bushwhack.

It took me a week to hike my ass out of the woods. Hiding and sneaking, shooting and running. Everything I ran into was diseased. Leena would smell them and growl. We finally had the trailhead in sight, I could see my beautiful old Kenworth parked in the lot. The houses around here appeared to be deserted, with the exception of old man Simpsons'. The only problem was halfway down the hill stood a small city of tents. Some youth group had camped between me and my ride. I decided to try and sneak around them as they milled in old man Simpsons' yard and around the tents. I followed a ditch, slowly creeping towards my goal. Leena stayed tight on my side.

I was just about to make a run for it when a noise came from the house. Loud Rock and Roll was blasting in his garage. I pulled my Hemphill bowie and figured it was time to run. With my bowie in one hand and my .45 in the other, it was game time. "Leena, Toc." Old man Simpson hollered out the window, "You damned kids get off my lawn! Jim, make your run when I start shooting." The mini munchers turned and sprinted towards his voice when he yelled. He started shooting and they charged toward the house.

Leena easily kept pace and we were in the truck in no time. I fired it up and by then the kids were all in the old guy's yard. The music was so loud they couldn't hear my truck until I popped it in gear and started running her up. Leena and I were safe for now and it was time to roll. I had a tear in my eye because the old guy couldn't run and I knew they would eventually get him. I recognized the music, "Swan Song."

III
On the Road

We blew through a couple of small towns on these little bitty two-lane blacktop roads. Going so fast nothing really had much of a chance to bother us. I had to use the big brush guard on the front a couple times to move a car and thump a zombie but no big deals. My AR and ammo were in the truck so I was fully armed. There was a barricade at one of the bridges with zombies milling around in uniforms. My AR is a .308 with a suppressor on it, great for coyote hunting. I just sat back and thinned the herd or pack or gaggle, whatever you call a bunch of the undead. I think I read a Chesser book that called them a horde. Kind of like the sound of that. Laid my cross hairs on their heads and squeezed the trigger, from 500 yards away. Their heads just kind of exploded with a funny looking mist behind them. It was more like a black goo than blood and brains. Being able to use my truck as a bench rest made it easy.

I pushed the barriers out of the way and made the sprint to the expressway. After I got on the road I saw an amazing sight. A weight station with trucks all around it. I pulled in and cradling my rifle, stared in awe. Trucks were coming and going, it looked like a damn truck stop. Some guys were getting fuel from tankers parked on the side. Trailers were parked all around and a couple guys were directing traffic. "I'm Kristopher, what's your load and does the scheduler know you're coming?" I thought out my brilliant response. "Ummm, ahhh, who?"

"Oh, new to the yard. You have to meet the scheduler. Go into the office and she can explain."

Now I didn't have a clue what was going on but figured it couldn't hurt to find out, so I headed inside. The last thing I expected was a good looking red head telling a bunch of truckers where to go. Her desk was covered in piles of notes. A pad of paper covered in notes sat in front of her. A map on the wall was covered with different colored pins. She looked at me as Leena walked over and put her head on her lap. "PUPPY!" a little girl ran from the back room and threw her arms around Leena. Leena stiffened for a second, took a sniff and decided it was a human puppy. Laughter came from everyone watching as a big tongue washed a jelly covered face. "Mom that crib midget keeps escaping and I'm getting tired of babysitting." The whine of a teenager came from the back room. "Go help your father in the yard and I'll deal with Miss Thing here."

"Welcome to the way station, I'm Valerie Lioudis and I run this nightmare. I was a load planner when all this shit hit the fan. Now, if you have a load you want to drop and maybe trade, we can hook you up. I have drivers bringing in anything and everything. If you come in with a load and want your own supplies we will trade, unless you're carrying something useless like nuclear waste. I know where all kinds of loads are and can have you get them if you want to build a couple survival loads." My jaw just dropped. "I have a load of clothing that I was going to drop." Valerie smiled and cuddled the little one. "What do you want for them?"

I thought for a second. "Food, ammo, water, blankets, fuel and generators."

"Standard survival load out is what you'll get then. Replacement trailer as good or better than what you drop ok?" "Hell yes, that piece of garbage company trailer cost me fuel."

In no time flat I was fueled up and had a new bright, shiny trailer. That gal ran a tight ship. I wished them all luck and hit the road. I had some tips on what roads were clear and what roads they didn't know about. After a couple hours it was time for lunch and I stopped in the middle of the road. I figured with a wall on each side and a good line of sight from the rise, it was a good place to stop and take a break.

I popped open a can of stew and put some down for Leena. After lunch I kind of sat on the hood having an after-lunch cigar. As I sat there I heard a rig slowing down. I dropped down and crouched by the front fender with Leena behind me, my AR trained on the tractor. The strange rig pulled up beside me. I couldn't help but admire the painting on the side, battle scenes of men in kilts, pretty cool stuff. The window rolled down and a gravelly voice with a Scottish burr to it yelled out, "Lad if ye're in the mood for a ride, we are onto a bit of a run. Me and a few friends that will be along shortly. Just ask for Gunny when they get here, I'm taking me a bit of a nap now."

That's how I met Gunny and Jock.

∼

T.D. Ricketts

T.D. Ricketts lives in Michigan. Married for 35 years, and his wife deserves a medal. Two beautiful daughters, a grandson and grand dog can be found running in and out of his home at any time. Hunting, fishing, motorcycles, camping and hanging out in the woods take up a lot of his time. A lifelong worker in various manufacturing and warehousing jobs, retirement figures prominently in his future.

T.D. will have seven short stories or more in various anthologies being released in fall of 2017.

Currently the plan is for his first novel to be released in Feb. of 2018.

T.D.'s first book "Release the Hounds: Dogging the Dead" will be out Feb. of 2018 via Amazon.

To find more information about T.D. Ricketts please follow him on Facebook. T.D. Ricketts - Author

Thanks to Tamra Crow for her editing skills.
Valerie Lioudis for giving a new scribbler a chance.
Michael Peirce for suggestions and reading rough drafts.
Christopher Artinian for his kind words of encouragement.

Hollywood

Sometimes someone is more
than they appear.
More than meets the eye.

12

JOHN THE BASTARD

GREG BENNETT

They called him John the Bastard. He didn't know if it was some slant to a biblical reference or not, he didn't care. He was a mean sum'bitch who took nuthin' from nobody.

Low supplies had forced him out on a recon trip, to explore some of the outer reaches of the city.

An abandoned strip mall had looked promising; most of the structure was still intact with no signs of major fire. Seeing it took his mind back to the fire fights and explosions in the early days of the battle; how he'd used his truck to mow down hundreds of zombies in his escape. They were fast, but not as fast as his Chevy. It was a miracle his radiator was still intact after all the arms and ribs that had been stuck in the grill.

To reduce his visibility, he'd hidden his truck behind a section of a broken wall and set out on foot.

Hearing zombies approaching, he took cover in the nearest shop. The sound was unmistakable. With missing feet or partial legs, their bones gave an unearthly clicking sound to their rapid shuffling and running on pavement. It reminded him of crickets or maybe frogs around his summer pond long ago. Once comforting, it was now the sound of death.

He waited several minutes after they had passed. Hearing nothing, he continued with his search.

Exploring the back of one of the other shops, he found a goldmine in a utility closet. Nails, a hammer, rolls of duct tape and, unbelievably, a propane torch with several spare cylinders. Other items appeared to be stored in boxes and he lost himself in exploration. In his haste and excitement, he failed to hear the distinct sound of shuffling coming from the front of the shop.

A crashing sound jarred his senses awake, but it was too late. Zombies filled the shop. He was trapped in the closet.

He grabbed the debris blocking the closet door and tried to close it, but a horribly disfigured woman managed to stick her head through the opening. Rotted, tattered skin hung in loose strips on her face; a face that could give him nightmares even in this world.

Her shredded mouth, what was left of it, appeared to be moving as if trying to speak.

That... wasn't... possible.

She was forming words........his name.........Joooooohhh-hhhhnnnnnnn......Jooooooohhhhhhhhnnnnnnn.

∽

"JOHN! Wake your lazy ass up and go get some wine from the supermarket. We're going to be late for the dinner party." His wife hurried away, her high heels clicking across the hardwood floors.

"Shit."

"Yes, Dear. Whatever you say."

13

MOTHER'S DAY BEHIND THE QUARANTINE FENCE

ROMA GRAY

Frank walked along the interior chain-link fence, carefully examining it for any breaches. Every few seconds his eyes darted past the open chain-link mesh to the outer fence, checking it for breaches as well. He adjusted his claustrophobic hazmat suit while continuing his task, resisting the urge to tear it off. The stiff fabric clung uncomfortably to his sweaty arms.

Damn, it's hot today, he thought to himself, checking his watch for the hundredth time.

It was boring work, no doubt about it, and on a hot day like this, downright unpleasant. But the two fences were all that separated the living from the infected...or 'the undead' as many now called them. The fate of everyone in the city—well, what was left of the city—depended on his diligence.

Still, it wasn't easy dragging himself out here every morning.

Day in and day out, inspecting this fence was all he did. Frank hated his job, yet he also felt guilty about his growing animosity toward it. In the zombie apocalypse, he had fared far better than most. A job was hard to come by these days, and he was damn lucky to have it. Yet somehow today he didn't feel very lucky or grateful. He almost wished the fence would get stormed just so he'd have something to think about.

Buzzzzzz

Startled out of his funk, Frank's hand automatically reached for a small black box attached to the sleeve of his suit and pushed a red button.

"Frank here. Over," he said quickly.

"Hey, Frank, this is Ramirez," crackled a voice over the device. "We're seeing a lot of activity over here on the east side. Looks like trouble. How's it looking over on your end? Over."

Frank felt his muscles tense. They hadn't seen any activity for months.

What if it's a full on assault like last time? he thought to himself, now regretting his earlier wish for a little excitement.

His eyes scanned the forest surrounding the outer fence, but he saw no movement. Sweat that had nothing to do with the heatwave prickled his forehead, and he once again damned his hazmat suit for preventing his hands from reaching it. It wouldn't be long before the acidic sweat dribbled into his eyes, and he blinked hard in anticipation of the all too familiar sting.

"I don't see anything," Frank nervously reported into the walkie-talkie. "Over."

"Just follow protocol, examine the area and remain where you are. I'm on my way over," returned Ramirez. "Over."

"Wh...why?" squawked Frank, alarmed at Ramirez's

announcement. "It's quiet over here and if they need you where you are, you should stay. Over."

"I have a fucking bad feeling, ok?" snapped back Ramirez, the shiny veneer of professionalism in his voice suddenly evaporating. "Double check everything! I'll be there in a couple minutes. Something's not right...I can feel it. Over."

"I'm at the far west corner, near the blackberry bushes," returned Frank. "I'll wait for your arrival. Over."

God, what's happening over there to freak him out like this? wondered Frank. *And why would he think there's something wrong on my side?*

Frank intently examined the long length of the interior and exterior fences that he had just passed, as well as the length of fencing ahead of him. *There are no breaches! It's fine...it's...*

His eyes paused at the blackberry bushes. The fence behind the bush was partly obscured. How many times had he walked past this point and not really given it a good look? The bush had grown so big over the past year it was difficult to see the fencing behind it. He used to check it more carefully in the old days, but lately it had grown so quiet he had become lazy and complacent.

Damn it! What's wrong with me?

Carefully, he edged forward and peered behind the bush. He swallowed hard at what he saw.

There were indeed two holes in the chain link on both the inner and outer fences. They were small and near the ground.

Nothing could get through that small gap, could it? His mind raced. Heck, even a dog could barely get through and then the bush mostly blocks it anyway...

"Grrrroooaaannn...," came a sound behind Frank.

Frank whirled around and a decayed hand reached for his face plate. Startled and completely unprepared for the encounter, Frank stumbled back in a panic. He didn't know what he stepped on, moss or mud or something else, all he knew was that in an instant both of his feet slipped out from under him, and he was falling helplessly to the ground.

The fall seemed to last an eternity, the bottom dropping out of his stomach while all he could see was the blue sky above.

The zombie! Where is it? Where is it? His mind reeled in terror.

He hit the ground hard, knocking his last breath out of his lungs and into his now fogged up face plate. Choking and gasping, he looked toward the last known location of his attacker. Through the white condensation on the thick Plexiglas, he saw the zombie of a very tall man with broad shoulders leaning over him, reaching out with its hand...

Scrambling back, Frank hit the blackberry bush and jerked away, realizing if the bush tore his suit, he could become infected simply by breathing the decay from the creature. He glanced back up and saw that the zombie was closing in on him fast. Altering his path, he scrambled along the edge of the blackberry bush, only to discover that his escape route had been cut off by several other zombies—six, seven, no...eight! They began to move toward him in a single massive wall of decayed flesh, the groans merging together into a chorus of the undead.

Pop! Pop, pop, pop!

The groans abruptly halted as several of the zombies turned to look in the direction of the new sound. Their bodies parted enough for Frank to see that it was Ramirez. He had a gun and was firing it into the air.

A new sound emerged: terrified mewling like the sound a baby calf would make if it had lost sight of its mother. The zombies ran off toward a larger herd of zombies several hundred yards away, deeper within the fenced area.

"Damn it Frank, how'd you get into this situation!" said Ramirez, helping him off the ground.

"I was startled, and I fell," said Frank, feeling his face blush. He remembered the defogging unit in his suit, and flipped the switch. His faceplate began to clear almost instantly. "I thought..." He didn't finish the sentence, too humiliated to reveal how scared he had actually been.

Ramirez glanced to the large group of zombies, still mewling and crying in terror. Other zombies in the massive herd appeared alarmed, but only briefly looked around before they returned to grazing on the grass.

"Well, me firing a gun to save your sorry ass risked sparking a stampede!" growled Ramirez, gripping and re-gripping the butt of the gun nervously. "You know how timid and skittish those things are. Next time, just stand up and shoo them away. It's not like they bite."

"I know, I know," stammered Frank. He thought of how the other guards would ridicule him after they heard about this. *Great, just great,* he mentally bemoaned. His job was about to turn even more unpleasant. "Zombies still freak me out. I keep remembering the zombies in the old movies when I was kid, you know?"

Ramirez nodded. "Yep. I saw them too. But this is the real world. You have to remember, the only danger from a zombie is that they can infect you with their illness or trample you to death if you scare them. Other than that..."

Suddenly, they heard a rush of feet at the fence and an almost banshee screaming. Frank whirled around and groaned. *Damn it!*

A group of men and women had arrived at the outer fence, all carrying signs and yelling. The signs displayed a variety of messages such as 'Vote for the Zombie Rights Act!', 'We demand humane treatment of the plague victims!" and 'Stop the cover up! The undead aren't really dead!'

"What do we want?" yelled the leader of the protestors.

"Humane treatment of the plague carriers!" cried all the protestors in unison.

"When do we want it?"

"NOW!!!"

The crowd repeated this chant several more times then broke down into chaos, different protestors yelling different slogans. One woman wasn't even bothering with a slogan, content to instead yell "Fucking bastards!" in a near shriek over and over again.

"Why won't you let families visit their sick relatives? Provide hazmat suits if they are truly contagious!" shouted a tall woman with short, black hair.

"That's because they're not really contagious," remarked another protestor. "It's a cover up!"

A blond woman slammed a clump of dirt against the outer fence. The chain-link metal rang out on impact, while the exploding dirt particles showered Frank and Ramirez. "If they're dead, why are they still moving around? Tell us the truth!"

"Why aren't they in hospitals being cared for?" demanded another man. "They're human beings, they have rights! You can't keep them in fields like cattle! Tell us why they aren't in hospitals."

Mostly due to lack of money and lack of resources, you idiot, thought Frank to himself, having answers for all of the protesters and their nagging comments. *Nearly 70% of the population has been infected and turned. We don't have enough hospitals, for shit's sake! Besides, all zombies want to do is graze in fields and don't seem to even notice if it's raining, snowing or hot as hell like today. If that's what they want, why fight it? And as far as them not being dead, well, they have no brain or heart activity. That says dead to me! And cover up? Fucking morons...*

The MP's finally arrived on the other side of the fence and began to push back the protestors.

"I knew they were up to something," said Ramirez to Frank as the protestors turned their attention on the MPs and stopped yelling at them. "They were trying to get our attention over to the other side of the fence so they could sneak in here. Did you see any gaps..."

"Hey!" yelled one of the MP's. "We have a breach! There's a gap in the bottom of the fence back here." He leaned over, grabbed something, then waved a piece of red cloth in the air. "Looks like someone has already gotten in."

Ramirez groaned. "Great, just great. One of the fucking protesters got in...no telling what kind of trouble they've already caused..."

Frank turned back toward the large herd of zombies, scanning the decayed bodies for something out of the ordinary. He spotted it. Moving away from them about waist high, he saw curly brown hair, bobbing up and down. Curly hair was wearing a red shirt too, he noted.

"There!" said Frank, pointing toward the intruder.

"Ah, hell," said Ramirez. "It's a kid. A damn kid!"

Ramirez and Frank walked quickly but calmly through the zombie herd so as not to alarm the creatures. A few close to the fence, already frightened by the protesters, sprinted away, looking fearfully back at the two men over their shoulders. In spite of this, the majority of the zombies remained calm and continued to graze on the grass. Fortunately for them, this group had grown accustomed to the presence of humans and had lost their natural fear.

"Hey, kid," called out Frank as he ran toward the boy.

As they approached, the boy finally heard them and turned to look their way. Then, apparently resigning himself to his punishment for being caught, he bowed his head and stared down at his feet. After a few seconds, he started to cry. Meanwhile, he continued to hold the hand of a woman zombie who was happily chewing away at a bouquet of flowers. "It's ok, kid, don't cry, don't cry," soothed Frank, slowing down as he approached the distraught child. "We're not going to yell at you. It's ok. What's your name?"

"Tommy," replied the boy, still sniffling.

"Well, it's nice to meet you, Tommy," continued Frank. "What are you doing out here?"

"My mom...I had to visit her, it's Mother's Day," said Tommy, looking up at the men and wiping his nose on his sleeve. "I used to bring her candy, but she prefers to eat the flowers now."

Frank nodded, looking at the boy's hand that was still clamped onto his mother's hand. His eyes followed along the boy's arm. Just under the long sleeve, he could see sores on his wrist, similar to the sores covering his mother.

Frank glanced up at Ramirez who returned a solemn nod—he had seen the sores as well. It was too hot of a day to be wearing a long sleeve shirt; the boy was clearly trying to hide the infection.

"You've been sneaking in for a while, haven't you?" asked Ramirez. Again, the boy looked alarmed, and Ramirez quickly waved it off and smiled. "No one is getting in trouble; we just need to know is all."

Tommy slowly nodded. "The government wouldn't let us in to see my mom, and she was right here, just a few blocks from our home. Dad told me to stay away, but I couldn't. She's my mom! She doesn't talk anymore, but I tell her about my day and stuff at home. I want her to know what's going on so when she gets well and comes home, she won't feel like she missed anything, you know?"

Ramirez and Frank nodded. As the boy looked up at them and told them his story, the sores around the collar of his shirt became more visible. He was in the later stages of the illness. Probably had a few hours or so left before he turned as well.

"Where's your dad?" asked Frank, trying to keep his voice steady, despite the tightening in his throat. *The poor kid can't be more than eight!* He hated to see anyone change, but someone so young... "Is he at home? Does he know you're out here now?"

Tommy shook his head. "Dad's at home. He's been really sick the past few days. Then this morning he refused to come out of his bedroom. I tried opening his bedroom door, but it was locked. I could hear him inside—he was groaning like mom does. I...I don't know why he won't come out of his room. I tried going to the neighbors for help, but...I couldn't get them to answer their door either."

A silence engulfed Frank and Ramirez, neither able to utter a word. It was one of the cruelties of the disease. It progressed faster in some people than in others, allowing some people to act as carriers, spreading the disease. No doubt, in this case, the boy had contracted it and took it home to his dad and his neighborhood.

How far has this innocent child spread the disease? Frank wondered. *If the father and the neighbors have it, it could end up being a very large outbreak.*

"Anyone else at home?" asked Ramirez. "Brothers, sisters, aunts, uncles, grandparents?"

This time the boy didn't answer right away, he stared down at his feet, grinding his right heel into the soft earth.

"Tommy?"

"No, they all came down sick like mom. They were taken to camps like this...I just don't know where."

Frank knew of three other facilities in the area. The army hadn't tried to keep families together in one camp. There was no point, really. The zombies weren't capable of recognition, they didn't care. Only the uninfected left behind cared, and that had turned into a different problem.

Frank knelt down so that he was almost eye to eye with Tommy. "Why don't you tell us where you live..."

Immediately, Tommy began to shake his head violently and grabbed onto his mother who had nearly finished eating the flowers. She didn't look down at Tommy; she only cared about the flowers and seemed quite happy munching away at them.

"We're not going to take you away, Tommy," continued Frank. "We just want to check up on your dad. In fact, I'll make you a deal. If you tell us, you can stay here with your mom. We won't make you leave, promise. You can stay as long as you want."

The boy's face lit up at this. "Really? I don't have to sneak in anymore?"

"Honest," said Frank, trying to hold back his own tears. "You can stay with your mom...forever and ever."

A vision of the next few weeks, the next few months, and the next few years flashed in Frank's mind. He could see it so clearly: taking his rounds in the quarantine area, seeing the undead boy wandering around in his red shirt. Frank knew he'd never forget this day or this conversation. His own words, 'You can stay with your mom forever and ever' echoed cruelly in his skull.

"We're at 2275 Humboldt St.," said Tommy, now smiling broadly. "The back door is open, but knock on the front door or my dad will get mad."

Frank stood up, and Ramirez motioned for them to leave.

"Enjoy your visit with your mom, son," said Ramirez, waving at the boy.

Tommy waved back as the two men departed. The relief and joy on his face would have been heartwarming if it had been under different circumstances.

Frank looked away quickly. *I need to hold onto that memory,* he told himself. *I need to remember that smile. Tonight, when I have trouble sleeping or tomorrow, when I encounter the turned boy...I have to hold onto that memory...*

Once the boy was out of ear shot, Ramirez called headquarters. In a hushed voice, he rapidly explained the situation. The words that were exchanged passed without Frank's notice. Unable to stop himself, he turned back around and watched Tommy. The boy, seeing that his mom had finished eating her flowers, quickly began to gather up buttercups. For every two buttercups that Tommy handed to his mother, he would pop one in his own mouth. Tommy didn't have much longer, probably less time than Frank had originally thought.

Much less.

After a short conversation, Ramirez signed off. He didn't say anything to Frank at first, and instead he turned away and watched the protestors leaving. Finally, he uttered quietly, "Damn it."

A queasy feeling rumbled through Frank's stomach. "It's big, isn't it?"

Ramirez nodded slowly. "This morning there was an outbreak at an elementary school, probably the one the boy was going to. That...that fucking vote to reopen public schools..." Frank said nothing. People wanted hope, wanted to believe things had changed. The law passed with a landslide vote, despite all the warnings from Homeland Security. "Our people were called in, and they found undead wandering everywhere, not just at the school, but at the nearby homes as well, and the homes of the kids, of course. They're thinking at least two hundred people were infected, maybe more."

"Two hundred?" gasped Frank.

Another long pause. Ramirez didn't continue, and Frank wondered if he was waiting for him to say more. He couldn't think of anything, so he just stood there, staring at his friend. After a while, it became clear that the gears were turning in Ramirez's head. A shadow seemed to pass over his features.

"You know what I've been thinking, Frank?"

"Umm...no..."

"I wish the zombies did bite, did attack people like in the movies," Ramirez answered. "If they did, we wouldn't have to worry about keeping humans away from them, people would just run away or kill the damn things or even pass legislation to kill them, rather than vote down the bill three damn times in as many years. But as it is, this..." he motioned towards the zombies walking past them, "...*this* will never end. People want to believe there's hope for the undead, they want to believe that their mom, dad, little sis, son or whatever is still alive, still waiting for them here in quarantine, waiting for a cure to be developed. They won't stay away, they will never, ever stay away. Tommy...the protestors...it's going to happen again, over and over and over again until we're all dead. That's what I think. I think our humanity will be the end of humanity. Ironic, right? We're dead, all of us. It's only a matter of time."

Frank didn't know what to say. He had reached this same conclusion months ago and had come to terms with it. It really should be obvious to anyone with half a brain. They were all going to die from this damn virus. Next year, next five years or the next ten. It didn't matter, every last one of them was going to get it eventually. It was inevitable. The only thing that surprised Frank was that Ramirez hadn't figured this out until now.

God, I hate this job, he thought to himself yet again.

Once more, he looked past the Plexiglas face plate on Ramirez's suit and saw a cold, blank stare, oddly similar to the expression worn by the zombies around them. He could see the despair and the depression taking hold of his friend, as deadly and cruel as the virus itself. Frank hated how the world clung to a false hope...but this... Something inside of Frank suddenly snapped.

"Ah, come on, don't get all melodramatic on me," said Frank, slapping his hand on his friend's shoulder and forcing a broad smile that he didn't feel on his face. "It's just a bad day, don't let it get to you. I don't want you being all sulky during poker tonight. Get over it. I mean it, I've been waiting for this night all week."

Ramirez looked startled at Frank's reaction. "Um...yeah, um...I think I'm going to skip..."

Pointing his finger at his friend's left eye as though it were a gun, Frank stated firmly, "You *are* coming to poker tonight, I'm not making excuses for you with the guys. You are coming...say it...say it..."

Finally, a light seemed to return to Ramirez's eyes, and he let out a short laugh. "Yeah, yeah, you're right. Just a bad day. Damn. This job really gets to you, doesn't it?"

Frank forced another laugh. In his own ears it sounded hollow, but Ramirez didn't seem to notice. "Let's finish our shift and get the hell out of here, what do you say? Just another half hour, am I right?"

"Around that," answered Ramirez, glancing down at his watch. "Ah, man, I've got to hustle if we're going to make it, though. I've got to file my report with the front office. See you at the guard house."

With a half run, Ramirez trotted off, their early discussion of the end of the world seemingly forgotten. *Wish I could forget... I wish...*

The words wouldn't come. He'd given up wishing and praying a long time ago.

Turning back around, he looked one last time at the boy. His mother had wandered away, but Tommy no longer noticed or cared. He simply sat in the grass, pulling up hunks of the vegetation—dirt-covered roots and all—and shoved them greedily into his mouth. Tommy stared off at a point on the horizon as he ate, dead to the world, and the world now dead to him.

∼

∼

Roma Gray

Roma Gray writes what she refers to as "Trick-or-Treat Thrillers", stories with a spooky, creepy, Halloween feel to them.

She currently has five published books: "Gray Shadows Under a Harvest Moon" (short story collection), "The Hunted Tribe: Declaration of War" (novel), "Celebration of Horror" (short story collection), "Jurassic Jackaroo: Jasper's Junction" (novel) and "Haunted House Harbor: Humanity's Hope" (novel). In addition to this, she has approximately 30 published short stories.

Roma lives in a haunted house in Oregon with her black cat, Chihuahua, and parrot.

Her books are available on Amazon.

Cobb

THE THREE FLAGS

The crotchety Vietnam Vet who owns The Three Flags Truck Stop and operates it as he sees fit. As long as he doesn't interfere with his wife's diner.

Scratch

Marine.
Lost his arm to an IED.
Hasn't slowed him down.
Runs freight in the 48
with a triple digit
Western Star
Large Car.

Sammy and his Mustang

JOSEPHINE

A Mach 1 Sammy built in his garage to escape the growing hordes of the undead.

14

MY CUP OF TEA

BY VALERIE LIOUDIS

I know I'm going to go to Hell for it, but God is it satisfying to stand here peering through the window while I drink my hot cup of tea and watch Laney get clawed to death. Every interaction I've had with her since moving to this suburban nightmare has been like having different versions of the same condescending conversation, one after another. It looks like my next-door neighbors, Mr. and Mrs. Adams, are trying to devour Laney, and while I should be questioning what in the world is happening, I am simply too fascinated by the scene unfolding outside. Instead, I stand there watching what has secretly been my only wish for six months play out in the cul-de-sac below.

"Mommy, it's getting late. Don't we have to leave for school?"

"Nope, they cancelled school today. You get to play Minecraft all day."

"Yes! Henry! Mom said no school, get your controller!" my son yelled excitedly as he ran off to find his brother.

I tell myself there is no reason to scare the children by telling them just yet. Really, I don't want this moment to end. This is the time of her comeuppance and I am going to savor every juicy bite of it. Her screams rip through the walls, yet I feel nothing. Well, not exactly nothing. A small smirk creeps across my face as I stare.

I am snapped back to reality as I realize that my phone has started to vibrate in my pocket.

"Hello," I answer, unable to pry my eyes away from the scene below.

"Honey, lock the doors and get the gun out of the safe! Something horrible is going on! People are rioting everywhere and killing everyone in their path! I'm heading home but I need you to hold down the fort until I get there," my husband spouts off in a panic.

"Sure, I can do that. But first I have to wait until Laney is dead."

"Wait, what? What do you mean 'wait until Laney is dead'? Is she coming after you and the kids? Chrissy, I will be home soon!" He sounds extremely worried.

"It's fine, Michael. We're fine. I sent the kids to play video games." I can feel the soothing warmth of the tea as it runs down the back of my throat. Speaking of throats, it occurs to me that Laney has finally stopped yelling. Mr. Adams has a good portion of her trachea sticking out of his mouth and is violently shaking his head back and forth like a dog with a rabbit between its teeth.

Blood spurts out of the giant hole he has chewed in her throat, covering his bald head with a bright red coating. He looks a lot like a shiny gumball from this height. I let out a giggle at the thought.

"What could possibly be funny, Chrissy?" Michael asks, irritated. "You need to take this seriously. You and the kids could die!"

"We'll be fine. I know what to do. You've been preparing

us and the house in case all Hell broke loose for as long as I can remember. I'm going to hang up. You focus on getting home to us. Be safe, Michael. I love you."

"I love you, too." He is barely able to get the words out before I press the red button.

"What a killjoy," I say to no one in particular.

Mr. Adams has moved on to his next victim, Laney's husband, James. He has made the rookie mistake of rushing out into the chaos to try to save his wife. He should have just let her die out there alone. Now he is being taken down by Mr. Adams in a terrifying burst of speed and ferocity that he would never have been capable of yesterday.

It is Mrs. Adams, however, who is my hero. She has no intention of leaving Laney in any type of recognizable state. At some point, each of the women on the block had been subject to Laney's personal brand of humblebrag and never-ending judgement. To the outside world, she came across as sweet as southern pecan pie, but once there were no witnesses around, Laney would tear you to shreds. Her emotional attacks were very akin to the physical attack that Mrs. Adams was carrying out against her that morning.

"Get her, Ann," I whispered as I took another sip of my tea. I was glad that I had opted for a spice tea that morning. It seemed like a more appropriate drink for observing a dismemberment than plain black tea. This *was* a special occasion after all.

"Mom, my controller isn't connecting to the game," my youngest whined as he walked up behind me.

"I'll be in to fix it in a minute," I said, perhaps a tad bit snippier than I intended.

Why wasn't the universe letting me relish this experience? We all have that one person in our life who wouldn't be around right now if murder was legal, and she was mine.

Yet here I was, gifted with a front row seat to her demise, and nobody could leave me alone for the five minutes it would take for her to be chewed right out of existence.

"Mom!"

"I swear on everything holy, if you two don't let me finish this cup of tea, I am going to make the apocalypse a living hell for you both!"

As soon as I turned back around, the unthinkable happened. Laney began to lift her half-eaten body off the ground. Mrs. Adams had now moved on, along with Mr. Adams. They were heading down the road, chasing what appeared to be a very scared and startled jogger. At least he had a chance of outrunning them, unlike most of the overweight couch potatoes that inhabited our neighborhood. Laney and her husband had decided to turn their attention towards our home. My dog was downstairs barking uncontrollably, which seemed to attract them.

I guess I would have to listen to Michael and go get our gun. The smirk that had been inhabiting my face turned into a full spread shit-eating grin. My fingers shook as I loaded the rifle, but not out of fear or anxiety. It was an overwhelming sense of anticipation that was making it hard for me to control my digits. If they attacked my family, I would have no choice but to put a bullet in each of their heads. No jury would ever convict a mother who was simply protecting her children.

I slid the window open and unlatched the screen. I pulled it out and slid it down onto the floor beside me. Lining her up in my sight, I yelled down to her.

"Laney! Get off my yard! If you don't stop, I'll be forced to shoot you!"

Please, God, let her keep coming.

Prayers don't always get answered immediately, but that

one did and it made me wonder if Laney had somehow managed to piss God off as much as she had the women on our street. She looked right up at me, let out a guttural growl, then sprinted towards the house. The grin turned to a giggle as I pulled the trigger.

I think it was my will alone that put the bullet square between her eyes.

Michael's truck was tearing ass up the street as her body fell onto the grass. He plowed right through James on his way into our driveway. I closed the window and slung the rifle over my shoulder, picking my tea back up as I went to greet him at the front door.

"Come on, boys. Pack up the PlayStation. We're heading down into the basement. Daddy's home from work early"

"The basement? Ugh, Mom, you said we could play all day."

"You can, but down in the safe room. There's a storm coming. Grab the dog on the way down. I am going to get the baby."

As Michael burst through the front door, wild-eyed and spouting off all of the atrocities he had witnessed on his short drive home, I gathered the few things we needed from upstairs and made my way down to the basement. The boys settled quickly with their game and the baby went right back to sleep. Michael, on the other hand, was losing his mind worrying about the problems we would face if anyone found our hiding spot.

I, however, felt calmer than I ever had in my entire life, the cup of tea still warm in my hands as I sat back and relaxed in my chair.

∼

Valerie Lioudis

Valerie is New Jersey born and bred. This has means that while she speaks English as her first language, sarcasm is a close second. Valerie is extremely active in the indie author community, especially with the ReanimatedWriters, a group with almost 200 zombie fiction authors. She is the co-author of the Aftershock Zombie Series, novelist of The Many Afterlives of John Robert Thompson, and featured in 9 anthologies, some released and some soon to be released, 2 of which she spearheaded. For more information on Valerie visit her Amazon page, follow her on Facebook or Twitter, or join the ReanimatedWriters Fan Page on Facebook.

15

SGT JOAN

BY GREG BENNETT

Her consciousness returning, Joan stirred, slowly opened her eyes and saw...nothing. The blackness was total and unnerving; it was as if her eyes had been dipped in printer's ink. Slowly and painfully working one arm free from the rubble, she moved her hand and, still seeing nothing, touched her face. *Shit...I'm blind.*

She was on a clean-up/recon mission with her squad. After the main artillery took out the larger zombie hordes; they would sweep the area, eliminate any stragglers and search for supplies. Food and supplies seemed to always run low at the outpost, especially since civilians were recently added. Marginal finds had forced them to look near some of the heaviest zombie concentrations. It was risky work, the zombies seemed to be faster than ever and could overtake a soldier in seconds.

They had been exploring an area on the outskirts of a small town when they found a business park with several warehouses. The warehouses appeared to be older construction with small side office buildings. Most were deserted and heavily damaged, but one appeared intact.

The warehouse windows were shaded and the standard walk-in doors locked. A couple of her squad members had started working to open a set of double doors when someone yelled that there were noises coming from inside. That's when all hell had broken loose. The double doors had burst open, surprising everyone. There weren't just a handful of zombies...there were 20 to 30 of them. Her squad had managed to take a few down with their weapons, but there were simply too many, too close.

The sudden wave of rushing death had forced her and her squad to seek cover in nearby buildings. A couple of the guys had been overtaken and hadn't made it, their screams merging with the zombie wails; deadly swan songs echoing between the warehouses.

She had run to an office section off to the side of the warehouse and managed to get the front door shut behind her. A few of the zombies had turned in her direction but she didn't know if they saw or followed her. The door seemed strong and would hold for a while, but not for too long. It needed reinforcement. As she had turned to run to the back of the office; the wood floor had given way beneath her. She had felt herself falling...then...darkness.

As her head cleared, she took an assessment of her situation. The darkness was total, she was either blind, completely covered in rubble or, as it had been late in the afternoon when they found the warehouse, simply enveloped in darkness. Partially rolled over and pinned down, she had several areas of bad pain, but it wasn't the sharp stabbing type she associated with broken bones. The side of her head throbbed, letting her know where she had hit it. *I guess that's what a knockout punch feels like.* She was lucky to not be injured worse.

She could hear what sounded like zombies wailing, but

it was indistinct, with no chance of telling how far away they were. She didn't smell the putrid, rotting stench associated with them. *At least I'm not sharing a hole with a meat-bag.*

She seemed to be dry. The basement, or whatever she had fallen into, was not flooded. There was no sound of running or dripping water.

But...there was something.

She could hear a faint sound, almost lost in the background noise from above.

Something like...scratching?

A wave of fear hit her like a thunderbolt.

Her mind flashed back to the gossip and bullshit with her squad at the outpost.

They'd heard rumors bout the work conducted in the China labs. That in their efforts in researching the outbreak, they'd discovered another possible threat. A threat involving...insects.

That some insects could possibly contract and transmit the virus by feeding on the zombies' saliva.

(It was at that exact moment she felt something crawling on her leg...something she couldn't reach...) Her training had not prepared her for this. She could feel the panic welling inside her, becoming an unheeding monster in her mind. The urge to move, to run, to get away was overpowering. The fact that she could barely move...

IT'S JUST A RUMOR! IT'S JUST A RUMOR!

(a second something had found her neck and was slowly making its way to her ear...)

Her panic had dissolved almost all traces of rational thought. Almost.

WHAT BITES? WHAT BITES? WHAT'S IN THE DARK? THINK! THINK!

(a third something had found her other leg and was

making its way up inside her pants. The fabric of her pants caused it to stop momentarily, but soon it found freedom... and continued. Pushing, crawling ever higher, tiny legs digging along her skin...)

Spiders? Yes, they were active at night and some could bite, but she didn't think they made much noise. Roaches? Yes, they were also active at night but she didn't think they could bite. Other night bugs she thought of were fliers and not crawlers.

What if they were centipedes? Could those bite or sting? What if they...

STOPPPPPPPPPP!

Using her free hand, she gripped her face tightly and shook her head in an effort to shift her attention. She forced herself to calm her fears and bring her mind back in focus. *Think dumbass. You haven't felt any bites or stings. They're probably just roaches. If there had been an insect breakout, you would have heard about it by now. Get your ass in gear and free yourself.*

As she slowly regained her composure, she came to realize how rapid her breathing was. *You are lucky you didn't hyperventilate. Get calm and focus. You can play Ants in Your Pants some other day.*

She listened. Aside from the faint scratching around her, she heard nothing.

She tried to ignore her crawling companions and focus back on freeing herself. Aside from her partially free arm, she was effectively pinned down. She felt that she was somewhat spread-eagled and turned on her side, probably facing downward.

She twisted her shoulder and arm and felt the debris with her hand. Some of the boards were thick and heavy, but some were small enough that they might be moved.

She slowly tested each piece she could reach, cautiously applying pressure. The last thing she needed was to start a cascade on herself, or worse, cause enough noise to attract the zombies.

After what seemed like an eternity, she finally moved enough boards to free her other arm. Her progress improved substantially; she was able to shift one of the larger pieces of debris away from her chest, allowing her some upper body mobility.

Now able to twist, she pulled on the large boards that held her right leg. The boards gave enough to let her ease her leg up toward her chest, free her foot and push against the boards holding her left leg.

She was free.

She still couldn't see.

She didn't smell the pungent, metallic odor of blood so commonly known to soldiers in the field. She ran her hands along her arms, neck, legs and body, searching for any gaping, bleeding wounds. She found none. She had painful areas, but none sharp. She wasn't feeling dizzy, so maybe the bump on her head wasn't a sign of a concussion.

She didn't have her utility belt, flashlight or rifle. They were likely covered by the debris.

Lifting herself into a somewhat crouching position, she tried to stand up and found she couldn't, the floor and debris completely covered her.

Dropping to her hands and knees, she began exploring her surroundings. She tried to ignore the occasional crunch of the scurrying things beneath her and still moving around in her clothes. Her initial panic over the creepy crawlies was still lurking in the back of her mind, waiting to lunge out again if given the chance. A cold shiver enveloped her. *I bet I have goosebumps on my tits.*

She decided she was on the bottom floor of the office, possibly in a basement. The smooth surface she crawled on didn't feel like it would give way or collapse.

She moved slowly on her hands and knees, stretching her arms and hands in front of her, advancing if the way was clear. The darkness was unnerving.

Her right knee landed on something soft.

Before she could react and shift her weight, there was a soft crunch, a sickening *POP*; then wetness slowly sliding down her face, neck and arms. The smell of decay was overpowering. It was the smell of death.

She muffled a scream and recoiled, rolling and hitting her head and arms on the debris above her. The beams and debris moaned and shifted, but nothing collapsed. Her breathing was rapid, her pulse racing. She felt the specter of panic rearing its ugly head again, ready to take control.

WHAT THE HELL WAS THAT?

The shock slowly left her and she checked herself for additional injuries. She found not just wetness but wet *things* stuck to her. She couldn't wipe them off fast enough.

She regained her composure enough to focus again. Listening intently, there were no sounds except for the same slight scurrying and scratching as before.

It must be some animal, maybe a rat, killed from the floor collapse. Wanting to avoid the sickening mess, she felt around and found a long, slender piece of wood and swung it side to side, just as a blind person would swing a cane.

She found the soft, mushy spot again and, based on its size, decided it was indeed a rat.

The smell was still strong; she didn't want to waste any further time there.

Keeping the piece of wood, she slowly worked her way

across the floor. Finding a somewhat open area, she swung the wood upward and hit...nothing. It was open.

She looked upward. It might be her imagination, but she thought she could see a faint, grayish blob high above her. She blinked and stared. There was definitely a grayish blob against the pitch-black darkness.

Maybe she wasn't blind after all.

She redoubled her efforts and soon found what appeared to be a wall. There was no debris here, she could stand upright. *It would be nice if they had a stair...* as she tripped... onto the first step of a staircase.

SHITTTTTTTTTTTTTTT!

Her shins protesting, she continued up the staircase, testing each step and remaining close to the wall.

Reaching a landing, she could see the grayish blob above her easier, but there wasn't enough light to see any objects nearby. She couldn't tell what condition the floor was in or how big an opening she'd fallen through.

Feeling along the wall and the side of the staircase, she found that the staircase continued higher, to another floor. Like before, she tested each step and remained close to the wall as she worked her way upward.

At the top, she found herself in the office room where she had started. There was faint light coming through a shaded window and around the front door. The front door was still thankfully closed. Again, her luck had been good, the zombies either hadn't seen her or had lost interest.

Surprisingly, her rifle and flashlight were near the corner of the room. Avoiding the weakened areas of the floor, she used her flashlight and peered into the smallish hole near the center. Cold chills embraced her with icy fingers. She'd fallen through this floor, through the second floor, and the second floor had collapsed in layers on top of her just like stacking cards. She was lucky to be alive and unhurt.

She didn't know the time, but based on the minimal daylight, it had to be near dusk. She couldn't yell or signal with her flashlight without possibly attracting the attention of the zombies. The zombies were attracted to loud, unnatural noises or bright lights.

She sat down and leaned against the wall, thinking about her squad. Did they survive? Were they hurt? Was she the only one left?

Her hand brushed against something in one of her pants pockets. It was one of the paratrooper "cricket" clickers they'd been issued and trained to use. They'd all thought the little gizmos were funny and some had thrown theirs away, but she had kept hers for some reason or another.

Hello beautiful.

She moved over near the door, listened for zombie activity and, not hearing any, slowly cracked the door open. With the clicker in her hand, she sounded the signal, "click click", pause, "click click", pause, "click". She listened and waited.

Off in the distance, she heard the reply, "click, click, click".

She felt her eyes welling with tears. Others were out there. Others who could help...or be helped. Others who were...alive.

For the first time that day, she felt...hope.

Kim-Li

Waitress at the Three Flags Truck Stop. Daughter of a Marine. Punches smiley faces in targets at 1,000 meters.

16

"SPARKY"

BY GRIVANTE

Sheila 11:44 p.m. *'You're supposed to be home by 11. You start your new job in the morning.'*

I looked at my buddy Jax as he flicked my lighter than glared back at my phone as it buzzed anew.

Sheila 11:45 p.m. *'Make sure you set your alarm for early. I got free bacon, so I'll be making breakfast.'*

I had as little interest in my nagging stepmother's reminder as I did her cooking. The last time she'd graced me with the experience it looked more like cooked roadkill than a meal. Still, I shook my head. "I gotta go, man."

Jax looked up. "Sheila?"

"Yeah." I put the joint we'd been smoking out and stuck it behind my ear. "See you after work tomorrow."

Of course, I didn't set my alarm, which is why I wasn't up in time for breakfast. I awoke to the crash of breaking glass but still grabbed my phone before moving to get out of bed. It was blowing up, vibrating all over my nightstand.

Tommy 8:02 a.m. *'Yo, Sparky! You believing this shit? I'm heading over to Jax's to stay low and smoke till this blows over!'*

Tracy 8:04 a.m. *'What'd we smoke last night? This can't be real.'*

Jax 8:07 a.m. *'They got Tommy, man. He was on my front porch and they just took him down. Tore him to shreds right before my eyes. You all right? Hit me back bro.'*

I hit the thumbs up button over and over, sending a quick, *'I'm okay'* to everyone I knew before getting out of bed, but I didn't leave my room. I didn't know what was going on, but if it's crazy out there and glass was breaking downstairs, the crazy might just be in here, too.

My shorts were still on, but my shirt was M.I.A. I grabbed another from my closet floor and crept over to my door. I heard noises below, definitely not my family talking, but not things breaking either. Someone enjoying a good meal? Maybe Sheila learned how to cook all of a sudden.

I slipped out my door and made my way down the hall. At the top of the stairs, I could see into the kitchen and dining area. Two plates of food sat untouched, my stepbrother Clancy's lay broken on the tile floor. Yet, I still heard someone eating.

I took two steps down and froze, spying Clancy crouched on top of his mother where she lay on the kitchen floor, a pool of red surrounding them both. Clancy's face was buried in her flesh, savagely tearing chunks from her neck and shoulder.

"What the f—" I muttered and Clancy turned to look at me, his eyes black as night. The guttural snarl he threw in my direction before leaping up and bounding for the stairs sent me scurrying. I hauled ass back to my room, slammed the door and knocked my mostly empty dresser over in front of it. Wishing, now, that I'd put my clothes away properly so that it had more weight to it.

Clancy smacked against the door, making me jump. Snarls and the sound of nails scratching against the hollow door echoed off the walls of my room.

"WTF?" I shouted to no one, then grabbed my phone.

Jax 8:11 a.m. *'ZOMBIES!'*

A short video clip followed his text, showing a bloody and partially decapitated Tommy getting up and walking away from Jax's porch. He was also missing his left arm.

I looked at the shaking door to my room, then to the window leading onto the roof. I'd snuck out that way so many times during high school to get stoned with my friends, there was literally a path worn in the composite roofing. Looks like I'd be using it again unless I wanted to become Clancy's second breakfast. Or make that third, the image of Sheila's dead form crept into my mind. What was happening? Zombies? Really?

I slid my shoes on, grabbed my phone charger; people always forget that shit in the movies and opened my window. I had one foot out before I realized I hadn't grabbed my stash.

I climbed back in, trying to remember where I'd put it. There was half a joint next to my keys on the nightstand, I grabbed it and stuck it behind my ear before searching my pockets for a lighter. I came up empty of course, remembering Jax flicking it while I had stared at my phone the night before. He loved reminding me of how I got my nickname by making sure I never had a light.

The door shook, this time making a cracking sound. My heart thundered and I wondered for a moment if weed, even 'the chronic', would be worth dying for. No. I shook my head. If you weren't around to smoke it, it wasn't worth it.

There'd always be more... I hoped! I climbed out the window and closed it behind me, rolling to the side and out of view just as Clancy crashed in.

I peered around the corner and watched him. His blood smeared visage scanned the room, hungry and confused.

"I'm no one's munchie. Not yet, anyway," I muttered and rolled back out of sight, whipping my phone out and texting Jax.

'Just escaped half-bro. He was about to eat me.' I hit send, then started a second message.

'I'll get in my car and...' That's where I'd left my weed! I reached down and patted my pocket. No keys.

I rolled back over and looked in my window. There, on the nightstand right next to where I'd picked up the half-smoked joint, lay my keys.

Fuck!

Movement in the room caught my attention and I turned to see Clancy running straight at the window. I screamed, fell over backward, and off the edge of the roof into the shrubs at the front of the house.

I woke up a few minutes later, laying on my back in the shrubs, phone clutched in my hand, my last unsent message still on the screen. Delete. I quickly sent a new one.

'Where is safe? I've got no wheels.'

A few deep breaths later, Jax replied.

Jax 8:21 a.m. *'Come here.'*

A moment later, a second message.

Jax 8:22 a.m. *'Bring your chronic. I'm out.'*

That was typical of Jax, he never had any of his own. On a day like today though, that didn't matter. Neither did I.

I sat up and looked around, the branches of the hedge

digging into my back. To my left stood the big bay window of my dad and step-mom's place, just inside was the dining table with its uneaten breakfast and... Sheila!

She stood facing into the kitchen, her clothes soaked in blood. I shook my head. It really was happening. If I wasn't seeing it, I wouldn't believe it.

I worked at quietly extricating myself from the bush, a feat that wasn't quite possible. The cracking and crunching attracted Sheila's attention. Her head snapped around at a grotesque angle and she ran toward the window, smashing herself against the glass. In the background, I saw Clancy run down the stairs to join her. I fell out of the bush onto the dry grass of the front lawn, stumbling over myself as I scrambled to my feet.

I reached up and touched the joint above my ear. Surprisingly, it was still there but after that fall, I decided I'd better keep it somewhere safe. I stuck it between my lips, then found my hand searching for my absent lighter. Maybe it wasn't safer there if I was just going to try to spark it up.

The quickest way to Jax's was through a dirt ravine that separated our neighborhoods and ran out to the highway. My old bike lay against the side of the garage. It was Clancy's now. My dad had made me give it to him after he bought me my car, but the little brat didn't even take care of it. I don't know if he even bothered to ride it. I wiped dust off the seat just as the crash of the front window shattering sent my adrenaline through the roof. Sheila and Clancy, large jagged shards of glass sticking out of them at weird angles, rushed for me.

I pinched the half-smoked doobie between my lips, muttered, "Shit" and tore out of there, the ravaged forms of my stepfamily in fast pursuit. I whipped out my cell phone as I rode, texting Jax.

'I'm coming in hot! Be ready!'

When I came up out of the ravine, dirt and dust flying behind me, I saw carnage lining Jax's street. People were screaming, a car rolled down the street, driverless, blood smeared across its side. A few yards away, two males had a small female form held to the ground as they tore into her flesh.

I turned and followed the car until it veered off the road and slammed into a light pole; knocking it over in a fury of sparks and one loud bang. Pedaling hard and breathing harder, I risked another glance behind me. Shit, shit, shit! Sheila and Clancy had just crested the top of the ravine and, without pausing, ran straight for me. The two men broke away from their feast and joined the pursuit.

A text came through from Jax.

'Come in through the garage!'

The houses on the street were alive with activity. Gunshots and screams filled the air; people, both living and dead, stared out windows. Even more of the zombies joined Sheila and Clancy. I felt like they wanted to catch me and make me a part of their insane little family. "No way," I muttered, "not when you were alive and sure as hell not now that you're dead."

I had a bit of an advantage now, Jax's house, well, his parents' house, sat at the bottom of a slope. His half-open garage door beckoned me to safety. A glance over my shoulder showed me that the dead were still close behind though and I pedaled even harder, wishing I'd had time to air up the tires, each rotation felt like I was going uphill rather than down. As I got closer, I saw that Jax was in the garage, peering out from underneath the half-open door. His long blond hair covered his plump cheeks. There were no cars inside or in the driveway which meant no one else was home. I had a clear shot, but because of how he had the door half-open I'd have to lay it down. Jax backed away from the opening as I neared, moving back to the door that led into the house, remote in his hand, ready to shut it as soon as I got inside.

I hit the driveway and saw the door begin to move downward and realized there must be biters right on my tail. I clamped down on the joint with my lips like a vice and laid the bike on its side, sliding under the closing door. Skin tore off my ankle and arm, but I made it inside with a cry of pain. A heartbeat later it sounded like a machine gun firing as my pursuers thudded into the steel closure.

"Whoo!" I breathed out, looking at the long-haired and wide-eyed form of my buddy, Jax. "Thank you!"

"Man am I glad to see you, Sparky. Let's get inside."

In the end, Jax coughed up his stash, a small baggie of mexi-weed and we spent the next two days smoking and watching the news in his dad's man cave.

He'd heard from his folks and sister early on the day it all started, then nothing more. I never heard from my dad, but that was nothing new. A number of our friends tried to make it to us, but they all went dark. Either out of juice or…

We'd go check out the upstairs windows every now and then and see the same crowd, Sheila and Clancy among them, milling about.

When the news channels became static and the few social feeds and websites that were active became nothing more than pleas for help we couldn't answer, we turned on the X-Box and played games. We had plenty to eat for now and all was well until two things happened; we smoked the last of Jax's weed and the power went out.

We still had the half-joint, again behind my ear, that we'd both agreed to save for last because it was the good stuff. We'd talked about what we'd do if the rescue we were initially sure would come didn't happen and we ran outta supplies. Running out of power and weed was not something we had prepared for and paranoia kicked in.

"We're gonna die, Sparky!" Jax said as he burned the ashen bowl one last time.

My own thoughts mirrored his, but I didn't voice them. "There's gotta be someplace safe."

We sat in the dark and silence a moment, then Jax had a halfway brilliant idea. "What about that truck stop you used to work at? The one where you got your nickname. Those guys had their own little compound and the truckers that used to hang out there, they were tough as nails. If anyone can survive this nightmare, it would be them."

"You're right man," I ran my fingers through my hair, "but I haven't been back there since Martha fired me."

Jax laughed. "You mean when she caught you lighting up in the walk-in freezer?"

"It wasn't the walk-in, it was the kitchen." He'd heard this story a million times before but he loved to hear me tell it. "It was my break and I wanted to hop out back to have a quick puff, but of course I couldn't find my damn lighter. So, I snuck into the kitchen to light it on one of the gas burners. Right as I leaned in to light my joint, she started yelling. I jumped and caught my eyebrows on fire." I rubbed them absently as he chuckled. They'd grown back but were much thinner than they used to be.

I ran out into the restaurant screaming that my face was on fire. Her old man, Cobb, was sitting at the end of the bar where the kitchen doors opened into the restaurant. He picked up his glass of water and threw it in my face, extinguishing my smoldering follicles.

"Settle down, Sparky," he said.

Martha, who was hot on my heels and prior to that moment had always called me by my full given name, Jonathon, came out behind me and adopted Cobb's new nickname for me. "You know work here no more, Sparky!"

I shook my head. "I deserved that, but you know what really sucked? The whole time I worked there I loved how the truckers had their nicknames and cool stories about how they got them. Now, I finally had one and I didn't get to hang out with them anymore. But you're right, that's exactly where we should go."

Jax who had been laughing, stopped and nodded. "Yeah, man, but how do we get there?"

I thought about it, fiddling with the still unsmoked joint. "Our bikes? We ride the ravine, it runs straight to the highway and from there, out of town."

His head bobbed in agreement, then shook side-to-side. "I can't outrun them. I'm not in that good of shape and, I'm pretty sure your step-mom and Clancy are still out there."

He was right, we'd never make it. They hadn't left. There could be hundreds out there. We'd need a distraction.

"Does your dad still have that old boom box?"

We had our bikes parked in the hallway by the front door. Tires pumped up, three layers of clothes and even helmets on. It was ninety-degrees outside, but we weren't taking any chances. Jax's mom would be losing her shit if she saw the bikes inside like this.

"Hey, let's smoke that before we do this." He pointed at the joint behind my ear.

"No way," I said. "We need our wits about us. Let's save it for when we get there."

Jax tilted his head and pursed his lips together. "Really?"

"Yeah." I nodded.

"Ok, but..." He pulled the lighter out of his pocket. "I'm hanging onto this, Sparky."

"No problem man," I laughed. "I won't smoke without you. Now let's put Operation: Garage Trap into action!"

We entered the garage via the door off the kitchen. Jax's dad had an old boom box he used out there that ran on batteries. I pressed play on the cassette and AC/DC's Hell's Bells came on already halfway through the song. I cranked it up and immediately from outside we heard the dead pounding on the metal door.

"You sure that garage door is gonna work?" he asked me.

"Yeah, man. You were the one who told me it still worked last year when we lost power during the big snow storm. It has a battery backup so that people don't get stuck and can't get out."

I closed and locked the kitchen door and we pushed the refrigerator in front of it.

Jax pushed the open button on the remote.

We heard them rush in, growling and snarling even louder than the rock-n-roll. We rushed back to the front of the house and peered from behind the curtains. Savage shapes came running from all over the neighborhood, their gore caked faces seeking out the source of the noise. At least two dozen of the damn things disappeared inside. We couldn't see the door from here, but we sure heard them.

"Ok," I said, "That looks like all of them."

He pushed the close button. "Let's hope they stay put."

"Let's get moving!" I opened the door and hopped onto my bike. We could still hear the electric whirring of the door and something in the back of my head screamed wait, but I was already rolling out, Jax on my tail.

As we rode down the driveway, I glanced back and saw the door was three-quarters closed, a mass of shuffling feet inside, the sounds of AC/DC fading. We pedaled our asses off, hitting the small hill and giving it everything we had.

We were halfway up when the sound of music grew louder again. I twisted my head around to see the door going back-up. I realized that with so many of them in there it hadn't been able to close. They must've set off one of those damn safety sensors. At least they hadn't noticed us, we'd be able to get away.

Jax followed my gaze. The song ended. In the pause between songs. Jax cried out. "Oh shit!"

My heart dropped into my stomach. We were far enough away to have a good head start, but when the heads snapped around in our direction, I knew we were fucked. The next song started as the hungry mass of dead ran from the garage in pursuit.

Our legs worked hard and fast, pounding the pedals. I made it to the top and looked back. Jax was only two-thirds of the way with the dead right behind him. They tackled him and he disappeared in a storm of bodies. I choked back a cry and hoped I'd have time to mourn him later, but I kept moving.

I hit the ravine without incident. My muscles ached but I kept going. Being out in the open wasn't safe and while the folks at Three Flags may have fired me, I didn't think they'd turn me away, I had to make it there.

A few cars dotted the highway with dead stuck inside, but luckily none on the open road. I was exhausted by the time I drew near the truck stop. I kept fingering the joint, daydreaming about when I'd get to smoke it. As soon as I got inside the Three Flags was my plan, but that fantasy was cut short by the blast of gunfire and the roar of straining semi engines.

Oh shit! Were they under attack?

I came over a rise and spotted the Three Flags, a string of armored semi's rolling out, plowing through the zombs and heading in the opposite direction. Those they hadn't flattened were chasing them.

There went my one shot at surviving. I stuck the joint in my mouth. Might as well smoke it.

It was then I remembered Jax had kept the lighter.

Dammit.

I recognized some of the trucks as they drove away. I even remembered the driver's names. Scratch, Pack-Rat, Gunny. I watched as the convoy disappeared, leaving carnage behind like a bloodbath on the blacktop.

I put the joint back behind my ear and started pedaling. Maybe I could catch them and maybe, just maybe, one of them would have a lighter.

∽

Grivante

Grivante writes sci-fi, fantasy, horror and post-apocalyptic fiction with a writing style that bounces between comedy and action-packed horror, most often mixing together to create things like Zombie Omelets and Spleen Soup.

Find more at Author.to/Grivante

Connect on Twitter, Facebook and Instagram under the name Grivante.

Stabby

Rock Star
Long Hair, Don't Care
Trapped in his beat-up old
tour bus in the Three Flags
parking lot when the end
of the world happens.

17

THE GLASS CITY ESCAPE

PHEOBE JACKSON AND EMILY STIVER

Moaning, the sound of shuffling, and the occasional thump penetrated the dark hiding place of the Glass City crew.

"In 1930 R.E.W was started by brothers Galen & Carroll Roush when they left C.R.Y. Freight," Pops whispered softly.

"For Christ's sake, Pops, shut your trap before you get us all killed!" Bugz said in a harsh whisper to the old man.

Pip tried hard to quietly make her way to where she though Pops was sitting in the old rusted truck trailer, the only sound came from the rustling of her coat and her boots on the dusty floor. Though barely audible, the sound was magnified in the rusty tin box and sounded like thunder to her.

Poor Pops is about 85 years old, as far as anyone can tell, and he spouts off facts about R.E.W. (Road Express Way Trucking Company) history when he is truly scared. Pip slid down the wall next to Pops and held his hand and told him they were ok. That seemed to calm him and his random fact reporting stopped.

They had hoped they could make it all the way back to the convoy of parked trucks, but then the horde was upon them and they had to find someplace to hide. Thank goodness there were some long-forgotten, broken-down cabs and trailers behind the garage of the Halfway truck stop.

They had lost track of how long they sat in the dark, dusty, suffocatingly hot tin box. At some point they had dozed off sitting with their backs against the wall, with heads on knees or curled in a ball with their head on an arm. Pip was still holding Pops' hand. It must be morning because daylight was spilling in through the many pin holes made from the oxidized metal being brutalized by the elements for years.

Pip (AKA Petenstine)

I could just make out Wrongway's Herculean form to the right of Pops, a huge man of few words, except when it counted most.

Squinting and wiping the dust and sleep from my eyes, I could see Indian Sue. She was a retired Air Force Special Ops gal who could read the sky and the secrets that it held.

Shutter Bug was next to her, sprawled out on the floor of the trailer sleeping like a rock, his head resting on his machete. That couldn't be comfy.

Comfort was one of those things we lost the day the world went to hell.

I couldn't make out the rest of the bodies in the box. I went to the door and listened for any sounds of the undead milling around. I just about jumped out of my skin when I felt a heavy hand land on my shoulder. I hadn't noticed I had been holding my breath till that moment, it worked in my favor as I was able to stifle a scream. Wrongway leaned forward and opened the door ever so slightly to peer into the brightness of the new day.

The horde must have just been passing through. Wrongway opened the door a little more and the hinges protested with a long squeak.

Now the rest of the crew were beginning to stir from their slumber and moving toward the doors.

"Are they gone?" Indian Sue asked. Wrongway nodded affirmative. Looking at the faces crowded around the sliver of daylight I asked, "Where are Pattycake and Tiny Bigman?".

Tiny Bigman has been a pain in my backside since he rolled into our truck stop. He has an issue with following a woman. The kind of guy with a tiny...brain and a big ole' mouth and prehistoric attitude. He thinks a man should be leading this group to safety. Ha!

Bugz spoke up and said, "Saw him shove Lil Pattycake into the office as we went through the garage. Didn't look like she wanted to go with him either."

"Son of a..." I murmured a line of curses under my breath, I looked at Wrongway and motioned for him to come with me. I swear, the first chance I get, I am going to feed Tiny Bigman to the man-eating shamblers as a pre-meal snack.

I told the others to grab their packs and get to their trucks as quietly as possible and not to start them up till we made it back to our truck. No sense in ringing the dinner bell till we were ready to vacate the area.

Wrongway and I went in search of the 'would be' kidnapper. We made our way across the lot toward the garage.

Strewn around were the cast offs from the horde that passed through last night. Bits of oozing, rotten flesh that had finally fallen off the undead it was attached to, a skeletal femur and a hand partially powdered by the trampling of feet, bits and pieces of rotted cloth lay where they had dropped, a shoe here and a finger there. All the tell-tale signs of a large horde passing through.

Trying not to step in the left behind goo, we made it back into the garage.

There were a few dead pounding on the door and walls of the office cubical.

I looked up at Wrongway, "Care to guess where they may be?" I asked. He rolled his eyes and shook his head as he picked up a length of steel piping sitting by the open overhead door. We had to sneak up behind the dead, that meant moving slowly and being silent in our approach. Let's hope our own stench doesn't give us away. We were just a few feet away from the dead when Tiny Bigman hit the glass and started shouting, "We're over here! Hey! Here we are!" *No kidding dumb ass, shut up!* I was shouting in my head. Putting my index finger up to my lips in a universal sigh for Quiet.

Just then the two dead in the rear turned to see what was exciting their morning meal. Wrongway let loose a solid swing of the pipe and brought one down with one blow to the top of the head, the spine went through the skull and came out through the top. I rushed the other before it could react. Its hands clawing and teeth snapping, I ducked and came up pushing my blade up through the soft spot under the chin. It started falling forward, I put my foot on its chest and kicked it backwards as I withdrew my knife.

Wrongway had dispatched two more in the time it took me to kill one. I pushed my blade into the ear of the next as Wrongway brought down the last one, knocking its head clean off its shoulders. Reminding myself not to get on the big man's bad side I looked up to see Tiny Bigman open the door with relief.

I rushed in, driving the man into the opposite wall. I had my knife to his throat "What the hell did you think you were doing? We had a plan as a group and you failed to follow instructions. Not only putting you and Pattycake in danger, but Wrongway and myself as well! Next time there will be no rescue party to save your sorry butt," I yelled in his face, looking over my shoulder, I asked how Pattycake was as I held the man in a vice-like grip pinning him to the wall with my forearm and full weight across his throat.

Wrongway was helping her up, her clothing was ripped and torn and she was sporting a new shiner on her left eye and bruises on her jaw and arm in the shape of finger prints. I head butted Tiny Bigman as hard as I could in the face, hoping to break his nose and let him go.

"If you ever go near Pattycake again, or man-handle any woman, I will kill you where you stand," I snarled, not sure if I was getting through to this Neanderthal, because I think I heard him mumble the c word. After a sharp knee to his balls, I let him slide down the wall and we were on our way. Wrongway carried Pattycake out to Indian Sue's truck. Them gals will take good care of her.

We safely deposited Pattycake into the sleeper compartment and we were on our way to meet up with Griz and his crew from the Three Flags Truck Stop that had made their way up from the south. We had plans of meeting in the middle as we were coming from the north east. The most beautiful sound in the world was the sound of more than two dozen trucks starting up in unison. I couldn't help but hum Jerry Reed's song, East Bound and Down, which lead into C.W. McCall's convoy. It was oddly comforting now, more so than it had been in the past. Not caring at the moment if that jerk was going to follow us out or not.

"Petenstine from T-town calling Wildcard Momma. Wildcard Momma what's your 20? How close are you to the rendezvous point? We have someone here that wants to give you a big 'Howdie Do', for saving their bacon back in Midland," I called into my handset.

"Thanks, Petenstine, for passing along our thanks. We thought we were going to die up on the roof of the Rockabilly Blue's Bar and grill. That convoy blew into town in the nick of time. Plucked us off the roof with the largest lineman truck I have ever seen. We were down to our last bottle of water for 6 people and had finished off our last jar of pickles two days ago. Thank you much, Wildcard Momma. We owe you our lives and hope to see you soon," Windy the Weathergirl said.

"Wildcard Momma how was it going from Texas to Oakly? How are the kiddos adapting to this new world? Be safe and Godspeed to you and the little ones. I have faith that the truckers will get you to Lakota, Oklahoma intact...Wildcard Momma?" I say and wait.

Wildcard Momma

"Wildcard Momma here, Petenstine, Windy the Weathergirl I'm glad we could help, come on back," I laugh at my use of the ridiculous trucker lingo through tears. Windy and her crew were in a bad way when Big Joe heard their cries over the CB and a crew of us went to their rescue. I'm glad she found her people...My people. Petenstine and her crew had quickly become my people. Then again any actually living people were my people now.

"How are the littles, Wildcard?" Petenstine's voice interrupts my thoughts before they can go dark.

"Rowdy and the Wild Bunch are just fine, Petenstine. Rowdy is in the back putting the Wild Bunch to bed as we speak." I look up to the mirror in time to see him step out of the bedroom our 5 kids are sharing and quietly shut the door. Rowdy looked to the windshield in time to catch me watching him in mirror of the RV, he winks at me and smiles. Thankful again that we were all together the day the world went dead.

"Pit stop Wildcard Momma," Big Joe says. I wonder where we're stopping, I'm 3 trucks behind Big Joe so I don't see anything but his back door and tail lights, but if the lead truck says pit stop, I won't argue.

"Petenstine, we're on 44 headed up but pulling off for a pit stop. Be safe, I'll talk to ya when we get moving again." I pull into a dark rest stop that used to have the golden arches blazing this time of night. Wondering if it's fuel for the barrels or our stomachs Big Joe is after.

After shutting off the engines we wait a minute to see how many lurchers we've attracted. "Only three right outside our door babe, you get one, I'll get the other two?" Rowdy says with a smirk. I'm out the side door, tire iron swinging into the first rotted head in my path before he's done being cocky. The second lurched and knocked my weapon from my hand. I grabbed its hair with my left hand and kept its mouth just out of reach of my skin, reaching behind me with my right hand I grabbed my knife out of its make-shift sheath and stuck it in the thing's ear. Rowdy put down the other one and started up the line of vehicles to see what we were doing.

I looked at the piles of flesh we just put down. An old lady with her arm chewed to the bone and gore all down the front of her, blood stained dentures knocked from her mouth when my tire iron connected with the side of her head. The second, a teen boy no more than 15 or 16, was the unlucky recipient of the ear cleaning with my trusty knife. He was worse off than Granny, his throat having been ripped to threads and his torso eviscerated and empty of all vital organs. Him being empty didn't do anything to lessen the sour smell of blood and poo and death that was clinging to all of the lurchers, a smell I was sickened to realize I was getting used to.

"A group is going in for food and the others are getting fuel and running interference with the lurchers. What do you want to do babe?" Rowdy asked as he came strolling back to me. "You ok?" he asked.

"Yeah, I'm good, I'll watch and run interference if needed," I say. "What are you gonna do?"

"I'm gonna go in with Big Joe. I'll get you some coffee and bagels and chocolate doughnuts," he says, bouncing his eyebrows at me. I laugh and kiss him before he runs back to the front.

A while later and we're all back in the vehicles. Another two large barrels of fuel in the back of the pick-up and a crap ton of gas station food for all of us and then some.

"Where you at Petenstine? Wildcard Momma here, we're rolling again, maybe an hour left to rendezvous. Out."

"10-4 Wildcard Momma, The Glass City Crew are about 2 hours out. We'll see you soon, Petenstine, out."

The rest of the trip was uneventful. If you count the lead trucks running down random lurchers after a horde or swerving around mounds of finally dead lurchers uneventful.

"We must be getting close," Rowdy says turning to me. " I don't think the mounds of finally dead lurchers is natural."

I laugh. "Lurchers aren't natural. But I think you're right, look." I point to the lights up ahead. "Looks like they have generators or something." There are runway lights, dim but they're like they were when the world was normal.

"Guess they aren't worried about being seen," Rowdy says, all joking aside.

"It's an army base. Soldiers and weapons, why would they be worried?" I ask, thinking it's silly to be worried about being seen by the living. Even if someone wanted what the base has no one could be stupid enough to mess with these guys.

"Petenstine, Wildcard Momma here, where you at? Over.

Petenstine

"Wildcard Momma, we ran into a weasel problem about an hour and a half outside our destination. Not sure how that angry little man 'Tiny Bigman' got in front of us but the triple dipped in crazy S.O.B was up on an overpass on 235 tossing something at the trucks. Turned out to be walkie talkies with the button taped down and magnets surrounding the housing with Alf Limbaugh on the channel spouting his hateful blast," I chirp. It figures that little twerp would idolize such a crackpot.

"Macky climbed up in the bucket truck and speared the S.O.B with a modified electrified pig sticker right through his heart. The ignoramus never saw it coming, since Macky was in the middle of the convoy. I do have to give Tiny Bigman points for originality. Heck, we can out smart, out run and exterminate the dead, it is the living that are the true threat now. Ya never know what crazy will do or what will set them off. It was a quick stop to remove the walkies and dispatch the dead that little stunt drew to us. We are now about 45 minutes from meeting up, pass word along to our old friend Griz. Petenstine, over and out," I signed off, excited to see Griz again and meet Wildcard Momma and her crew.

~

Griz

Marine
Contractor
Two-Fisted Fighter
Trucker
Don't mistake his kindness for weakness

18

THE HIGHLANDER

W.J. WATT

He had the pedal to the floor in his Kenworth W900 when he heard a trucker going by the name of Gunny calling out to other drivers in the vicinity of the Three Flags truck stop on route 395. He couldn't make out all of the conversation, but made out the words "Don't .... Haji bac.., it f.... you up."

"I wouldn't eat that stuff if you paid me," Jock Fraser muttered to himself, in fact he refused to eat any food from the middle east. Especially after seeing the horrors of war in Iraq and Afghanistan with the Highlanders, one of five Scottish infantry regiments which had served in the sand box. He had seen too many deaths due to the insurgents that tried to stop the West from winning the war against the Caliphate.

Anyone who saw the lorry motoring down the highway on a normal day would have admired the artwork on the double sleeper cab Jock called home, an old army bagpiper playing the pipes on the battlefield. The idea came from the cover of a book of his regimental piping tunes called the Pipers Day.

When he arrived in America, it was his plan to work in the oil fields of Texas until he saved the money to buy his own tractor unit. He arrived in Austin with all of his possessions in his Bergen and kitbag and pounded the streets until he got a job as a roughneck on a drilling derrick.

Jock arrived just in time to begin drilling on a rig that had to drill 14 wells in four months. He saved enough money for his tractor and left the tool pusher on good terms with a pocket full of cash, enough to pay the $48k asking price.

When he saw the rig, he knew he wanted something different, so he had some bodywork done. A picture of Piper Kenneth McKay, 79th Cameron Highlanders at Waterloo on one side of the sleeper cab. A picture of the 79th at the River Escaut, Belgium, May 1940, (this was the last time that the kilt was worn in action) on the other side. The Queen's own Highlanders cap badge was painted on the hood and on each of the exhaust covers he had the battle honours, finally, the air dam was decorated with the Scottish Saltire, that had been three years earlier.

Jock eased back on the speed as he saw a human being running toward him at what he thought was a fast rate of knots. "Still using fisherman's words," he said slowly to himself. "Dammit, where the hell have you..." as he heard a bang on the side of the 18-wheeler. Applying the brakes, he coasted to a halt and when the vehicle finally stopped, Jock opened the glove compartment and extracted his Browning 9mm Hi Power automatic pistol and two of his 13 round magazines.

Feeling pensive, he climbed down until he stepped onto the hard surface of the road, he loaded a magazine and made the gun ready. Taking a second to survey his surroundings, Jock couldn't see what had caused the bang.

He started walking down the side of the trailer, his Cameron of Erracht kilt fluttering in the warm breeze as he stepped heel to toe down the side of the road. "Where the hell is that bloody nutter?" Jock muttered quietly to himself.

Noticing some blood splatter on the road the ex-soldier took a knee on the tarmac, looking at the undercarriage of his trailer to make sure that what or whoever hit him wasn't trapped below the 44 tonne vehicle. Seeing nothing, Jock looked down the embankment at the side of the highway and what he saw startled him. The battered body of a human was starting to stand up when it should have been dead, it looked up and gave a tremendous roar and started to make its way up to him. Jock had seen enough awful injuries in Afghanistan and Iraq during his time in the British armed forces to notice that the compound fracture in its leg should have been enough to incapacitate the average person, so when it was jogging up the 20-degree incline Jock thought he was seeing things. It wasn't until he noticed the lifeless eyes, ten feet away, staring back at him that he realized he was in trouble.

"Halt, or I'll shoot," he said in his gruff highland Scottish accent, the warning was just a standard that he had used if a suspect was running from him in Ulster. It was because of his dialect and wearing his old army kilt, that other drivers who met him in a storage depot on his first run gave him the nickname of the Highlander.

From four feet away, the average sized adult leapt at Jock, which caused him to drop the Browning onto the black top as he scrambled back out of the way, before landing on his back on the road. The former humans' teeth were snapping together just inches from his face and Jock was using all his strength just trying to keep it from causing him damage. Not knowing what to do, he tried reaching for his pistol but it was just out of his reach. Tiring fast, Jock went for the second-best choice, his fingers clasping round the handle of his dirk. It was a long-bladed dagger that had seen active service in America when his ancestor had fought in the seven-year war as an officer in the 78th Fraser Highlanders. Extracting the dagger, he held the monster at bay with one hand around its neck and plunged the blade into its temple, as it was the only target left.

The thing stopped immediately, and its head slumped down and its dead weight pinned Jock down and it took all of his strength to roll it off. Jock had a long lineage of soldiers in his family tree, his Great Great Grandfather was Simon Fraser, the 15th Earl of Lovat who formed the Lovat Scouts, the first commando style regiment in the world. His Gt Uncle, David Stirling formed the Special Air Service in WWII and every male had served with distinction as an officer since those times. Jock enlisted as a private in the British Army even though he could have joined as an officer but he didn't like the politics his father put up with.

Jock's military career ended the day an IED exploded as the Land Rover Snatch Wagon he was in passed over the culvert the device was hidden in. His unit was driving on a patrol in Helmand province when he lost his leg after being trapped in the rear of the lightly armoured vehicle designed for the streets of Northern Ireland. The result being he was left with a prosthetic leg that would remind him of that fateful day for the rest of his life.

Jock started drinking everyday and when his former wife gave him an ultimatum between her and the drink, Jock went to the nearest off license and bought another bottle of Glenmorangie, his favourite malt. By the time he had limped back to his house, his rucksack and kit bag were lying on the front lawn and it sent him into a downward spiral. It wasn't until he ended up in hospital with pneumonia that he finally admitted he had a problem but by then he had lost his job, wife and family.

Lying in the hospital, he started watching a TV and on it was a documentary about drillers and it caught Jocks eye. He had nothing to stay in the UK for and thought to himself about emigrating to the states for some work. The day he was discharged from the hospital he contacted some guys he had served with at J-Bad and one put him in contact with Black Dog Drilling, which had been set up by a veteran to help give other veterans a chance instead of wallowing in a bar feeling sorry for themselves.

Jock arrived in Texas thinking he would have to work for a few years before he could start his driving career, but within ten months he had bought himself a Kenworth W900, and the reason he bought this make was because of the film Convoy.

Jock stood up from the hard top and saw four more humans sprinting toward him and he made for his 9mm, which was lying 8 feet away from him, picking it up as he started a limping jog back to his cab. Jock chanced a look over his shoulder and saw that the "creatures" were gaining fast. Placing his prosthetic on the first step Jock started to clamber up the steps to the cab.

Opening the door, the sound of footsteps padding on the road surface gave Jock a sense of urgency, *whatever the hell is going on behind me is not a good thing*, he thought to himself before glancing over his shoulder as he clambered onto his seat. Seeing four more runners coming at him like Kenyan sprinters, he slammed his door shut as one leapt the last ten feet slamming into metal, which had been where an open door had been seconds before.

The creature fell to the ground and its head hit the road

with a sickening thud before it sprang to its feet again. It was looking at the strange mechanical beast, trying to work out how to get to the food looking back at it. Its soulless eyes gave Jock the shivers, like the former person was looking into the depths of his soul, searching his thoughts. Letting out an ear ripping shriek, it padded off out of his direct view and Jock followed it from his rear facing mirrors and watched it scramble up between the cab and the trailer.

The Scotsman locked the door and turned the key in the ignition, starting the throaty rumble of the Kenworth as he wound up the window in his door, wishing he had bought a rig with the electric wind up windows as the winder was stiff to turn. As he let the engine warm up to temperature again, Jock heard scrabbling coming from the roof behind him

"Dammit, wont those bitches give up?" he said as he pounded the steering wheel of his rig with the open palm of his hand. He stretched over to the glovebox where he kept some boxes of 9mm Hydra Shock. Grabbing three boxes, he began loading up two ProMag 32 round magazines, he was beginning to worry about having enough ammo for his pistol. He had 500 rounds of mixed types of hollow point, mostly Sig Sauer 147gr rounds but he reckoned he still had 5 more boxes of the lower grained rounds he was now filling up.

He also had 1500 rounds for his illegal assault rifle, the Heckler Koch SA80a2 that he had bought from the boot of an arms dealer's car in Canada. He had been delivering a load of goods in Saskatoon to the dealer's legal business, Shooter's Paradise, a Walmart sized hunting goods store in Saskatoon, the largest in the nation.

Jock wanted an SA80 for one reason, he had used it daily when in the British Army, and its bullpup design kept it small. Although it was much maligned due to the failings of the original model, Heckler and Koch redesigned it and made some small changes. That had sorted the problems of the a1 and kept the good points, including the accuracy and the ability to change direction of aim very easily due to the bullpup design. It was also easily hidden in the confines of a lorry but due to the design and lack of availability, it was also a head turner when out performing at 800 metres on the range, the AR-15 could only dream of that.

Jock engaged the gearshift into drive and the big engine growled in protest as it started under strain as it pulled the laden trailer from a stop, accelerating slowly as the gears engaged at the correct RPMs. Jock hit the brakes and the creature that was on top of the sleeper slid from the roof, over the hood of the lorry and hit the ground but as he accelerated again he felt the bump as the tractor unit's wheels rolled over the zombie, flattening it like a roadkill Red Deer from back home in Scotland.

"Take that bitch!" he yelled in delight before he ran through his iPod songs list and selected one of the many tunes he had downloaded from the internet over the years. The slow start to Hell Bound Train came on, the organ work before a lone chanter started, pumping out from his 300 watt speakers.

Jock thought back to when he was a bagpiper in the Highlanders, one of a few proud Scottish regiments left. From the day the Drum Major of the Pipes and Drums school looked for willing volunteers to attend the school and having played the chanter for a short time in the small two classroom school in the village he was brought up in, he thought why not and signed up to become a piper in the British Army.

As he put some miles down on the road Jock noticed a large congregation of zombies surrounding a house 300 metres from the roadside and started decelerating using the gears to bring his lorry to a stop.

Some of the creatures turned to face him after the noise of the Caterpillar caught their attention. Jock knew he couldn't just drive away and leave the occupants to the fate of being attacked. He made his way through to the sleeper unit where he grabbed his L85a2 from the bracket under his bunk and four 30 round AR magazines that he preferred to use instead of the inferior spring issue mags that came with the assault rifle.

Climbing back through to the passenger seat, he rolled down the window far enough to get a sight picture through the SUSAT x4 scope and easily found the first of his targets.

Taking carefully aimed shots he managed to whittle the group down to single numbers before he expended all of his loaded magazines, but doing a quick head count he saw seven zombies left standing. Others were crawling about but he wasn't worried about them, a 9mm to the head would cure that.

He started to load a magazine up when he heard the crash of a door hitting the backstop and a child started screaming in terror.

"To hell with this clusterfuck, that wee one needs help," Jock said to himself, no-one else was within hearing range anyway. He grabbed the one item he knew would help him, his custom-made Claymore that he bought from a traditional blade smith from the Highlands of Scotland. The sword was made in the traditional manner, along with a basket hilted broadsword and cost a small fortune, and both came with custom scabbards from the same artisan.

Jock slipped his arms through the leather straps of his back mounted scabbard and sheathed the claymore, then slipped the broadsword scabbard through the belt mounted frog that he always wore, before checking his dirk and Sgian Dubh were in place.

Jock started to work himself up as he climbed out of the cab and the first of the zombies noticed him, letting out a keening cry to the horde members still able to attack. Jock drew his sword and let the tip drag in the dirt as the first of the group neared him. As a female zombie closed to thirty meters, Jock took a firm grip of the double handed sword and prepared himself mentally to swing at the female zombie that was clad in rags, which luckily covered the woman's modesty.

Remembering that ISIS warriors used the females of their groups as warriors and Jock had faced more than a few, had even shot one who had a suicide vest strapped over her burka, which had numbed Jock from the thoughts of killing a female. It was always in self-defense and this time would be no different. The Scotsman swung the sword left to right and as the torso dropped, its heads whirled in a graceful loop before joining the rest of the body on the ground.

The sword was not a mantelpiece ornament, it was razor sharp after hours on a whetstone. He had honed the blade so that it would cut if brushed against, unlike most swords on the market which were cheap clones of yesteryear or used in commemorative war games.

Seeing two more of the things approaching fast the Highlander swung again taking the head from another but the third creature was only partially wounded. The sword buried itself into the creature's shoulder and stuck fast. Pulling the broadsword from its sheath Jock thrust forward and the sword impaled deeply into the suited creature's head.

All this time Jock could hear a child crying from the small two-story timber clad house and it helped build his resolve to try and save someone and get the feeling of self-worth again.

Jock advanced, slashing through the small throng of zombies, having retrieved his Claymore from the shoulder of the eyeless dead creature. Hacking away at those who were formerly human, arms and hands joined the heads littering the green garden grass. Not seeing anything that would pose a danger, Jock entered the house and after hearing the whimpering of a child, took off up the stairs after searching the ground floor and finding nothing.

Checking both bedrooms, he couldn't understand where the child had gone and seeing the last door was closed he decided to sheath the sword. He kept his hand on the grip of his pistol before entering the bathroom, he gave it a cursory look and once again the room was empty, this room only had the utilities that every bathroom had, a sink, toilet and bath. Jock started to leave the room to recheck the children's bedroom.

"Please don't go mister, I don't have anyone left," called out a voice, "But you are covered in blood and look like a monster."

"I am not going anywhere if that is what you want little one, why don't you come out and tell me what happened to your mum and dad," replied Jock, as he headed over to the sink top mirror.

Wow I am covered in blood, I look a fucking mess, he thought as he ran the taps. After what seemed like an hour but in reality was less than ten minutes, he was ready to dry his upper body.

"You missed a bit, but you look a lot nicer, why do you talk funny, and wear a skirt?" the youngster asked, and after Jock turned around, he could see a young boy standing in front of the bath tub.

"I speak funny because I come from another country, one called Scotland, and this isn't a skirt, this is a kilt, a skirt is what you wear if you have underwear on underneath it," Jock said, starting to laugh at the child's inquisitive questions. "What's your name laddie, and what happened to your parents?" the Scotsman asked, this time squatting down to the boy's height.

"My name is Andrew MacLeod, mister, my mum and dad turned like the rest of them, my big brother left to try and get some help and those scary people hurt him real bad. What is your name, and can I come with you, I don't have anyone else to look after me?" Andrew begged, he looked about 5 years old to Jock and the final question caught him off guard.

"Your name means your family came from Scotland, in fact the name MacLeod is from the Scottish islands, mainly where I come from, an island called Skye. As for you coming with me, look at me, I am falling to bits as it is and I can hardly look after myself. Don't you have aunts or uncles that you could stay with?" asked Jock, who didn't want to be lumbered with a child any more than he didn't want his leg blown off in a country far from home.

"My uncle Seoras stays in New York, we were going to go to a place called Dunvegas in England for a holiday, my mom showed me pictures of a castle beside a lake, and it had a flag made by fairies and islands with seals on them that we were going to see," the youngster said to Jock. "I don't think I will get to see any of them now," said Andrew, who was starting to tear up again.

"Don't cry Andrew, and I think you mean Dunvegan Castle, that was 8 miles from where I was born. If I can get back to Scotland, I will try and take you with me so that we can see the Fairy Flag, the Seals and even the Fairy Pools and Fairy Glen, would you like that?" Jock asked, not knowing if he would ever get back home to Scotland, never mind seeing the small back house he called home.

"Does that mean I can come with you in your lorry, you were like the Viking we were learning about in our first-grade class, they were bearjerkers I think the word was," the small boy informed the gruff highlander.

"I think the word you are thinking of is Berserker, and I wasn't that bad, but I do have Viking blood in me. My grandfather met my grannie in Norway when they were fighting the Germans in World War II but aye, you can come with me," laughed the Scotsman, who was knocked down by the ferocity of a small child running and leaping at him, catching him off guard and sending him sprawling on his back. "Go get some clothes together and remember to pack your toothbrush and comb, no dragon breath and bed heads allowed in my lorry," he said as Andrew gave him a big hug then scampered off to his room.

After five minutes, Jock went through to his room after searching the house for anything he might need, grabbing tins of food and juice for the child. He saw the boy must have packed the biggest suitcase with all of his belongings. Jock unzipped it and checked to see what the boy had packed and was impressed that it was a variety of clothes but at the very top he saw a family photo, with two boys, and what must have been Andrew's parents, a good-looking woman and a handsome man in a Ranger uniform.

Grabbing the suitcase Jock made for the door when he heard the small child.

"Wait, you forgot my other bag, and I need this one, too," said Andrew solemnly.

Jock picked up the holdall and, surprised by the weight, put it back down and opened this one up as well. When he saw a wooden box and cars he told the youngster to make a choice, either lose the weight or struggle, but Andrew would be carrying it to the lorry. Andrew dumped almost everything out, keeping some of what looked like Star Wars action figures and the small wooden box. The toy cars got emptied out on the floor and as the pair were about to walk out the door Andrew stopped in front of the wood paneling beside the door jamb.

He pointed at the panel and told Jock to open it up, which Jock did, and got a surprise, the false wall hid a small armoury, an M4, Ruger 10/22 which had a sling sized for a boy, a bullpup shotgun, two Colt.45 pistols with pearl grips and a Beretta .32 pistol and small cardboard boxes of ammo. Jock noticed the pelican case that would fit the two rifles and the pistols and upon opening it he found a camouflaged stock which he was about to take out and leave when he felt and heard movement from inside and magazines for the weapons which were already loaded and four smaller .22 magazines.

He tried to see what was inside the stock but couldn't work out how until the young boy tried prizing off the rubber butt plate. When Jock tried he found a complete takedown rifle but wasn't sure how to assemble it yet, and when he asked the boy, he just shrugged his shoulder so Jock ruffled his hair and told him it was time to leave.

"Nice one kiddo, that we can certainly do with," Jock said messing up the kids hair and the small child looked up with a smile but his eyes told Jock a different story, they had the look of a veteran with shell shock, the thousand metre stare, one which looked right through you.

Jock glanced out the door quickly and saw that some of the zombies were surrounding the wraparound porch and he knew that his next move could prove fatal to both of them, so he grabbed the suitcase full of clothes and the holdall and threw them over the carpet of zombies who were crawling about the ground. Next he shouldered the weapons using the slings and picked the boy up and took a running jump, clearing the undead, but when he landed it was on his false leg and he collapsed to the ground. "Run for the lorry and pull the door open but don't close it," Jock said, pushing the boy in the direction of his rig. The boy took off as fast as he could, only stopping to pick up the holdall. *Smart bairn* Jock thought as he sorted his false leg and started limping toward the Kenworth again *This shit is getting really old now* he thought, knowing it was only an hour before when he had hit the first of these creatures.

After he climbed back up into the tractor, he started driving down the road, after 300 metres he passed the small town of Sutcliffe on the shores of Pyramid Lake. The sign said the population was 283, Jock reckoned it was now zero, another ghost town which would be reclaimed by nature eventually.

"Breaker, Breaker, any other survivors out there come in," the CB suddenly burst to life. Jock fumbled with the handset of the radio before finding the key.

"Station calling this is Highlander, just passing Sutcliffe in a Kenworth, heading for Hawthorne Depot come back," Jock replied, hearing static for thirty seconds.

"Highlander, are you the dude that drives the Kenworth 900 with the Piper on the sleeper, over," replied the unknown voice breaking through the tinny sounding speaker.

"That's a big 10-4 good buddy, who am I speaking to, over," he replied, puzzled that the man had an idea who he was.

"This here is Cobb over at Three Flags, we are about to

bug out heading for Lakota, if you are fast, try and join us on I-80, and I hope you were hauling a load to Hawthorne and not running empty after a delivery over," replied Cobb, the last part of the message had Jock wondering if Cobb knew what might be in the trailer.

"Foot will be hard to the floor Cobb, and do you know what I am carrying? I just picked up a laden trailer and was running down to the depot, it's a new run for me, but got a contract for two more trailers after this one," replied Jock, forgoing the over at the end, as it got boring fast.

"Hell boy, do you limeys know nothing, if you are heavy and heading for Hawthorne, then you are likely carrying surplus rounds back for storage that have come from the sandbox. Don't bother heading there, we heard from Cheyenne that Hawthorne has been lost and we sure could do with the load especially if you have any spare 5.56 in there, over," Cobb informed Jock, who was surprised that they would allow a civilian trucker a load like this.

"If you have shooting irons that will use what I have then you are welcome to it, will see you on the road, keep me posted, Highlander out," Jock ended the conversation, wanting to find a cutting torch to burn through the heavy grade pad lock used to secure the doors of the trailer

Knowing the route he had to take, Jock plugged in the final destination of his new route into the GPS unit, and seeing 1800 miles he knew he was in for a long trip that would probably involve chatting to an inquisitive passenger. Remembering he had one, Jock glanced quickly into the sleeper and what he saw didn't really surprise him, the young boy was crashed on his bunk, snoring softly while sucking his thumb. *Oh, to be that age again, without a care in the world* Jock thought before remembering the young lad would probably be better sleeping than thinking of his family and what he had seen since his brother left him alone.

Jock didn't see anyone else, living or dead on the route until he hit Nixon for the turn off onto to route 447, and the dead were very prolific. *What the hell did the first shout on the C.B. radio say* Jock wondered, *something about Hajjis and it sounded like fucking you up, the only hajji's I saw were over in the Stan, has it something to do with that new meat processing company?*

A group of zombies started running at the lorry and Jock did not touch the brakes, in fact, accelerating as fast as he could Jock hit the group of twenty at sixty-five kilometres per hour and bodies flew everywhere. It was like hitting ten pins and getting a strike in the bowling alley. Jock pumped his arm and did a half dab in salute to his endeavour until he saw the 80 junior high aged kids just waiting in front of the store at the junction of 446 and 447.

"How the hell do I get past those brats?" he asked himself, already knowing the answer but the voice from behind him gave him another idea.

"Hey, Mr. Jock, you could drive behind the store and onto that other road. "Andrew said quietly, afraid that the bad people who attacked his house would hear him in the lorry and come after him again.

"Great idea, I haven't been on this road before so I don't know my way round this whole area, but thanks kid, you don't know how much I appreciate this" Jock said to the small child who looked very pale and was trembling with fear, Jock offered his fist to be bumped which the kid duly did and drew his hand back, making an exploding noise while opening his fist wide.

Driving slowly toward the junction, Jock kept the gears low before suddenly pressing down on the accelerator and hauling the wheel over to the right and driving down the dirt parking area at the rear of the store.

As Jock pulled out onto route 447, a blind on the blue and white trailer across the road opened slightly as he passed and Jock swore he saw someone giving him the thumbs up. The kids started to gain until Jock's speed started to climb to 40kph a mile from the store when the green Trans Am from the trailer overtook the articulated lorry at a high speed. *Stupid bloody fool will crash at that speed* Jock thought to himself and two minutes later, after turning a corner, the car was on its side and steam was billowing from the engine bay.

Jock looked in the wing mirror and saw that the children were not far behind him and closing, due to him slowing down for the bend. Making a split-second decision he down shifted before taking the whole lorry off the road to see if anyone was hurt without having to leave the tractor.

As he drew closer he heard someone shouting so he turned toward the trunk and gave it a nudge, which caused the car to right. The driver, an older man who was covered in blood, struggled out from the seat belt and staggered out of the open door. Jock opened his door and extended a hand to the clearly injured driver, but he went to the trunk and popped it open. Grabbing a pump action shotgun and what looked like an AR-10 platform and two boxes of ammo before hobbling to the passenger door, which Jock opened for the man after closing his own.

The ammo cans were placed on the floor area before Jock saw the elderly man, who appeared to be a Native American, climb up and sit down, catching his breath. "Thank you, my friend," he started off. "I am Joe Hashké Dilwo'ii of the Navajo nation, first I must thank you for moving those weird kids, and secondly for getting me away from that car. the seatbelt wouldn't release due to the tension until you flipped the car back on its wheels," the Native American informed Jock.

"No thanks needed Joe, and I can always use a second pair of hands, I take it you know how to use those weapons? Did you ever serve?" Jock asked in return, as he started to drive the 18-wheeler up the small incline to get back on the black top.

"You speak mighty funny but if your rig has anything to do with it, I would say you are from England mister," Joe informed Jock, who spat out the coffee he had been drinking from an insulated travel mug, the coffee was long cold but Jock was dry.

"Close, Joe but no biscuit. I am from Scotland it's north of England. Many people, especially from here in the states, think Scotland is a state in England and not the country that it is. By the way, forgive me for being rude, but my name is Jock, or Highlander is my callsign," replied Jock who knew a lot of people outside the UK thought the same way, in fact many from England thought like that, too.

"Forgive me then friend, but how did you end up driving big rigs over here in Nevada instead of staying where you would call home. And as to your earlier question, I was in the service in Nam, in fact I served with Colonel Hal Moore at La Drang back in '65. That was some bad juju that few days, went on to join the Teams back in '68 and was in-country until '71, left then and just drifted about from one place to another, whether I was moved on or left voluntarily," Joe had paused, thinking back to that first battle he had fought in and the hell of the morning after.

Sensing the American had stopped talking for the moment, Jock carried on, "Well, why did I move to the states? I lost my leg in the Stan to an IED and living on a disability pension from Her Majesty's British army wasn't easy, so I packed a kit bag and a Bergen and flew to Texas to see if I could roughneck for a few months. Just enough to buy a rig and work from home, if you dig my meaning, anyway after four months I bought my home and been trucking ever since." Jock informed the Navajo veteran, as he noticed they were coming into another built up area, "Stay frosty my friend and make sure you have one up the pipe, this place looks slightly bigger than Nixon and I know here even less than there, too."

"Don't worry, I have been locked and loaded since I left my house. This baby isn't stock by the way, it has three selections single, 3 round burst and full auto. It's 7.62 so you don't need to spray and pray, single shot will take out just as many and from further away," Joe winked as he informed Jock. "Just don't tell the ATF will ya," he finished off laughing, knowing the ATF were the least of their worries.

"What direction are you needing to go, and I can take you to the correct on ramp faster?" Joe enquired, knowing his local knowledge would help the stranger out better than the small GPS screen.

"We are making for Lakota, Oklahoma. I had been speaking to a Mr. Cobb who was at the Three Flags services up by White Lake but they have all bugged out, and I am hoping to tail end Charlie them until we catch up," replied Jock whose head was like a radar, moving left to right all the time, looking for any trouble in this larger town.

"You need to be heading east then, Jock, take a left on 4th St and just keep heading on straight and it will take you to the on ramp. This place looks very strange, too quiet. There should be some niłch'i bida'iiniziinii but the place looks empty," Joe announced, then jumped as Andrew brushed against him.

"Damn, I forgot about you kid, how are you hanging there Andrew? Say hi to Joe, by the way and stop being rude," Joe told the youngster, and Andrew complied, even shaking the elderly man's hand and calling him sir.

"Your child is very polite Jock, you must be so proud. I wish I could say the same about mine but the eldest died in Desert Storm, killed by our own Warthog pilots, my other son is your usual white man's version of the Indian, an alcoholic. My daughter is a neurosurgeon at the Walter Reed National Military Medical Center in D.C., helping our service personnel who return from far off battlefields, usually with an injury that's life threatening, to say the least," Joe spoke of his children, even the alcoholic, with a sense of love. "I hope they are all surviving this century's version of the Book of Revelations."

"Andrew isn't my son Joe, I saw over 100 of those demons surrounding a house north of Nixon, killed or injured every one and found the small child by himself. If I had left him, I might as well have put a bullet in his head, as he would have died by the end of the week. Yes, he is a very polite young man and I will look after him if I have to," Jock said in front of a smiling Andrew who suddenly interrupted the men.

"And he told me he would take me to Scotland, and see Nessie, and castles with fairy flags and fairy swimming pools, too," were the excited words from the small child's mouth.

"Hang a left here and don't stop until you hit the onramp, onto the Dwight D Eisenhower and then from there on it's pretty much on the interstate all the way to McAlester and Lakota," Joe told Jock, who was looking at him quizzically. "Is something up mister?" Joe inquired, not understanding the trucker's worried expression.

"I just thought we would be on 80 all the way, didn't

realize that we would be on another highway," Jock told the old man, who started laughing after noting the confusion on Jock's face.

"It's the same road Jock, don't worry, the Eisenhower Highway is just the old name for the road from pre-interstate days," replied Joe, "and take your time along 4th St, I took you this way because the junction from 447 onto Main St is sharp and you would have to slow down, this way you can keep going at a faster clip when joining Main St.

Jock carried on down NV-427 until he saw the over pass of I-80 ahead of them and before he knew it, he hauled hard on the wheel and took them up the off ramp onto the interstate.

"Hold on Andrew, we are about to shunt some cars over to the verge." Doing so seconds after he gave the youngster a warning, the car an old Chrysler like Jock's father once had. The car gave the tractor little resistance and flipped over the concrete barrier where it landed on its chassis and rolled down the embankment. Seeing no further cars on the off ramp, Jock gunned the engine and started on the long crosscountry route that would hopefully lead them to a safe zone.

It was roughly 820 miles to Elk Mountain, near the Medicine Bow national forest, where Mr. Cobb had told Jock to try and catch up with the convoy first. Most of the towns along the route were small, but they had to get past Salt Lake City first.

"Hey kiddo, go into the locker above the bunk and grab that road atlas and find us a truck stop where we can top up the fuel tanks, I want plenty of fuel before we have to pick our way past Salt Lake," Jock told Andrew, knowing the youngster needed distracting after losing his family.

"You got it da.. Jock," he said, climbing up and opening the small hatch where Jock kept some useful items easily at hand. The road atlas being one of them that he checked his routes when he pulled up at a truck stop for a rest when he got tired, it helped him picture the route on a larger scale than the dash mounted GPS unit allowed. Being an old school soldier, he knew that the old acronym he had used daily spoke truth. The 7 Ps, which stood for Proper Planning and Preparation Prevents Piss Poor Performance, would always make sure he knew how to get somewhere if the satellites up in space failed to send a strong enough signal or that if his GPS unit broke he had a back up method, GPS mk1 or the Paper map.

Jock heard the youngster sobbing and started to brake when the old native caught his attention and shook his head. "Leave him be, he needs time to grieve in his own way," Joe said quietly and Jock nodded his head in agreement, knowing that the young boy would be hurting in ways he didn't know.

10 minutes later the boy stuck his head between the seats, his cheeks still showing the dampness of tears, but in his hands he held the book that was used for the task Jock set for him.

"I have found one, but I can only spell it, the word is difficult, C-O-S-G-R-O-V-E exit 158," Andrew informed the two grown-ups who were amazed he found what they were looking for so quickly until he followed up with, "It had the picture of the things gas comes from."

Both men laughed and congratulated him and the older one picked Andrew up and sat him on his knee so that he could see what was going on in front of them.

Jock thought this was like driving a car back home in the highlands of Scotland on a Sunday, or the sabbath as it was generally called in the islands off of the west coast of Scotland, before the tourist horde had arrived in May. The roads were empty, and you would be forgiven for thinking that you were on a county road rather than the interstate.

The only thing off was the amount of cars just sat on the road with doors open or, looking more closely, the smashed windows and the pools of blood. Thankfully Andrew never noticed those, as the boy usually questioned the Scotsman or the elderly Navajo who was busy telling the youngster old native a folk tale involving a Coyote killing a giant.

It was just outside Imlay that there appeared to be hundreds, if not thousands, of dead bodies littering the road, even the carrion birds that usually flit about the battlefields were not touching the corpses.

"Get in the back Andrew and draw the curtain," Jock told the youngster, who started to question Jock until a quick glance out of the windscreen elicited a sharp intake of breath and Andrew duly climbed into the sleeper

"Get that SA80 and AR-10 ready, we might have a need for them sooner rather than later if this is the dead here. We are sure to see some living if they follow the convoy from Three Flags," Jock instructed Joe, who started getting his AR ready, screwing a black cylindrical tube onto the threaded end of the barrel.

"Might be better leaving the shooting to me Jock, the suppressor will help keep the noise down and I will be able to touch them further out than your British pile of buffalo dung," the old man said, trying and failing to stop himself from laughing at the Scotsman's expense. The L85a2 was better than the previous rifle of the same designation, the a1, which was prone to bits falling from it when the rifle was first introduced to the British army in the 80's.

"Very bloody funny *old* man," Jock replied, drawing out the word old to emphasize it. "This is the best rifle for doing house clearances, one of the reasons the Brits chose it was the need for a carbine sized rifle, but this one has a similar barrel length as your AR-10. The can is probably a good idea, I will have to get one to fit my rifle, will just need to take off the flash eliminator," Jock informed Joe, who looked shocked at the revelation over the assault rifle.

"That may be so but I will stick to my heavy hitter to take them things down compared to your bb gun, and talking of them things watch out to your 11 o'clock," Joe indicated toward the town in the distance where four human forms were sprinting at the vehicle. "Stop when you can, I feel like these things should be taken out from as far away as we can."

Jock started to hit the brakes gently, slowing down the large vehicle and angling toward the centre reservation on an overpass while Joe started to wind down his window. "Why didn't you get electric windows mister?" he complained, catching his breath as he got himself into a shooting position sitting in the cab seat. "Plug your ears Andrew, this might be louder than usual," Joe said over his shoulder before looking down the Trijicon Accupower RS22 scope, after he fired one shot he moved slightly. The noise was significantly decreased but louder in the confines of the cab, he took 3 more shots dropping each of the former humans.

"Damn Joe, that was some good shooting, you got four headshots for four there!" Jock exclaimed, clapping the man on the shoulder in congratulations.

"What do you mean headshots? I went for centre of mass, why try and hit a head at this range?" he replied, turning to face Jock with a curious look on his face.

"That's why Joe, damn I thought you knew," Jock said, pointing over to the zombies who were starting to rise to their feet again.

"Damn demons, won't make that mistake again," Joe muttered as he sighted on the group who had started their wonky run again, Joe fired twice dropping the first one, its head had a cloud of read mist exploding from the rear of the skull before repeating three more times. "That was harder than I thought it would be," he said, after the fourth dropped within 400 metres of the lorry.

Jock started the drive again, straightening out for the next 11 miles. When they pulled into the rest area, Jock climbed down and checked the fuel station and Jock and Andrew kept a look out but nothing stirred, not even a mouse. 25 minutes later they were back on the road when they heard an Englishman's voice, that Jock was sure he had heard before, breaking through on the CB.

"Scratch here, to any other truckers out there, the convoy has pulled off at Exit 194 Golconda and Midas and set up a perimeter, if you are looking for safety in numbers look us up," the London accent broke over the radio.

"Hang on a minute Sassenach till we find out where we are, Highlander is just down the road a bit and looking for company," Jock replied to the Englishman.

"Bloody hell, a sweaty sock over here, I thought you would be in a doorway drinking from a bottle wrapped in a brown paper bag mate."

"Jock, what is a Sassenach and a sweaty sock?" asked the young boy whose head stuck out from between the two front seats.

"A Sassenach is just an Englishman, a sweaty sock is what they call us Scotsmen, Cockney rhyming slang, Sweaty Sock is a Jock," replied the trucker.

"But how did he know your name was Jock?" Andrew continued his line of questioning.

"Look kid, are you a bloody lawyer? Scotsmen also get

called Jock and hold on a minute, I need to let them know where we are," Jock replied, glancing at the Exit sign they just passed.

"Sassenach, we are not far behind, expect us in before darkness falls. We are just passing 180 now, think we are about 17 miles from your position," Jock informed the Englishman of their rough ETA.

"Look Highlander, my name ain't Sassenach, its Scratchy, but I am sure Gunny and Cobb will be happy to have you tag along with us on our merry journey. You might see a truck coming toward you on the wrong side of the road, don't worry about it, we will just be clearing our area to allow us to bury some of our fallen brothers when we get a chance."

Jock cocked an eyebrow hearing this but didn't think anything more until he passed Exit 192, when a lorry resembling a Highland Council Foden snowplough passed them on the outside lane. To top it off, a lunatic was hanging out of the passenger window with a set of gloves that looked like Wolverine's claws headbanging to some raucous music being pumped of the tractor unit's sound system.

"I take it you are the bloody Scotchman I have been chatting away with?" Scratchy sounded back to Jock, "Stabby says he loves the artwork, got to admit it does look bloody smart. Anyway let us turn around and we will take the lead and direct you to the … wait a minute.......laager as Stabby called it, I didn't see no brewery there though," Scratchy carried on and the tractor unit with the blade overtook Jock's Kenworth, the driver in the other tractor just nodded as they passed and took the lead 100 metres in front.

Scratchy, Stabby, what the bloody hell type of handles are those? Jock thought to himself as they drove the last few miles down the road, but that Englishman looked familiar, had Jock seen him the last time he was home in the UK? He looked like he was a rock star or something, probably saw him in one of the tabloid newspapers in Scotland, either that or Crime Watch.

Jock saw a group of lorries all parked up, but the scene looked very sombre when he opened his door and climbed down, the two men from the plough walked over to him and introduced themselves.

"Where did you lose your leg?" the American asked, Jock noticed the prosthetic hand and he explained his story as another Trucker walked over.

"Hey Highlander, welcome to the convoy of destruction, call me Gunny. This fine fellow is Stabby but don't let him hear you call him that or he will show you why he got the nickname, that idiot from your country is Scratchy, a bloody singer with Freddy Kruger gloves. Sorry I can't hang around, but we lost some guys filling up at Cosgrove and it is time to lay them to rest," Gunny said as he shook Jock's hand. He didn't even mention the false leg that Jock limped with.

"Gunny, in my country at funerals, we often play a lament to the fallen, for allowing us to travel with you, please let me get my bagpipes out and do likewise here?" Jock requested, every army did similar, the Buglers played The Last Post, 21-gun salutes and in the Scottish regiments, they played the pipes.

"Sure thing Highlander, give us ten minutes to get the graves finished, they won't be deep as it is hard going but we would be grateful if you could do that," replied the very obvious veteran, Jock reckoned the equivalent of a Company Sergeant Major, at the very least.

25 minutes later, there wasn't a dry eye in the group of men, women and children as Jock began with Amazing

Grace, followed by The Flowers of the Forest and finished up with the Sands of Kuwait.

When he returned his pipes to the sleeper, Scratchy followed him and shook his hand once again.

"That brought a tear to a glass eye mate, better than that bloody Highland Cathedral, but to tell you the truth, glad to have another Brit here, I don't suppose you have any Tetley Tea in that wagon of yours do ya?" the Englishman enquired.

"Nope, I only drink Scottish Blend, but I do have plenty of that as I received three boxes just before I left to go on that last run, do you want a cuppa?" Jock asked as he switched the kettle on in his cab.

"Bloody right I do, getting a bit sick of coffee now," replied Scratchy, who had earlier confirmed he was the lead singer for a rock band on tour of the USA from England.

∽

W.J. Watt

W.J. is from Scotland, having settled in a remote region of the Highlands. After leaving school at sixteen, and going to work on the family fishing boat, he discovered reading for enjoyment in his downtime between deck shifts. Leaving for the army shortly after, he saw service initially as an engineer before qualifying as an infantry specialist with the Queen's Own Highlanders. Sadly, his military career was cut short after being injured in active service; an injury which plagues him to this day. Having left the armed forces, he returned home to work on the boats but the injury forced him ashore.

W.J. is an avid reader and has become so enamored with

the post-apocalyptic genre that his own ideas formed into a story which found its way to paper. He is a true indie author networker, and has gained inspiration from writer's such as Devon C Ford, Boyd Craven, David A. Simpson and many others too numerous to list.

W.J.'s debut trilogy launched in 2017, beginning with 'Highland Hunger: Call To Arms' in Spring followed by Patriots Rising in August. He is currently working on another sequel to this series, and two post-apocalyptic series, another set in Scotland and one set in Europe along with a "Lone wolf" terror campaign set in the US all hopefully to be released in 2018.

His books can be found on Amazon.

19

THE MIDLAND CREW

EMILY STIVER

"I can't take the kid, Em. Tell him sorry for me and I'll be there in 2 weeks." I read the text from my ex again.

"He bailed on Josh again." I shoot a quick text to my husband now that he's off work.

"Figures, guess he'll have to go on our 'dumb road trip' after all." Is Dave's quick response.

Dave took two weeks off and borrowed his buddy Dan's RV so we could take a road trip across New Mexico and Arizona, and my son begged to stay with his Dad instead of go with us. He's far too cool to hang out with his Mom and four little sisters.

"Hey Ma...what's the look for?" Josh asks, getting in the van.

I hand him my phone with the text from his Dad open. "Sorry kid, you're stuck with us for 2 weeks," I say, grabbing his chin and shaking it playfully.

"I wonder what this one's name is," he says, putting my phone in the diaper bag between us. He sets his jaw and looks at me with a smile. "Don't tell Dad but I really want to see the caverns and Roswell!" he laughs.

"Dad?" I ask simply, blinking. I must have missed something. I turn right out of the parking lot, waiting.

"Dave. It's about time I cut the crap, don't you think? He's taken care of me since I was what, 5? He deserves it, he's earned it," he says, and with that he changes my radio station and starts singing while looking out the window.

The next morning we wake up early, load up a few last minute things and carry the girls to their bunks. Josh walks out looking as grumpy as I feel and climbs on to the bunk with Riley. There are two sets of bunk beds in the bedroom at the back of the RV, with rails so no one will fall out, but Josh volunteered to share with the baby. He doesn't toss and turn like the girls do, so he's less likely to squish her and I need a baby break. His words, exactly. So Kati, Mia and Alayna get their own bunks and Dave and I will use the full size bed shoved in the closet size second bedroom.

I get in and buckle up as Dave runs back in the house. He runs back out a minute later with the safe he keeps the 9mm in. "Don't look at me like that. The kids don't know I have it and it's better to have it and not need it..." he says, putting the little safe in the driver's seat hidey hole.

"Than need it and not have it," I finish for him. It's been my mantra for the pistol since he bought it. I don't like guns that aren't for hunting. It makes me nervous even in the safe. I know how to use it, even have my open carry permit, but I still don't like it.

"I'll stop at the truck stop, top up on fuel and you can go in and get coffee. We'll drive for a few hours and eat breakfast before we go explore the Caverns," he says to me.

I used the last of my energy finishing my mantra for him, so he gets a "Sure". It's the best I can do this early.

"Shit! I need to take this to the yard, or the guys won't be able to fix my truck," he says, holding up a key. The mechanics at the yard are taking the two weeks we're going to be gone to fix the winch and shocks on his work truck. Finally.

"First coffee, if you're going to keep talking to me," I grumble. I am not a morning person.

Smirking, he replies, "Good for you, making a whole sentence like a big girl!" I wanna slap the smirk off his face, but flipping him the bird takes less effort. It makes him laugh, and he turns the radio up. "Find something that isn't talk radio," he says, paying attention to the road. I flip through stations, and everyone is a morning show host going on about the Muslims and their peace pork stunt. I roll my eyes and turn it way down. "I'll stick to my usual brand of bacon," I say and cross my arms, looking out the window. The haji bastards tried to kill my brother and cousin, they both came home seriously messed up by what they had seen overseas. Despite what our government and the Salaam company said, I would never trust anything out of the middle east. It's a sore subject for a lot of people.

"I wouldn't touch that stuff with someone else's mouth," Dave says, totally serious.

"Mom," Josh whispers from behind me.

I jump and turn. "What's wrong Bear, why aren't you sleeping?" I ask.

"Riley stinks and I'm not changing her," he says and sits at the table.

I laugh, "I got her." I grab the diaper bag and head to the room. The other girls are sound asleep so I hurry and change the baby and lay her back down.

"Dad says we're going to stop and fuel up and get coffee. Can I have a pop?" Josh asks as he climbs back on the bunk. "I'll get you one but I want you to stay back here with the girls when we stop, ok?" I say. "Ok, can I get a yogurt too?" he asks with a smile. I squint my eyes at him and go back up front as we pull into the station.

Dave gets out and starts pumping. I grab my bag and look around. The station is packed, mostly big Oilfield trucks, their drivers stopping to get a Ma & Pa breakfast at the little diner inside, and a few pickups. The gas station across the road is packed too, but they have a Golden Arch attached, so they're always busy. I get out and walk around the RV, "Hey do..." is all I get out before all hell breaks loose from across the street.

There is an ear-splitting scream, followed by the sound of breaking glass and howls that make my hair stand on end. Dave looks over my shoulder and I spin around. The sight is worse than the sounds and I freeze.

The big window that only a minute ago had the Golden Arch logo splayed across most of it is shattered. There are people jumping out of the new opening, the ones in front with huge shards of glass sticking out at odd angles, chasing other people who are running to their cars, and tackling and biting the ones who are to slow. "What the..." I start as Dave grabs me around the middle and throws the side door of the camper open. He tosses me in like a rag-doll, follows me in and slams the door. He leaps over me and jumps in the driver seat. "Lock that door Em!" he yells as he speeds away from the pump. I lean over and hit the lock, dazed. What the hell just happened?

"What's going on Mom?" Josh asks, scared.

"We're not getting coffee there. Go back to the room, please, I need to talk to your Dad," "Did you see what I saw or have I fully lost my mind?" I add, hoping for the first time that I'm nuts.

"You're not crazy, babe, I saw more than you did," he says in a low growl. "And I saw you freeze. Sorry for tossing you like that, but we had to get out of there. What if one came after us or got to the kids," he says a bit softer, risking a side-look at me. "We're going to the yard and leaving, ASAP," he finishes, squeezing my hand and flying down the road, away from the craziness.

I have my phone out in an instant, dialing 911...busy. I try again. Busy. I try six more times...busy every time. I dial the non-emergency police number and someone answers.

"Midland Police, please hold!" a friendly female voice says quickly.

"I don't have time to hold!" I say, wanting to scream.

"Midland Police," a gruff male voice says this time.

"I was just at the truck stop across from the Golden Arch on 1788, something bad is going down there, you need to send people. There were people attacking other people and biting them!!" I say faster than I thought possible.

"Sir, did you get that?" I ask. Click and then nothing.

"What the hell!! He hung up on me!" I screech at Dave as we pull into the parking lot at the yard. Dave leans out his window and punches in his code to open the gate. I turn the radio up a little.

"Reports are coming in of riots across the country taking place at all retailers serving Salaam pork products this morning. We here in Midland are no exception, MPD, State highway patrol and the Texas Sheriff's office are responding to trouble at Golden Arch's across the area. You are advised to stay away and do not approach if you are out and near." The usually perky morning show host reports. "So, please, if you are headed to work be safe and call us with any hot spots you may see." She continues, giving the number for the Citizen Warrior line for the station.

"Guess they already knew to expect something, maybe that's why he hung up. Probably got 300 of the same calls,"

Dave says as the chainlink gate rattles shut behind us. "I'll be right back. And then we're going," he says as he shuts off the engine and hops down. He hustled to the door and disappeared a second later.

My head still spinning from all the bs before coffee, I look around. This time of day it should only be the big boss Ben, his secretary Nancy, 3 dispatchers and a few mechanics, but the yard is still full of trucks.

"What are we doing here, where's Dad?" Josh asks, scaring a squeak out of me. "Are you ok Mom?"

"I'm fine, just edgy over some protesters we saw at Golden Arch," I turn to tell him. "Dad just has to drop his truck key off and we're going. See, there he is now," I say, turning back around. Dave is at the shop door waving his arms, a look of horror on his face. I go to open the door, until a screaming bloody mechanic running right for me changes my mind. I lock the door instead and fall out of my seat trying to back away as he slams into the door. Bloody hands hit the window and I scream. "Go in back with your sisters, now and block the door!" I bark at my son as I grab the safe from the hidey hole.

HONK, HONK, HONK "Over here!" there's a yell from somewhere out of sight. The mechanic tears off around the building, and Dave is running from the shop door pointing wildly at the driver door. I lean over and unlock it a second before he gets to it and climbs in. "We're going in, no questions," he says out of breath and I notice the shop door is open. He pulls in and the overhead door shuts faster than I thought possible. "Get the kids and come on," he says grabbing the safe. "MOVE!" he shouts when I just look at him. I jump up and run to the back. Josh already has Kati and Mia up and is rushing to Dave, I grab Alayna and Riley and run back to the side door. I see Dave hand the safe to Ben before he reaches for Alayna. Nancy meets us at the door, "Kids are in Ben's office, first door to the right," she says, pointing it out to Josh.

I follow him in. "You're in charge dude," I say as I put Riley down and Alayna runs to my legs. "Dad and I need to figure out what's going on," I say and tip my head down the hall toward the raised voices in the reception area. "I will be back in a few, I love you," I say and kiss five heads before I turn to leave. I hear Nancy ask if they want to watch cartoons, and feel a little better that there's an adult in there, too.

As I walk toward the raised voices I can hear them better.

"Why aren't they calling them what they are... Zombies!" one guy yells.

"Zombies aren't real you crackpot! They are just hopped up on something," a different guy yells.

"Bullshit! Jimmy shot Andy point blank in the heart and the bastard still tore his throat out!" the first guy yells again.

I walk up to Dave. Everyone is around a small radio, ignoring the morning show host giving the station's number out again. There are only five drivers I don't know, Ben, Dave and I in here. And Nancy with the kids and whoever yelled outside. "Where is everyone?" I ask.

"Turned or never came in," Ben said sadly. "Apparently one of the mechanics had gone crazy and bit Andy's back and tore off a chunk and then headed for the trucks. Andy went crazy a little later and bit a few other drivers as they came in to get their keys, before going after Jimmy and being shot. Me, Nancy and the guys hid in my office until it was quiet," he says, looking through the floor.

A shriek came from his office, where my kids are, my mind screamed at me. I ran as fast as my legs would go, and came up short at what I saw. Andy had crashed through Ben's office window and was crunching on Nancy's left shoulder. I still had the gun in my bag and without thought, grabbed it and sent a 9mm bullet through her head and into his. I've read and watched enough Zombie horror to know it's a head shot. If he wasn't a zombie no court will put me in jail for killing the nut job eating a woman just feet from my babies. My babies! I turn and kneel and all five of my kids just stare, open mouthed, at their Mom who just shot two people. Josh was holding Riley and Kati had Alyna. Josh blinked and then ran to me, and Kati and Mia did the same.

I would never freeze again!! Kill or be killed. In the span of a scream everything clicked. I had to buck up and protect these five, whatever it took. My family was together when the world went to shit, I'm at least thankful for that.

∼

"The first days were bad. We worked together and cleared the yard. Taking head shots until we realized it drew more to the weak chainlink fence. Then we used tire irons to crush skulls and screwdrivers to stab through eyes. The guys used the frac tanks in the yard and braced them inside the gates and fence line. The food we had in the RV went quickly, so a few of the crew went on raids to the few houses and the little store on the corner. We were fine for water, but we found good knives, a HAM radio and more guns. We set up a guard and only lost two more people. Then we heard Sargent Meadows on the radio and decided to head to Lakota'" I finish telling our story to the group we just plucked off the roof. Wiping the rotted gray matter from my knife. Smashing heads and stabbing soft spots is second nature now, but they need to know I wasn't always like this. Or maybe I need to know that.

"Big Joe was the voice that drew that mechanic away from my babies! He saw a horde surrounding this little dive and figured we should stop," I add, so they know who to thank instead of me. Who I thank, constantly, for saving our bacon.

∼

Looking at it now, I'm glad our trip didn't go as planned, and that we were all together. "I don't know that we would have made it," I say, seemingly out of nowhere. Windy gives me a weird look but hugs me again. She's headed North to find her people, with Ben and a few others from our growing group. Most of us are headed straight for Lakota, Oklahoma and they'll meet us there once they have answers.

"They call me Wildcard. Or Wildcard Momma. Feel free to chat with me if you get lonely and stick with Ben. He's a good man. Look us up!" I say and hug Windy again before they leave.

"Why do they call you that?" she asks.

I smirk, "Because I don't look like much, but I killed more shamblers than the men did on our raids. The more I kill, the less there are to hurt my babies. Hence, I'm a wildcard." I laugh and head for the RV, with "Rowdy" Dave sitting shotgun. He embraced the skull crushing with ease and made a game of it after we knew what was going on.

Emily Stiver

I love reading and wanted to try my hand at writing. I was a food delivery driver and nursing assistant before becoming a full time stay at home Mommy of 5 crazy kids, who keep me busy !!!

I'm hoping to keep writing and eventually go back to school for nursing.

Bridget

Starlet
Social Butterfly
A tall drink of water that traded lipstick tubes in shades of red for hard caliber ballers that dealt in lead.

20

THE PRISON

R.L. CHAMBERS

"Daddy, Daddy, I hit one," Lilly said, the excitement in her voice was easy to hear.

Ricky looked through the scope on the sniper rifle, and could see the zombie stood there, covered in dried blood, it's lower jaw missing and tongue hanging down. "That's great princess, but you need to hit it in the head, take another go."

"Okay, Daddy," Lilly said as she looked through the scope, she lined the shot up, aiming just a little above its head to allow for drop, held her breath, and pulled the trigger.

The bullet flew through the air, crashed into the zombie's skull, ripped through its brain, and exited the other side, its now lifeless body crumpled to the ground.

"That was a great shot, it won't be long until you're on guard duty," Ricky said as he smiled at his daughter.

"That's an important job, isn't it?" Lilly asked, her light brown eyes full of excitement.

"It is, we need to keep the survivors here safe, this prison is the best place to make that happen, and the guards are the most important people to ensure that we all stay safe."

The Prison | 239

"I can do it, Daddy," Lilly said, as she swept her light brunette hair from her eyes.

"I'm sure you can, but we need to make sure you're hitting the mark every shot, the bullets will run out eventually, so we need to make sure we make them count," Ricky said, he looked Lilly in the eyes, everyone said that she looked like him, but he couldn't see it, every time he looked at her all he could see was her mother. His eyes began to water, and he quickly wiped at them, not letting Lilly see the tears.

"Daddy, I'm hungry," Lilly said, as she rubbed her belly.

"Let's get you something to eat," Ricky said. He placed his hand around his daughter, and they walked to the prison food hall, where they stored all the food they had.

He looked through the various boxes of canned food that they had, and settled on two cans of chicken and mushroom soup. He grabbed a pan, pulled the lever on the small gas canister, placed a match to the small hob, and warmed up the soup.

"Here you go princess, you make sure that you eat every little bit, then you can go find Zelda and Scott, and play for a bit," he said as he placed the can of warm soup in front of her. He sat beside her with a can for himself and started to eat.

He was just about to finish his can when a short guy, with a half-shaved head and hair dyed purple and needing a touch up, came up to him.

"What's up, Tom?" Ricky said, as he placed the last spoonful of soup into his mouth.

"We found the prisoner files," Tom answered.

"Cell block Z?" he asked, wiping at his mouth.

"Yes, we've got them for all the cell blocks."

"I'll be there in five minutes," Ricky said, Tom turned around and walked back to where he came from.

"Daddy, what's cell block Z?" Lilly asked, as she was still eating.

"It's the basement of the prison, somewhere you should never go, unless I tell you so, okay princess?" he said, as he looked her in the eyes with all the seriousness in the world.

"Yes, Daddy."

"You finish, and go find your friends, I'll be back later," he got up, and walked in the direction Tom had gone moments earlier.

Ricky walked to a steel door, the letter Z was engraved into it, he pushed it open and walked down the concrete stairs. As soon as he got to the other steel door at the bottom, he took a deep breath, knowing the shouts and screams he was about to be assaulted with.

"Hey cock sucker, you can't keep us locked in here," one gruff voice shouted.

"Let me out, I shouldn't be here in the first place," another yelled.

Ricky ignored them all, and walked to the only occupied cell with no sound coming from it. He looked inside, the occupant was sat on his thin cot, just staring at the wall.

"You ready to tell us what you're in for?" Ricky asked.

There was no answer.

"We have the prisoner files."

The occupant looked at Ricky, but still stayed quiet.

"It'll be easier if you just tell us."

The occupant stood up, and walked toward the thick steel bars, staring Ricky down. As Ricky held his gaze, there was a gunshot from behind him, and the occupant's head violently whipped back; blood, skull fragments, and brains splattered the back of the cell.

"What the fuck?!" Ricky yelled as he turned, seeing a petite blond still holding the smoking gun.

"Here," she shoved a file into his chest, and walked off.

"Tina, wait," he yelled, but she just kept walking.

Ricky opened the file, and could see the mugshot of the cell's now dead occupant. He read out loud, "Ken Drimmel, seven counts of kidnapping, rape, child abuse, six counts of murder, and one for attempted murder, all victims under the age of ten," he could feel a rage building inside of him. He would have loved to torture the sick fuck, and make his death a slow, drawn out process.

He dropped the file to the floor, and shouted at the top of his voice, "If any of you sick fucks have lied about what you are in here for, now is the time to speak up. There's a reason you lot weren't evacuated with the rest of the prisoners above and if it's like his, all I can say is you better hope you get a bullet through the skull, because I'll make that seem like child's play."

The cells were all silent, and Ricky left to find Tina. He found her in a small room filled to the brim with filing cabinets, she was leaning against them, a cigarette in hand.

"Mind if I steal one of those?" he asked as he walked in, he had a full pack in his pocket, but needed something to break the ice.

She didn't say anything, just passed him her pack, he removed a smoke, and brought a lighter to it.

"I'm sorry, I didn't mean to yell, but I almost shit myself," he said as he took a pull from the cigarette.

Tina had a grin on her face, "Shot a cunt, and almost made you shit yourself, not a bad day."

"You been through the rest of the files?"

"Some, it's mainly murders, he was literally the worst of the lot. The rest may be useful, if we can trust them," Tina said, as she blew smoke rings into the air. "You know this means Shipman was right."

"Fuck Shipman, that crazy twat thought just because he was a doctor, he could perform experiments on people, that's the only reason he suggested coming here, he knew there'd be a secluded wing," Ricky said, as he flicked the butt of his cigarette into the corner of the room.

"So, you think we did right? Telling him to get lost?"

"We gave him a gun and some food, if he couldn't figure out how to survive, that's his own problem. My priority is Lilly, and the other survivors who legitimately want to help."

"How do you keep going?" Tina asked as she sparked up another cigarette, and handed it to Ricky.

"What do you mean?" he said as he took a drag and handed it back.

"I lost my shit before you guys found me, I was a wreck if you remember, how do you cope?" She took a pull and passed it back.

"I just do, it's for Lilly, but there were times at the start that I cried myself to sleep, but I'd never let Lilly see that."

"So, what's the plan?"

"You know I'm not the leader of you lot, right?" he said, as he took his last pull from the cigarette and passed it back to Tina.

"Like hell you're not, you pulled most of us out the shit and gave us a purpose, you got us here, and this is the safest we have been," she flicked the cigarette butt to the ground.

"Coming here wasn't actually my idea, it was Shipman's."

"But you still got us here after we cast him off."

"The plan right now is to stay here as long as possible, maybe sort out a team to go out for supplies."

"I volunteer," Tina said without hesitation.

Ricky smiled, "I have another job for you, I will be on the

team, and more than likely so will Tom, I want you to watch over Lilly and Zelda while we're gone."

"You can fuck off with that idea."

"Please? The girls like, and look up to you, and I wouldn't trust anyone else with them."

"Fine, but the second Tom wants a day off, you tell me and I'll take his place," she said, and Ricky knew she was serious.

"It's a deal, get someone to sort these files out according to severity of the crimes, and we'll see if there's any hope in here," Ricky said.

"Alright, I'll let you know when it's done."

"Thank you," Ricky said as he left the room and went back up to the main part of the prison.

He went back up to the food hall of the prison where he found Lilly, Zelda, and a few other kids he didn't know the names of, drawing pictures at a table.

"Daddy, I made this for you," Lilly said as she lifted the picture up for him to see.

His eyes started to water when he realized what was in front of him, the picture showed him and Lilly, standing watch over the prison, with her mother in the clouds watching over them.

"What's the matter, Daddy, do you not like it?" Lilly asked, a hint of sadness was in her voice.

"I love it princess, it's just that I miss mummy."

Lilly threw her arms around him, and squeezed as tightly as she could, "I do, too, Daddy."

He wiped at his eyes before returning her embrace. She let go, and returned to the table with the other kids, and started to color in her picture.

He walked over to the corner where they kept the coffee, and his ears began to ring. Everyone in the room looked around confused, the loud old alarm bell echoed through the whole prison.

"What the fuck's happening?" Ricky yelled out the closest barred window.

"Runners, Rick, a fucking lot of them," a voice came back, just barely loud enough to hear.

"Right," he yelled, "this is not a drill, every capable person, get a gun, some ammo, and get to the guard stations, don't stop firing unless they are all dead."

People scrambled to the janitor's closet where all the guns were kept and loaded up.

"Daddy, what do you want me to do?" Lilly asked.

"I need you to wait in our room, take the other kids and shut the door. If you see a zombie in the prison, you take this key and lock yourself in until someone comes to get you," Ricky said, and handed Lilly a key.

"Okay, Daddy," Lilly said, as she took the key and ushered the other kids to the cells they used as personal rooms.

Tina and Tom ran past Ricky, guns at the ready, and he followed them up to the guard station. He looked through the scope of his sniper rifle and could see a horde quickly running in the direction of the prison.

People had already started to shoot at the horde and Ricky joined them, pulling the trigger, watching the zombie he was aiming for collapse to the ground missing the back of its head. The zombies behind it tripped over their now dead comrade, tumbling to the ground.

He kept lining up shots, dropping zombie after zombie, but the horde didn't seem to be thinning, every time one fell, two others would take its place.

"What I wouldn't do for a grenade, or ten, right about now," he said to Tom.

"You and me both," Tom replied, as he kept shooting.

"They're going to be at the walls at any moment, is the entrance locked?"

"Yeah, it's locked, hasn't been unlocked since we moved in."

"Well, at least they won't be able to get in then." Ricky got back to shooting.

The battle continued, the zombie horde relentless in its pursuit of food. Ricky looked through the scope. "What the fuck is that?"

Tom looked in the same direction, seeing a red truck speeding down the street, heading straight toward the horde. "It's either some brave soul, or a crazy motherfucker."

They continued to watch the truck as it closed the gap between itself and the zombies. As the front of the truck hit the first few zombies, the backend began to swing out.

"No fucking way he's going to power slide that thing. It's going to roll for sure," Tom said as he watched in awe.

The backend of the truck slammed into the horde, and the truck tipped and rolled over the dead in its way.

"Get some covering fire on that truck!" Ricky yelled, as he started to shoot the zombies closest to the cab of the truck.

The survivors defended the truck as best they could; dead bodies, blood, and brains littered the area around the cab, as the other zombies had reached the prison walls.

"Rick, I don't think the driver made it, it's been five minutes, and there's been no sign," Tom said as he kept firing.

"We still need to dispatch these fuckers though, we're going to need more people, it's like the whole city turned."

"Do you want me to see if they've sorted through the prisoners yet, one or two of them might actually be useful, the others can rot," Tom said, he stopped shooting, waiting for a response.

Ricky weighed up the idea in his head, he didn't like the thought of having mass murderers running around with guns, but he knew that without extra help it would take hours to dispatch all the zombies. "Fuck it, but only the lowest of crimes in there, I don't really trust any of them."

"Yeah, me neither, but needs be as the devil drives." Tom ran off.

"Be quick Tom," Ricky yelled after him.

∽

Tom ran to the steel door of cell block Z and unlocked it, he quickly walked down the concrete stairs, pushing through the door at the bottom.

"What the fuck?" Tom said, as he looked around the cells, blood drenched the floor, cells that were once occupied now had nothing but puddles of blood.

He walked to the room where the prison files were kept, pushed the door open and was almost sick from the sight. Bodies had been dumped in there, throats had been cut, guts removed and some had even been scalped.

Tom dropped his gun to the floor as he doubled over, throwing up the noodles he had eaten earlier.

"It's about time one of you cock suckers got down here," a voice behind him said. Tom tried to right himself, but could feel the cold steel of a knife pressed against his neck.

"What do you want?" Tom looked at his gun, and cursed at himself for dropping it.

"I want to see you bleed."

Tom felt the knife slice through his neck, deeply, blood started to pour from the open wound. He held his hand up to neck, trying to stop the bleeding, but the blood seeped through his fingers.

"You thought the zombies were bad, I promise, you haven't seen anything yet," the guy whispered into Tom's ear, before running his tongue up his cheek, and then leaving him to die.

∽

"What's taking him so long?" Ricky asked Tina, as they continued firing into the horde.

"I don't know, want me to check?"

"No, I'll go, you keep firing." Ricky left his gun with Tina, and headed into the prison.

He walked through the dinner hall and could hear shouting in the distance, it sounded like the children, and they sounded scared. He started to sprint to the cell he and Lilly called their room.

"Let me in you little shits!" Ricky could hear a voice yell.

He rounded the corner and could see a blood covered man standing at the cell, a knife in hand, trying to shake the cell door. The children were all cowering in the far corner, screaming and crying.

"Get away from them," Ricky yelled, as he sprinted for the man.

"Oh look, another cock sucker," the man said, as he turned to see a charging Ricky sprinting straight for him.

Ricky recognized the bald head, and cold blue eyes, as one of the prisoners from cell block Z.

The man side stepped Ricky's charge, throwing a punch into his stomach. Ricky gripped the bars of the cell as he doubled over, the wind leaving his body.

"Oh, this is too easy," the man said. He stood behind Ricky, and held the knife to his neck.

"Lilly, under the mattress," Ricky said, before the man sent him to the ground with a punch to the back of the head.

Lilly lifted the mattress, underneath was a small pistol; she had only been shown how to use a rifle, but was sure she could figure it out.

"Oh look, the little bitch has a gun," the man said sarcastically.

Ricky used the distraction and swung his fist into the man's knee, there was a cracking sound, and the man fell to one knee with a scream. Ricky tried to get back to his feet, but a searing pain fired down his calf, he turned to see the source of the pain.

The man pulled the knife out of Ricky's leg, licking the blood off it, and dragging Ricky back toward him. Ricky tried to fight him off, but was met with the hilt of the knife crashing into the back of his head. The edges of his world started to fade, he could see Lilly stood with the gun pointed, her hands trembling from fear.

"You can do it," he said, before the man brought the knife down onto the back of his neck.

"Daddy, no!" Lilly shouted as she started to pull the trigger, the first bullet crashed into the man's neck, severing his jugular, the second and third hit his chest and head, sending blood and bone fragments through the air.

Lilly unlocked the cell door as quickly as possible and rushed over to her dad, he was clutching at the back of his neck, but the blood continued to pour.

"Daddy, please don't go," Lilly said, tears were already falling down her face.

"I'm sorry princess, it's my time to go see your mummy

again, now you go find Tina, and make sure you do everything she tells you, okay?" Ricky said, tears ran down the side of his face, and he let go of his neck. "Daddy loves you."

"I love you, too." Lilly wrapped her arms around her dad, and cried as he took his final breath.

∼

R.L. Chambers

R.L. Chambers is a British freelance writer and poet. He has been obsessed with horror, and the post apocalyptic genre for more than a decade, and started to write in early 2014. He currently resides in Chesterfield, England with his fiancée and their daughter.

His books can be found on Amazon.

Casey

A Man of particularly low moral values.

21

THE VEGAN

CODY MANN

Some people think selling weed is for uneducated lowlifes but that's not always the case. Take me for instance. I was raised in a good two parent home. My Mom was a homemaker and my Dad was a drill sergeant in the United States Army. We lived in a three-bedroom house in a good neighborhood.

My father wanted me to follow in his footsteps but I have been playing football since I was eleven. After graduating high school, I accepted a scholarship to Baylor University to play Division-1 ball. After a blown-out knee in my senior year, I left school and found marijuana to deal with the pain, not wanting to become addicted to pain pills.

I fell in love with the magical herb. Selling some on the side so I could smoke for free was the next logical step, so I moved into a shitty little apartment close to the campus, off the freeway. I had been living in the small studio apartment on the fifth floor for about three months when the end of the world happened. The only reason I'm still alive is because I was trying to impress the vegan chick down the hall with the big tits, so I had given up meat in hopes of getting in between those gigantic chesticles.

It was late afternoon when the sound of sirens and gunfire woke me from my stoned haze, after staying up most of the night smoking some new Maui Wowie I'd just got and playing Call of Duty. Peeling my eyes open, I groaned and rolled off the couch headed for the bathroom when a crash sounded through the wall. I live on the top floor of the Texas Arms Apartment Complex. There are three apartments per floor and five floors. I'm sandwiched between a hot vegan freshman and three typical college douche bags in a studio apartment but they are my best customers.

The crash came from the douche bags' apartment so I figured they were in the middle of one of their raging parties. As I flushed the toilet I heard a piercing scream through the walls and thought that's not normal but it's best not to get involved. Flopping down on my worn leather sofa and reaching for my trusty bong so I could wake and bake, I froze when someone shrieked again, followed by wet gurgling and sobbing.

I got up from the couch and went to check through the peephole, seeing nothing unusual I cracked the door and looked both directions. I noticed the vegan's door was open and looking the other way, I noticed the douche bags' door laying splintered on the floor. Hearing strange squelching noises coming from the douche bags' door, I slowly crept down the hall on shaky legs to the threshold of their doorway.

Suddenly aware that I was only wearing some tattered boxers and no shoes, I peeked around the door frame, slowly taking in the scene of destruction. It appeared like a normal college student's apartment after a party, with furniture strewn about but the growing pool of blood drew my eyes to the feet sticking out from behind an overturned couch.

"Hello," I said in a shaky voice when suddenly the vegan's blonde head prairie dogged up from behind the couch to slowly swivel in my direction like an owl. Her eyes were milky white and the lower half of her face was covered in gore, I could see bits of flesh stuck in her teeth. She exploded off the floor like a running back through the hole and bowled over the couch in her zeal to get to me so I backpedaled until my back was against the rail above the courtyard.

She was up and after me in the blink of an eye, charging, arms outstretched. Her pendulous breasts were covered in blood and were not at all how I had imagined them during my long lonely showers. Vegan's charge was punctuated by shrill howling and as she reached for me I did the only thing I could think of and that was to move aside at the last second and let vegan's momentum carry her over the balcony to crash to the courtyard below. She landed hard, feet first, breaking both legs and probably her back but after a second she looked up at me with hate filled eyes and started crawling toward the sounds of life on the lower floors.

There was suddenly a groaning behind me so I spun on my heels and found douche-bag number one standing in the middle of his living room. When he turned toward me, I saw that his throat had been torn out and I could clearly see the white of his spine and that's when, I'm not ashamed to say, I pissed myself. Turning and running back to the safety of my apartment, I slammed the door and leaned shakily against it when the pounding started.

My mind was spinning and I was having a hard time processing everything. Are zombies real? Did I just kill my neighbor? Am I going to have to kill this one? If zombie movies have taught me anything it's to go for the head. My thoughts instantly went to the pistol in my nightstand. It's a .410 Judge five shot revolver that shoots shotgun rounds, my dad had bought it for me when I left for school telling me I needed something for protection.

The door is a solid core door and I knew it would hold for a minute but I was more worried about the noise he was making. Wrenching my nightstand open and scattering the contents across my floor, I spotted the shiny glint of steel peeking out from a pile of unused condoms and other detritus. Snatching up the deadly revolver and checking the cylinder with a practiced hand, I snapped it closed and ran back to the front door. It now sounded like there were more than one out there.

Checking the peephole, my blood ran cold at the sight of all three douche-bag neighbors attacking my door, and they were indeed dead. I had to come up with a plan, and soon, before the douche bag brothers brought more of the dead to my doorstep or worse, knocked the door down. So, I ran to my closet to put on my heavy Carhart jacket, thick Levis and my mil spec combat boots for protection. The plan is to crack the door and when they poke their heads through the gap, I am going to pop them in turn but someone once said a plan only lasts until first contact, or something like that.

I put my shoulder into the door and unlocked the deadbolt, fully expecting them to open the door and charge me but I guess they can't open doors. I cautiously turned the doorknob and was instantly bowled over by the combined weight of the douche bags and fell to my backside when the first gory body charged into the room looking for fresh meat.

I lined up the sights like I had been taught and pulled the trigger. His head exploded into a pink mist and he pitched forward. The second and third douche bags honed in on me instantly. When I acquired a new target, I pulled the trigger a second time and was rewarded with another exploding head. Douche bag number three dove at me and my third shot went harmlessly over his head when he violently collided with me. He was trying to relieve me of my nose and I didn't have a shot. It was all I could do to keep him at bay with one hand under his chin and my gun hand pushing him back.

I angled my gun hand toward his head and let another round fly but it only tore off the side of his face. That seemed to only enrage him further and he redoubled his efforts to eat my face off. Pressing the Judge directly under his chin and squeezing the trigger, I watched as the top of his head exploded, raining bits of brain and bone down on us. Pushing off his body, I emptied my stomach on my floor, adding to the ungodly smell emanating from the dead douche bags.

I immediately dragged the dead bodies out into the hallway, fear driving my actions. I checked that the door to the fire stairs was closed and moved to the small elevator, pondering my next move. I decided not to push my luck at not knowing what was in the elevator and ran back to my apartment, slamming the door and locking it.

With shaking hands, I took a long pull off my bong to plan my next move. I knew that information was key so I turned on the tv and started scanning the channels. Finding only the emergency broadcast alert on all the channels, I threw the remote across the room and took another pull off my bong to help me think. Looking out the window at the scene below was like something out of a horror movie. Packs of the undead were running down the living who were trying to flee the carnage.

I watched as cars were overrun by mobs of the undead, swarming for the living flesh within. They seemed to be drawn to sound, had an uncanny ability to sense the living, an increased sense of smell and were faster than they had been in life, never tiring or needing rest.

Taking stock of my supplies, I was a little worried at not having very much on hand so I was going to have to scavenge from my neighbors and leaving the security of my apartment terrified me. I decided to check the douche bags' assortment first, not wanting to eat nasty vegan food during the end of the world. So I slowly peeked out my door, checking to make sure no one was waiting to jump me.

Turning left, I hustled to the douche bags' apartment and went straight to the fridge, carefully avoiding the pools of gore. Pulling it open, I was shocked to find only five 4 Locos, a half a bottle of mustard, and a moldy piece of pizza. Groaning, I started pulling open cupboards. Finding nothing, I silently cursed the douche bags. I guess it's vegan food for the apocalypse, I grumbled as I hustled to the vegan's apartment.

Walking in, I was shocked to see a half-eaten BLT on the floor and a pan of bacon grease on the stove. Well, well, well, it looks like Miss vegan was just flexing for the gram and wasn't even vegan. In the fridge, there was lunch meat and cheese as well as an assortment of canned meat and vegetables in the cupboard. It took three trips to lug my bounty home but in the end, I was set for a few weeks until things die down. Things were ok for a while inside my apartment with the power still on, for now. I spent as much time as I could at the windows in the back that overlooked the neighborhood so I could learn all I can.

There is the freeway, two truck stops beyond that, then it's just the industrial district. The picture was bleak outside. These zombies aren't the Romero 'Night of the Living Dead' shamblers. No, these fuckers are fast, like Walter Peyton in the open fast and Jerome Bettis hitting the #3 hole strong. I'm a big guy at six foot two and two hundred seventy-five pounds. I can run the forty-yard dash in 4.4 seconds but after those forty yards I'm done and my shitty Honda Civic is in the shop anyway.

I had a Sharper Image hand crank world radio in the back of my closet and wound it daily. As I listened, I began losing hope as stations slowly went off the air after reporting on the horrors from the U.S. and beyond. The middle east was eerily silent, not broadcasting much but calls to prayer and gibberish to my untrained ears. One day ran into the next with the monotony. This ritual was only broken by the winding of the radio once an hour and scanning through, listening to the static. When suddenly it locked on a strong channel broadcasting loud and clear, I listened to the end of the message. As it repeated, my blood ran cold.

The authoritative voice on the machine said, "This is Sergeant First Class Meadows of the first special forces operational group, recording this message on the 22nd day of September. I don't need to tell anyone listening what is happening. You already know. We figured out that the contamination is in the meat. So, if you have any throw it away. What you may not realize though, is that you are all in danger of radioactive fallout from the failing nuclear power plants scattered around this country. You have less than a week to get out of the danger areas. That's a best-case scenario. You may only have hours. There is a region the United States government has determined as a safe zone in Oklahoma and the president is relocating there. It is lightly populated so we will be able to eradicate any of the undead easily. There is a large group of us leaving Crow City in Kansas and heading to the town of Lakota, Oklahoma".

So that's how the vegan got infected. I chuckled to myself, thinking my dick might just have saved my life, if I wasn't trying to screw the hot vegan I would have definitely tried some of that cheap halal bacon.

~

It wasn't until week three when the power went out that I started to worry. My supplies were running low. Those things are everywhere out there and I got a measly 17 shells for my gun, I'm fucked. I was eating my last can of green beans when I heard an old familiar rumble. I had been working nights in the parts department of the tits and ass travel center, as the truckers love to call it, so I knew the sound of a Peterbilt 379.

The 379 is an extended hood conventional cab truck with an oversized sleeper, perfect for over the road, designed for owner operators. They are great for taking punishment and relatively easy to work on. This one was murdered out. It had a black paint job and all its shiny bits looked to be spray painted black. There was a large plow blade attached to the front, bars on the windows and it looked like snow chains hanging in the wheel wells. It was clearing a path down the freeway and trailing the dead like the pied piper, rolling coal at a rate that would give an environmentalist a coronary.

The thing that made me blink and do a double take was the rice rocket with an exoskeleton attached, leading the grizzly procession. The guy driving was wrapped in a leather racing suit that I couldn't believe he fit those enormous balls into and dodging the outstretched hands of the dead. They took the exit for the 'Flying Shithook' and the bike continued on while the truck turned around and plowed into the line of hundreds and hundreds of dead. Driving back and forth several times, the truck came to a stop under the cover of the truck stop with a loud hiss of air.

A large convoy of mixed Mad Max looking semis with everything from flatbed low boys, reefer trailers, and there was even a set of pups mixed in, charged down the highway. There were cars and what looked like a fancy RV or tour bus in the middle. The convoy followed the path cleared by the war wagon into the truck stop and orderly lined up while the passengers swarmed from the various vehicles and formed a perimeter.

The people had a mix of firearms and bludgeoning weapons but had a very familiar military air about them and I think I spotted a hook on someone's hand. By the looks of the POW/MIA You are not forgotten stickers and various American and military flags adorning the trucks and trailers, I'm assuming they are a convoy of Veterans. They appeared to be refilling and bugging out so I knew if I wanted out of here, this was probably my best shot. Now, how am I going to get their attention without drawing every zombie to me?

~

~

~

Cody Mann

Cody Mann was born and raised in a small town in the foothills of Northern California about 45 minutes outside of Sacramento called Placerville. After accepting a scholarship to the University of Houston and graduating with a degree in Communications and advertising his love and passion for cooking led him to be a chef where he has cooked in some of the best and worst restaurants in the country but now he is the head chef of the Placerville Brewing Company in Placerville California and lives with his wife Tonya, their dog Little Girl and their crazy cat Bullet!

22

TRUCKERS DILEMMA
MICHAEL PEIRCE

"Just where do you think you're going with all those guns? You just got home." Jennifer was more than mildly annoyed. It seemed to Evan sometimes that she was always annoyed.

He'd just run into the house, grabbed his guns and told her to pack a bag and be ready to bug out in five minutes.

She had her hands on her hips and hadn't done any packing. "We need to talk. You're acting like a crazy person."

"Bobby is out there in his truck, this may be our only chance to get out of here in one piece. For God's sake woman, haven't you been watching the news?" Evan didn't have time for this, and while Jennifer didn't know it, she didn't have time for it either.

"Are you afraid rioters in some city hundreds of miles from here are going to attack us? I've asked you a hundred times to see a counselor about this PTSD business, but no..." She was wound up and ready to launch into full bitch mode but was interrupted by a loud blast on the horn. Bobby was getting impatient.

"Wonderful, now you'll have the homeowner's association on our asses. You are truly the gift that keeps on giving. Tell your drunken friend to go home and then I want to hear what you're going to do to sort yourself out.

There was a continuous sound of sirens, some of them fairly close. Some muffled gunshots.

"Is that idiot firing a gun out there? What is wrong with you two?" She angrily opened the front door in time to see Bobby fire several shots at a woman who shrieked and ran toward him, ignoring the rounds that impacted her in the chest. Then his gun jammed...

"That does it, I'm calling the cops!" She grabbed her cell phone but was unable to get a connection. "Now what?" She tried the landline but it didn't work either.

Evan ran out the door with that silly looking 'black rifle' he'd purchased without even discussing it with her. He knew she hated guns.

Evan fired two shots; one of them hit the female creature in the side of the head and dropped it. He turned to an ashen faced Jennifer, "There is no more time for your shit. You saw that thing take hits that would kill a normal person. They are eating folks! Now get in the damned truck or I'm taking off without you."

Jennifer was trembling and backing away from him, "You're crazy...I'm not going anywhere with you. Get out, go away..."

Evan grabbed his guns and his kit and jogged out to the truck and threw his stuff in the back. Bobby asked, "Where's Jennifer? She's taking her damn time and those things are coming on fast."

Evan said coolly, "She doesn't believe in zombies...I'm tired of her shit anyway. Let's roll."

∼

Michael Peirce

Mike has been a musician and songwriter as well as a soldier in an African War and private security agent. His "Red Dirt Zombies" trilogy started life as a musical and draws on his experiences in those other areas. The TV show "The Walking Dead" shows the consequences of losing the war against the Zs. Peirce's books focus on the consequences of winning.

The "Red Dirt Zombies" series is available on Amazon as paperback or Kindle as well as several short stories plus links to various anthologies where he has a story. Coming soon a non-fiction book called "African Days and Hollywood Nights" is in the works as well as several additional short stories. You can find his books on Amazon.

23

BATTLE FOR WAREHOUSE 3

WESLEY R. NORRIS

"Dad, they're back, worse than ever, I counted fifteen this morning." Gage told the tired looking man in front of him. His dad looked up at him from the list he was making and ran scarred fingers through his hair. He was looking every bit of his 40 years and this was just another in a long list of things they weren't prepared to deal with. But it was fast becoming an issue. There was enough death and disease outside the wall without risking infection inside too.

"Let me take care of it Dad. I can do it. I've been shooting since I was a kid. I've got a plan and a list of stuff for the scavenging guys to get. Please, come on Uncle Scott says it's cool. Me and Timbo and some of the other boys wanna help. You tell all the new people everyone has a job to do if we are gonna make it so please please let us do this."

Rob smiled at his son. "Since you were a kid? You're nine years old. You are a kid, but fine give me the list and I'll see what I can do."

Gage pumped his fist. *Yes!* dropped the list and headed off to find Timbo and his friends.

Timbo, Booger, Mikey, Catfish, Hambone and of course Lizzy were hanging out by the wall.

Why was she always hanging around? Why couldn't she play with the other girls? Gage thought to himself. She was always telling them why their ideas were stupid and they would just be Zom bait outside the wall and wouldn't last a minute. Mom says because she was "sweet" on him but that was just gross. This was the zombie apocalypse, not some romance book like his Mom read when she wasn't teaching him and the other thirty-five kids in the compound.

Gage strutted up to his friends, "Booger, knock that off!"

Booger was at least two knuckles deep up his left nostril hunting a trophy.

"What?" Booger asked, wiping his finger and the result of his treasure hunt on his jeans.

"Never mind. Look, Dad gave me the ok. My uncles are gonna get us what we need when they hit the Walmart and hardware store today. Operation Kill Them All is a go!" Gage said.

High fives all around, except Lizzy. "That's the dumbest name I ever heard." She snorted.

Gage glared at her. "You in or out? I'm sure there's a Barbie needing her hair done somewhere else."

Lizzy glared right back at him. "I'm in, but it's still a dumb name."

His uncles had come through even better than he had hoped Gage thought as he surveyed the arsenal in front of him.

He could hardly sit in his seat in the makeshift classroom when the Humvees came rolling through the gate two days ago. Stern looks from his mother did nothing to keep him on the lesson plan she was going through. Outside the walls was a warzone. Who cared about Abraham Lincoln crossing the Delaware? Gage had a mission to fulfill, he was finally going to fight, and he was going to win. Protect the survivors like his Dad and Uncles and the other men, maybe even be a legend once all the Zoms were dead, again. After Catfish claimed he had to pee, followed by Timbo, Hambone, Booger, and then Mikey, Mom finally decided they and she had enough and dismissed them. The six boys tore out of the room and headed for the hanger where the Humvees were. Lizzy rolled her eyes at Gage's mom, boys are so stupid. But as soon as she was out of the room she yelled "wait for me" and tore off after the boys.

When they reached the hangar, Uncle Roy was coordinating the unloading of the Humvees. He was bloody and tired looking. All of the adults always looked so tired to Gage. "Lost Riggins and Lockhart. " He heard Uncle Roy tell his Dad and the people assembled to unload and sort through the scavenged items. Gage and his friends stood quietly as he watched his Dad shake his head and Gage was certain he saw wetness in the corner of his Dad's eyes.

Dad was a hero. He had fought in what he called The Sandbox when Gage was just a baby. He was driving big rigs and training Cub Scouts when the world ended. He saved all these people. 189 people, now 187. When the Zoms came the National Guard was sent out to help. They never came back. His Dad and Uncle Scott had found the Armory deserted. Big buildings, warehouses full of food and weapons and fenced in with high fences and razor wire. They had quickly claimed the facility and got Uncle Roy involved in fortifying the place. Big shipping containers stacked 3 high ringed the place and armed guards patrolled around the clock.

At first it was just his uncles, aunts and cousins, but people started drifting in and Dad wouldn't turn them away. Gage saw his first boob when he was supposed to be in class but was instead on a scouting mission for his "Operation". People turned quickly if bitten or scratched, so Dad insisted that the Doctor and his nurse/ wife inspect every one before they were allowed to join the group. Hambone didn't believe him when he told the guys about the boobie, but that's why Hambone was a private and he was a General, Gage decided.

Uncle Scott saw him and waved him over. Uncle Scott was his favorite, always quick to laugh and didn't treat him like a little kid. He always told the boys dirty jokes and even gave them a cigarette once. Made them all sick, but still, a cigarette. Mom said he was incorrigible, whatever that meant, but she always said it with a smile so it couldn't be all bad..

Scott looked at the boys, a smile creasing the corners of his mouth. Even with all the death outside the wall it was good to see kids excited. Six scruffy looking boys and a girl, all knees and elbows, stood in front of him bursting at the seams with anticipation. "Booger, stop that." Scott said.

Geez, that kid is gonna be elbow deep in his own nose soon, he thought then yelled "Alright you maggots," in his best drill sergeant imitation, "form a straight line, shoulder to shoulder and prepare for inspection."

The kids shuffled around and formed sort of a line. Scott reached in his pack and pulled out a handful of candy bars. "Don't eat these until after supper. Lawrence, (Booger's given name) make sure you wash your hands."

"Yes sir." Booger answered.

"I can't hear you maggot!" Scott yelled.

"Yes sir! "Booger screamed.

Scott laughed. "Ok kids, I heard what you have planned. I think it's a great idea and one we never anticipated having to deal with. However, I don't wanna see you guys hurt so we are gonna do some training and you are gonna prove to me you have what it takes or I'm pulling the plug, ya hear me?"

"Yes sir!" seven enthusiastic voices yelled back.

Scott flashed his trademark grin at them. "Let's do this."

Gage reflected on the past two days as he looked at his arsenal. His troops were gathered around. Eyes alight with anticipation of the coming battle. Uncle Scott had made them practice their gun handling skills over and over. Sharpened up their marksmanship, drilled safety into them. They were ready. Stupid Lizzy was the best shot. She'd never even held a gun but flat out slayed those aluminum cans Uncle Scott had them shooting at. That really got on Gage's nerves. She was a girl! Girls couldn't shoot.

Gage gazed with pride at the table in front of him. Uncle Scott was the man, no doubt. Seven solid black rifles. Matte finished. *No shiny surfaces to give their element of surprise away* Gage thought appreciatively. Each had a picatinny rail Uncle Scott had mounted to the side to carry a tactical light. Empty Skoal cans that Gage had been hoarding were filled to the rims with hollow point ammo. It was going to be a slaughter.

"Alright guys," Gage started, "This is it. We fight, we win. Take no prisoners, show no mercy."

He eyed each of them with a hard look in his eyes. Mikey stared up at a butterfly fluttering away. Hambone scratched his ass. Timbo couldn't take his eyes off the rifles. Booger, well Booger did what Booger was always doing. Lizzy just looked bored.

"Guys, this is serious. We are going to war. Booger stop that." Gage looked at his friends. "Arm up. We are going in."

Standing in front of the warehouse, Gage looked over his assembled army one last time. Some of them might not make it back. "Last chance anyone wants to chicken out." He said.

No one spoke, no one ran. "Let's do this" Gage told them channeling Uncle Scott's catchphrase.

The plan was simple. Gage was going left through the door to Warehouse 3 with Timbo. Uncle Scott insisted on a buddy system for the entry teams so one man (or girl, apparently) could shoot while the others reloaded. Lizzy and Booger, who was a surprisingly good shot when he kept his finger on the trigger and out of his nose, were going right. Mikey and Hambone would go up the middle. Catfish was to guard the door to keep any non-essential personnel out and pick off any of the enemy that got by the teams. Each carried a rifle and a backpack of booby traps to set as they eased their way through.

Gage walked quietly down the left side of the warehouse. He knew they were here in number. He panned his tactical light slowly through the corners and across the shelves, eyes focused intently. Timbo beside him covered the areas he missed. *Slow and steady* he heard Uncle Scott in his head. *Watch your muzzle, know what's behind your target, finger off the trigger until you are ready to shoot. Make it in and back out safely.*

Timbo tugged at his sleeve and pointed to an opening between cases of macaroni and cheese. Gage nodded, provided cover while Timbo laid the first trap. They crept forward slowly, stopping often to set their deceives.

There! Gage saw a reflection from a set of beady eyes. Swinging his rifle on target he calmed his breathing, squeezed the trigger just like Dad and Uncle Scott taught him and heard the shot. The eyes disappeared, followed by the soft thump of a body hitting the floor. Gage reloaded the rifle. Timbo wanted to shout in victory, but Gage silenced his friend as they advanced on their fallen enemy. *Who knows? Might still be alive* Gage thought.

"He's a big son of a bitch" Timbo whispered softly as they stared at the corpse. "Look at those teeth. You drilled him right in the damn eye."

Gage proudly responded, "Uncle Scott says head shots are the only way to be sure."

He looked at his kill. No remorse, no pity, just a soldier doing his job.

"Let's go Timbo, there's hundreds more where that one came from."

They left the body where it lay.

The shelves were lined with food. Cases and cases of MRE's held in reserve for natural disasters or other crises. Pallets of water lined the walls. Additionally, items scavenged from the stores and restaurants that had a long shelf life were stored here. Enough food to feed an army, or a desperate group of survivors for a long time. Another army had laid claim to it too though. Rats. Big, buck toothed, hairy, disgusting rats. Along with their much cuter field mice cousins, they were slowly but steadily starting to eat into the supplies. Along with their droppings and the diseases they often carried, they were as real a threat as anything outside of the wall. Gage had seen them peeking out from behind crates, peering over the tops of cans of rutabagas and turnips like they owned the place whenever he was helping move items from the scavenging runs into storage. The adults were always so busy, so worried they paid little attention to the invaders, but Gage had learned all about the rat and his long history of spreading disease in biology class before the Zoms came. He knew what had to be done and he was the man for the job.

Still feeling the high of firing the first kill shot in the war Gage spared a glance at his rifle. It was a Ruger pellet gun. Single shot break action, powerful with its .177 hollow point pellet, Uncle Scott assured him it was the right tool for the job. Uncle Scott was always right.

Gage snapped back to attention as he heard the whoompf of Timbo firing. Another rat down. This was too easy. They set a few more rat traps baited with peanuts and continued on. Rat after rat fell to their guns. It was a slaughter. Hopefully the other teams were doing as well. All except Lizzy that is, he hoped she was getting a few but not more than the boys.

Gage was unprepared for the screams from the center of the warehouse. Someone was in trouble! He and Timbo took off.

"Hambone, Mikey!" they yelled in unison.

No answer. Tearing ass around the corner Gage was shocked to see Mikey in a pool of blood. Hambone stood by having dropped his rifle and stood there crying.

"*What the hell happened?*" Gage screamed at Hambone.

"*It was a giant rat! It got Mikey. We gotta go, we gotta go. He needs help!*" Hambone blubbered.

Lizzy and Booger arrived seconds later.

"Oh my God!" exclaimed Lizzy. "We've gotta get him a doctor!"

Hambone, with a thousand-yard stare common to

combat veterans, said "It was huge, it was massive, big as a dog. Just came out of nowhere. Ran up Mikey's leg and took him out. Just took him out man, he got off a shot but it was too late. It killed him! Man, it killed him and it's gonna get us too."

"*Nobody is dying today!*" Screamed Gage. "*WE ARE ALL GETTING OUT OF HERE ALIVE! Help me get him up.*"

Booger and Timbo got the bloody boy to his feet, supported between them. The glow of the exit doorway seemingly miles away through enemy infested territory.

Meanwhile, the giant rat watched confused or amused (either one) from a shelf a few feet away. It was a big one. Easily the size of a house cat. It twitched its nose at the aroma from the saturated boy as it watched the humans. A rat his size didn't fear much and certainly nothing in this warehouse of which it was king. He watched with hungry anticipation as the screaming kids dragged their unconscious friend away. He was really looking forward to tasting that red pool on the floor.

Lizzy and Gage watched constantly around them. The giant creature was still there somewhere waiting to take them out. Who knew who would be next to fall under its claws and fangs? Hambone, dragging his rifle by the barrel behind him, had checked out. He followed dazedly behind Timbo and Booger who were carrying Mikey's dead body. Catfish heard the yelling from his friends, saw Mikey's limp form, and dashed to go get help.

Gage yelled at him "Get Uncle Scott and Dad and the doc!"

Hambone, still disoriented and in shock at the death of his friend turned at the skittering noise behind him he knew would haunt him until the day he died. He lifted his rifle and yelled "NO!" and fired from the hip. The Rottweiler sized rat was drinking Mikey's blood!

At the shot Gage and Lizzie both spun. The pellet from Hambone's rifle missed the rat by a mile. The rat had slipped down from his hiding place and was hungrily lapping up the red liquid on the floor. Gage raised his rifle, fighting down his rage, and fired hurriedly. The pellet hit the large rat in the shoulder and spun it around. The rat, who just wanted to eat and go back to his rat business, squealed in terror and instead of running away, in his pain and confusion ran toward the terrified kids. Lizzie squeezed off her round and hit the rat in the head. The dying rat skidded to a stop at a shocked Gage's feet. Gage looked at her with new respect and felt something he'd never felt before when he looked at a girl.

"Thanks, nice shot." He said meekly cheeks burning red.

Lizzy broke open her rifle, loaded another pellet and smiled. "Load your gun General. Mikey needs us."

The kids burst through the darkened doorway into the afternoon sun. Catfish, Dad, Uncle Scott and the Doc rushed up to them. Dad grabbed Mikey from the boys and laid him out. Doc leaned over him checking his vitals.

Dad turned to the breathless kids. "Gage what the hell happened?"

Six different versions of the story came rushing out at once. Scott unnoticed, slipped through the door and threw the switch for the lights. Scott walked the thirty or so odd feet into the building. Dead rats and set mouse traps were everywhere. He shook his head. Those kids were dead serious. He approached the big corpse on the floor in the red puddle where Mikey fell. A decent sized rat lay there. About the size of a house cat. A rat that size would wreak havoc on their supplies for sure. He looked at the red pool on the floor and then looked up on the upper shelf. A smile and then a laugh lit up his face. Shaking his head he made his way back outside.

Mikey was sitting up. Doc was scratching his head. Dad just stood there wondering what the hell the big deal was. Kid fainted. Sure he was covered in red liquid but he was fine. Dad headed back to his office. He was speaking with a group of survivors in Oklahoma on the radio, making plans to join up with them.

Scott walked up to the group still laughing. "Who killed the tomato juice?" He asked.

Hambone having recovered somewhat after Mikey's resurrection said "Wasn't me."

Gage and Lizzy looked at each other. "He was like that when we got to him. We thought it was blood." Scott nodded in Mikey's direction. "Apparently when Rambo over there fainted, he pulled the trigger and shot a hole in a gallon of tomato juice and it ran out on him. That was a big rat though so I'm gonna cut you some slack, soldier. You kids go get cleaned up and put those rifles away. I think you've made quite an impression on the rat population today."

Scott laughed as the kids gathered up their gear and headed for the living quarters. "Gage hold up."

Gage, a little embarrassed over that revelation walked back to Uncle Scott. Putting his hand on his shoulder Uncle Scott looked him in the eye.

"Gage, I know it wasn't what you were expecting in there today. Shit got real for you in a hurry but you didn't quit. You got your people out, did what you set out to do and you will fight another day. I'm proud of you. In this new world that's the way it is. Anything can happen and you've got to adapt or perish. You did just fine. Hold your head up. This is gonna make a hell of a story to tell the other kids."

Gage looked up at his Uncle. "Uncle Scott, I'll never quit fighting. This thing between me and them is just getting started. You worry about the Zoms, I'll deal with the rats. Now if you're all done talking, I've gotta girl I think I want to kiss."

∼

Wesley R. Norris

Wesley is an Air Force veteran, full time Industrial Mechanic and part time gunsmith. He lives with his beautiful bride, children and granddaughter in South Georgia. He loves Jeeping, paddling his wife around in a kayak, hunting, fishing, large caliber guns and all things Bigfoot.

Most of his writing can be found on bathroom walls in Sharpie.

24

TRUCKING IN PINK

ALINA IONESCU

I had been trapped in that toilet stall for five hours now... With all the screaming and the noise outside, I admit that I had not dared to leave the safety of the rather dirty rest stop bathroom ...

I had no idea really what was going on, but with all the murders and terrorists, who could really know. So, there I was, in the imaginary safety of the quiet place, my shoes on the floor and me doing my best imitation of a tiger crouch on the toilet. The window was too small for me to go through and I had seen some of them in the parking lot, too.

This was the way I would spend my last few hours.

After all the screaming and shooting started, I climbed up on the toilet and watched what was going on outside, I also looked longingly at the safety of my rather impressive truck. I was new in the business, but I came from a trucker family, both my dad and my brother did this work. I'd had my license since forever, so when the economy started to go downward and I lost my fancy job at the bank, the bills started to pile up. Then I remembered how much fun I had driving down the open roads with dad. After trying my best to get hired as a trucker and being politely refused because of my lack of experience, or let's be honest, because of the fact that I was a woman. I used my last savings and a line of credit, sold my car, sold everything that I could and got myself a brand new (well, for me it was) old truck and started my own business. I called a few of Dad's old contacts and they first offered me small jobs because they were ashamed to turn me down, but after seeing that I do the job same as the guys and that I am no diva, they started recommending me, so the trucking actually went well. A great plus is that the ladies toilet in most of the trucking restrooms is always empty.

The guys where mostly ok, there was a joke now and then, but I would say something shitty back, and we would end up drinking some coffee together and talking trash about something else. There was always another topic to pick at from sports to new cars to a pretty new waitress. Even if here, in the middle of fucking nowhere, I was hoping that we were rather safe from terrorist attacks, this was an open carry area, where everyone was packing. Talks about guns and knives were a regular thing.

My Glock 43 was tucked in the back of my jeans, brought it out from my purse but my nicer stuff was …you guessed it, in my truck. And my truck was so so far away, I could see my beautiful truck in the middle of the parking lot, what would have been a 5-minute walk now looked like a few hours because these fuckers were everywhere!

I noticed that there was a pattern, if there was no noise they would just walk around, slowly, like in the old zombie movies, but as soon as they heard something, they jumped, sprinted and attacked. Like rabid dogs. They bite a victim a few times and lose interest, after a few minutes the bitten starts twitching and acts the same way as their attacker. I always was a fan of horror, but are these creatures zombies, vampires, or a cross between them? I have no fucking idea but you have to know your enemy in order to beat him. It, not him, I say it because they could not be alive. One of the first that I started to look at was a grizzly looking trucker that I had known. His name was Joe, he was one hell of a nice guy, always ready to help anyone in need and always with a joke and a smile on his face. Joe was missing half his face and his rather large frame was split open. Guts and gore were hanging out from his Metallica t-shirt. His trucking cap was still on his head, and pieces of his blood encrusted skin where sticking to it. It, I could not say him anymore, because Joe could not be alive the way he was. Others in the parking lot looked similar to him.

The noise from the restaurant was calming down, but I could hear movement and things bumping into each other, into furniture, it was eerie. What could have caused this? When I stopped to grab a bite everything was normal, the waitress recommended a burger special, but I had to lose a few pounds. All that trucking made my ass grow in size, so I had ordered a salad with grilled chicken and a Diet Coke. I will not become Miss Trucking, but I still liked to be able to run and tie my own shoe laces and stuff like that. So, while waiting for my order, I was walking to the restroom. Then all hell broke loose, there were a few screams, and then shooting and more screams. After about an hour and a half the screaming died down and these things started pouring through the parking lot, each of them hunting down new people that where stopping to get a break. Was that just happening here? The fact that my phone had no service, and I could not use my tablet to get online, made me believe that this wasn't just regional but nation-wide because of the speed ... well... fuck it! I had no time to dwell on it, I was captive in a fucking restroom. I had water and I locked the door (found the key, lucky me) but this door was thin plywood, so if one of those things heard me and decided that I was a juicy meal, they could break it down in a few seconds. All I had was my Glock and a small knife, not really much of an arsenal to beat these things. I was also not sure how to defeat them, no one had yet, as far as I could tell...

I just wanted to get to my truck, get on the radio, find some of the guys and warn them. Maybe if I could reach a few people they will stay safe...or get armed.

Time to get moving. I had a feeling that I would go crazy in here. Something had to be done, and my gut told me that there would be no help coming any time soon.

I started taking one of the plastic doors to the toilet stall out using my knife as a screwdriver, I saw that guy in 28 Days Later but he had riot gear, maybe I could use the light plastic door as a shield. It was a farfetched plan, but a plan nevertheless. After building something that resembled a shield with the straps from my purse, super glue and the door, with my gun in my hand, I felt armed enough to try and see what was out there. My plan was to get to the kitchen and make my way out through the back. Not much of a plan, but it was the best that I had. The kitchen entrance was just a few feet away, and I was going to be silent, maybe if they didn't notice me I could sneak away. Shooting would ruin my ninja style approach, well ninja was maybe the wrong word for a 5'7", 180-pound female but I could at least try. I refused to go down without a fight, or starve to death in the toilet while drinking tap water and eating tic-tacs. Fuck it!

The hallway showed me what I had been fearing, the entire restaurant was overrun by the people that had eaten lunch there. There was blood, so much blood... on the floor, on the walls, on their clothing. Some had limbs missing, a few were crawling on the floor, others had chunks of their flesh ripped out, and hanging guts seemed like a popular injury.

And I actually did it, hidden behind my door, crouched low, I crawled to the kitchen. I know, it was not very dignified and I will not write it down in my memoirs but it worked, motherfuckers!

The kitchen looked empty and the first thing that I had in mind was closing the door behind me. I knew that it would make a noise but I could not bear the idea that those things were there and could just step through with no warning. The door was not massive but it was loud, and my closing it had gotten a roaring scream from the restaurant area... I had never heard anything like that, ever. It was like the roar of a wounded and hungry animal. I never thought that a human throat was capable of producing such a gruesome sound. The sound was followed by the first thud on the door... Fuck, fuck, fuck!

Ok, so I was smart enough to make it into the kitchen and now all I had to do was outrun about 20 monsters in the parking lot, reach my truck and lock the doors, all the doors. Who needed a really good plan if you had a plan, any plan? I had about 10 minutes before the door was going to give in, so I grabbed a piece of pie and started to eat it. Hey, I was hungry and this might have been my last meal... ever. Blueberry pie, no cream, it was still yummy.

While I was bingeing out on my pie, I heard this small noise, like a sniffling and a hiccup, it came from the kitchen cabinet.

"Hello, who is there?" As if some of the zombies would say back, "Hello I am a zombie and I want to rip your guts out and tie them in a bow." I can be stupid now and then... But there was a voice, a human voice and the sound of the cabinet doors opening. It was the young waitress that took my order.

"You ok?" She was just looking at me, her lips quivering and tears flowing freely to stain her cheeks, shaking all over her petite body. "They just turned... they had a few bites...and ...blood...so much blood..." and then she started crying again.

This young lady would not be of much use, but I could not leave her behind, she was too pretty to die. If I could get us out of there, who knew how the world would look, and I could not bring myself to hush her back into the cabinet and close the door. Not knowing that she would be a monster's lunch in a few minutes. So, after shaking her shoulders a bit I looked deep into her eyes, "Ok, no matter what we do next, you can't scream! Noise attracts them. We have to be quiet and maybe we'll get a chance to live. I won't leave you behind. Just shake your head if you understood."

A small smile tugged on the corner of her mouth and she nodded, "Ok."

"Just follow me." There was a name tag on her blood-stained uniform, it said 'Wendy'. "Ok, Wendy, let's go." I was gripping my Glock for dear life, there was no way in hell I would let loose of it. If I would have been bitten I wanted to blow my brains out ... I didn't want to become one of them, stumble over my intestines and lose the little sanity that I still owned.

The kitchen entrance was about to give in, so I focused on the back door, cracking it open I could see the rear parking lot, where the people working here would park their cars.

"Wendy, do you have a car here?"

Wendy handed me a set of keys with something fluffy and pink hanging from them, and pointed towards a small Golf. Great, just fucking great, could she not drive a Hummer???

Ok, so there were a few of them mingling in the parking lot, absently staring around and occasionally bumping into each other.

I knew that as soon as they heard the noise from the kitchen they would come to us, fast, and then we will be like a slice of ham between two parts of the same bun, trapped.

I motioned to Wendy, who in the meantime got herself a big butcher's knife, good girl, that we have to sprint to her car as fast as we can. And sprint we did. I was sending prayers to all the Gods that I could think of, I didn't want to die that day! Not that I had many plans, or a family that would miss me. ..or even a cat, but I just didn't want to die!

The zombies saw us and started sprinting toward us before I could react. One tackled Wendy and she was down, I could see her trying to defend herself with her knife but another two of the walking speedy dead were on her faster than I believed could be possible.

I reached the car, it looked like they were all attracted by the screams of poor Wendy and I was not that interesting anymore. From the safety of her Golf I noticed the moment when her human life left her, and she started twitching, immediately the greedy undead stepped away and turned toward me. Start the car, stupid, start the car! I got the key in the ignition and the stupid thing just made a gurgling noise, in a second the zombies were hitting it from all sides like rhinos in a National Geographic documentary. My plan was to get to my truck, it was higher and safer, I had weapons in it. The windshield started to crack, that thing was hitting it with its forehead, oh my God, I was going to die just like

Wendy who, by the way, was absently pushing her pretty face to the side window. The former guy on the windshield was making me worry. Ok, ok...breathe...breathe... you will not end up with your face peeled off in a junky piece of crap old car...

I closed my eyes and made a last effort to turn the key in the ignition, and it worked! It actually worked. The motor hummed to life and I could put it in drive and I started pushing the monsters away. I had quite a following, nothing like the 4 followers I used to have on twitter. Is twitter still a thing? Doesn't matter now.

I could see chunks of flesh between their broken teeth, and there was so much hatred. I had never experienced that level of hate on someone's face. Even Wendy's pretty face was a mask of hatred and horror, blood dripping from the wounds on her forehead.

I had to plan on the go, this thing only had about a quarter of a tank. All I could think of was to drive away from there, go anywhere else, there was a small town not far away from there. Maybe that was not overrun and I could get some help from the people there, and guns. Now that the car was working and I had put a bit of distance between me and the monsters, I opened my window and tried to shoot one of them... I hit it center mass in its chest, but that thing kept coming, that was not possible. Each and every zompoc movie came back to me, aim for the head, shoot for the head. I am a decent shot, but try to hit a running target right in the forehead, if you have shaking hands. I shot its neck and I think that I hit its spine because now its neck broke, it looked as if the head was held up with just the skin and muscle tissues. It fell down, the body paralyzed, but the fucker wasn't dead, the teeth were still snapping. Only then I had the courage to step out of the car and try a head shot and I killed my first zombies. Even if in the long run it was a mistake, as I was down to just 2 bullets and I had attracted a horde with all the noise, knowing that these things could be killed, and they were not invincible, made me feel good.

I stopped wasting time and jumped into the car with the running engine and started to drive to the next town, with a nice bunch of zombies running after me.

I was thinking that if they didn't see me anymore I would be safe and they would stop following me, because the last thing that I wanted was to attract a horde of crazy undead into the next town with me.

This piece of junk could be pushed a bit more, just a few more miles faster. On the side of the road was a sign: Greentown 10 miles. Who would call a place here Greentown, and what would await me there?

I was lost in my own thoughts when I felt the impact, I was driving fast and could feel that shitty piece of crap losing traction, spinning like crazy out of control. Last thing on my mind was that deer are not common in this area and I had never seen a deer that wore a white nightgown.

Something warm and sticky was making my eyes burn.

Long Dawg was driving around and trying to find as much useful information as possible, there were a few cars that lay in ditches. He was not sure if the drivers had turned while behind the wheel, or maybe someone in the car had turned and attacked them, but he knew that each and every one of those cars had a story and there was the end of someone's human life connected to it.

∾

Alina Ionescu

Alina Ionescu likes watching horror movies and driving a bit too fast. She is a self employed fashion designer that has her workspace at home and creates fabulous and scandalous looks. After she found out about the indie zompoc scene a few years ago, she became hooked and follows most of the new releases.

Alina was born and lives in Romania....yeah, Dracula's country.

Jessie

Son of Gunny and Lacy, Jessie finds himself facing the Zombie Apocalypse with only a few friends from school.

25

SCARECROWS

DAVID A. SIMPSON

Five Years After the Fall

Jessie needed fuel.

The old chop top Mercury, if it could still be called that, idled into the little town of Cattle Creek, South Carolina. He was way deep in no-man's land, far inside the territories where no one else ventured, and he kept his guard up. He spotted what he was looking for on the outskirts and pulled into the gas station. This town was well above sea level, but he still looked for tell-tale signs of muddy high-water marks. The hurricane that came through a few years ago had effectively destroyed any fuel still in the ground near the shore with the storm surge and flooding. He was a good fifty miles from the ocean, and although he could see visible signs of the squall, this town hadn't been flooded.

He bumped up over the fallen Kwiky Mart sign, not concerned about a stray nail or sharp piece of metal with the run-flat tires, and parked near the underground tanks. He looked around again, checking for followers before he shut the diesel down. It wasn't like the old days when those undead things were wicked fast and could chase you for miles. Now, most of them were over five years old and being dead hadn't been kind to them. They were slow and plodding, barely even dangerous anymore unless a fresh one surprised you or you managed to get yourself surrounded by a horde of them.

He pulled out his M-4 and carefully checked his perimeter, looking for anything coming towards him, especially something dragging itself along the ground. Those were the most dangerous now, they were old and slow and perfectly camouflaged after years of crawling in the dirt. He'd even seen them with grass, weeds and other plants growing out of them, looking like an animated ghillie suit. They would drag their way towards you, and you'd never hear or see them until they were taking a bite out of your ankle.

The area was clear. There was nothing around him, and the birds had started singing again as he opened the door and got out. He stretched, dug out his collapsible fuel stick and opened the lid to the underground diesel tank. He dipped it in, cautious not to stir up the contents, then pulled it back out. He was careful not to shake the attached baby food jar as he held it up to the sun to see how it looked.

It'll do, he thought. It wasn't exactly a pure golden liquid, but the algae buildup wasn't bad. He'd used worse. The triple filters on the fuel line would catch any contaminants before it got to the motor. He dumped a few quarts of diesel treatment into the oversized tanks mounted in the trunk and dragged his hoses out to start refueling. The pump was a quiet 12-volt model that he had permanently attached to the tanks, all he had to do was drop one end of the hose in the underground tank and flip the switch.

Jessie leaned against the car and pulled out his poke to

roll a cigarette. It was a habit he'd picked up from his dad those months he'd spent in Lakota, the new Capital City of the States. It was a nice enough town; walled, secure and offering most of the comforts they'd had before the poison-laced meats had wiped everyone out. That's where he'd built this car, along with his old man's help. It used to be his dad's, but after he had managed to drive it all the way from Atlanta when the outbreak was fresh and the undead were unbelievably strong and fast, his dad had given it to him. Said he'd earned it.

Life was great for a while after he finally completed the thousand-mile trip but then he got bored. He was seventeen and had just battled his way through countless skirmishes, close calls and narrow escapes. He'd lived on the edge for months, done things no teenager should ever have to do and now he was supposed to go back to school and learn a vocation. He would rather join the Army and go after the people who did this to the world. The radical Islamists that finally had one of their terrorist plans succeed and it had nearly killed everyone, themselves included. There had been thousands of them in the States, and they needed to be eliminated, but his mom had insisted he heal properly before he did any more adventuring.

Jessie hadn't put up too much of a fight, he was about done in. The months on the road had been rough. The doc's had to re-break his arm where he'd set it badly, he had picked up a nasty parasite somewhere, and it took a while for the antibiotics to work. They didn't know what to do about his face. The SS sisters told him to grow a beard to cover most of the scar and keep a handkerchief in his pocket to wipe away the drool. They didn't have plastic surgeons, but he wasn't very vain, anyway. It uglied him up some but he didn't spend much time looking in the mirror. There weren't any girls to try to look good for anyway. All of them were already with someone or had a bunch of men lined up, waiting for dates. With his face, he didn't even try to compete.

He'd spent a few months recuperating and working at Tommy's shop, trying to adjust to a normal life again. A life where you didn't have to kill or be killed every day. He beefed up the old Mercury, setting the body on the running gear from a 4x4 diesel pickup. He wasn't sure what he was going to do when he was healed up but it wouldn't be hanging around behind the wall and becoming a farmer. Maybe he could join the raiding parties that went into small towns, cleaned out the undead and brought back truckloads of goods from the hardware or shoe stores. By the time he finished his car and was feeling better, there was no use joining the army, most of the jihadis had already been eliminated. The survivors of the zombie virus had been fast and vicious in their retaliation as soon as they knew who had caused it.

He thought about becoming a bounty hunter and trying to find any of the remaining Muslim enclaves that went into hiding but he didn't really want to hunt humans. Maybe he could join the sheriff's posse or the Convoy guards. There were plenty of jobs to do, most of them dangerous enough to keep you on your toes.

In the end, he decided he wanted to be a Retriever and chase down those items people would pay well for. It got him out of town, away from the stares and the whispers. It wasn't as if people didn't like him, they did, but he got the feeling that most of them felt sorry for him. He hated it. Everyone had a horror story to tell but his had lasted for months, not days. Besides, the Retrievers had the best stories to tell down at Pretty Boy Floyd's. They were always having mix-ups with the undead and sometimes Casey's raiders, the gang that had escaped from prison, ruled in the West and made trouble for the new society. There were other settlements popping up, some small, some with hundreds of people. Other fortified towns and trading posts. Some were safe and clean with a working government and police force, others were shady and dangerous that were ruled by the law of the gun.

The Retrievers lived on the edge. They went into areas where everyone had fled and recovered all kinds of things. People would pay good New American coin for photo albums and other keepsakes they had left behind in their panicked escapes from overrun towns. They paid for safe transport to other outposts or for the rescue of loved ones from some of the outlaw towns.

Jessie needed that adventure.

The heart thumping excitement of close calls.

The thrill of living.

The long days behind the wheel, constantly seeing new things.

He could never settle down and become an electrician or mechanic after all he'd lived through. He had to feel that adrenaline coursing through his veins once in a while. Something had happened to him during those months on the road by himself. Something deep inside him had changed. He'd only been sixteen when it all started but that child was long gone. Probably had been since he'd made a single mistake that had gotten his friends killed. Or maybe when he saw people he'd rescued slaughtered and stacked in a pile. After that, he was just... different. Colder, perhaps. He couldn't stand being around ordinary people for very long. He didn't have anything to talk about with them.

He had to get out of the little paradise his dad had established and just roam the roads. He had chased money for a while but what good was money if you didn't need anything? Jessie delivered the mail to different outposts and had done a lot of retrievals for folks wanting certain pieces of jewelry or grandma's handmade quilt or other cherished keepsakes from their old homes. They wanted reminders and remembrances of who they had been. Family history.

He earned a reputation as a man who didn't fail. He had never come back empty-handed with a story of how it was too dangerous or too many infected were in the area. He even crossed the Mississippi and went into the Eastern Lands, something only a handful of men would try. Too many had made the crossing and were never heard from again. He recovered the various things his clients wanted and he'd even raided a few museums for the town's collection, the curator trying to preserve the priceless art. Paintings were being destroyed by the heat, cold and dampness of buildings with no electricity and damaged by storms or neglect. Those had been tough jobs in the heart of the dead cities and he'd gone in with a team of other guys.

He'd still take on odd jobs sometimes, if someone could convince him or make it worth his time. Usually, he would recommend one of the other Retrievers to them, one of the handful of guys or gals that specialized in whatever part of the country the items were in. The truth was, if the retrieval was boring, if it wasn't dangerous enough, he'd pass on it. He went after the hard-to-get things the others deemed too risky. He wanted the challenge and having a destination, a goal, was much better than just wandering aimlessly through the wastelands.

The majority of the people had quickly become accustomed to the security of the walls and few wandered out past them on their own. The truckers still made weekly runs to raid warehouses for various supplies but they ran like a military operation. Loud, heavy and with plenty of firepower.

For the last few years, Jessie had just been rambling. His tentative 'mission' was to let any survivors he came across know that the nation had been reestablished and the lands West of the Mississippi and East of the Rockies were relatively safe territories. Teams had been eliminating the undead for years in those areas and there were scores of walled towns who would always welcome newcomers. He was also supposed to note any significant changes to the landscape. Collapsed bridges, dams or levees that had failed, areas that were nearly impassable from hurricanes and which cities had burned to the ground. He kept notes, checked in occasionally on the Ham radio but mostly he just drove. He would go weeks, sometimes months, without coming across outposts of survivors, without speaking.

Jessie tossed the cigarette when the diesel started flowing out of the neck of the oversized fuel tank. He flipped the switch on the pump, reeled up his hoses and stowed everything before walking towards the store. Not much was still good after all this time except Twinkies and jerky. Canned goods were usually still fit, as long as you gave them a good sniff after you opened them. Sometimes they had spoiled but most of the time not.

Jessie sat on the hood, leaned back against the bars welded across the windshield, munching on teriyaki jerky and sipping a warm soda. Rule number one. If you're stationary, keep your body off the ground. The crawlers could slither out of anywhere, unseen and unheard until it was too late.

He was trying to decide where to go from here. The hurricane that blew in a few years back had trees and power poles down everywhere and it was getting harder to maneuver around them. He wanted to make it to the ocean, only a handful of people could claim to see the Atlantic or the Pacific since the fall, but this was slow going. Maybe he'd angle back up north for a hundred miles or so, then cut in.

He heard a flock of crows take flight somewhere off to his left, cawing noisily at each other and whatever had frightened them. Might be shamblers. He listened intently, trying to hear the tell-tale sign of their dry and crusty moans. You could hear for a long distance now. There were no noises other than the breeze rustling the leaves and the sounds of insects. Anything unnatural stood out, easily identified as something that didn't belong in this land where no humans dwelled. He heard the faintest tinkle of breaking glass and sat up quickly. The undead didn't break glass unless they were after someone. Any windows that could be broken by simply bumping into them accidentally had long since been shattered. It could be something else, like a branch falling from a tree, but he doubted it. Not when it came from the same direction that flock of crows had just swarmed up from. Then he heard them, that unmistakable keening sound of zombies on the chase.

After a fast check of the ground, he rolled off the car. He grabbed a couple of spare magazines from the holder mounted inside the door and shoved them in his back pockets. Whatever was happening was close, no use taking the car and letting the whole world know he was coming. He had good mufflers, but it was still a diesel. It was noisy. He didn't know if whoever being chased was friend or foe and he wanted to see them before they saw him. He considered his armor for a second but it was hot and he hadn't had any close calls in quite a while. The undead were just too dead to be a real risk anymore if you were careful. They no longer leaped and ran and screamed. They bumbled along in unsteady gaits or dragged themselves along the ground.

He flipped the hidden switches on the Merc so the motor couldn't be started and took off towards the sound, stepping around the debris littering the parking lot. Shredded plastic bags caught in the fences still fluttered listlessly with the light breeze. As he went up the street, he kept his head on a swivel, looking for danger and also signs of life. He didn't understand why survivors would fortify a house in the suburbs and stay in it, but he'd seen it more than once. People grew attached to a community or a family home and just wouldn't give it up. He stayed in the middle of the road and set a brisk pace towards the town center. A half mile later, he saw what had stirred up the crows.

In the parking lot of the Piggly Wiggly grocery store, a dozen or more zombies were half-leaping and clawing at someone trapped on the roof of an RV. She was little, just a kid, with an unruly mop of black hair. The undead were fairly fresh ones, they still moved fast and jumped and they all had clothes on. They must have been stuck inside the store, out of the weather and the baking sun all these years. That kid on the roof, or whoever she was with, had set them free. They'd probably been trapped in a break room or something. Maybe he should have brought his armor. Too many of them to take on with his blades, not without protection. He'd have to use the carbine and be quick about it because anything within blocks was already on the way, following the keening of the undead. Once he started shooting, every crawler, shambler and runner within a mile would be headed towards him as fast as it could.

He dropped to a knee, shouldered the M-4 and started popping heads. They turned, saw the fresh meat, and ran towards him as fast as they could. They were in better shape than most he'd come across recently but still, they'd been dead for a long time. Fourteen became twelve became ten. They were closing the distance too fast and he wasn't getting enough head shots. Their uneven gait made their ugly, open-mouthed heads bob and weave. This was gonna be close. Even above the sound of the rifle double tapping and their breathless screams, he heard more glass shatter across the street behind him. He'd have company from one of the houses lurching for his blood.

This plan sucked. He needed a plan B. He emptied the magazine and sprang to his feet, sprinting towards the RV. He dodged around the six still running for him and smashed the stock of his rifle into a mummified store clerk's face as he dashed by. The jawbone shattered and teeth went skittering across the parking lot as Jessie kept going, not even breaking stride. He leaped for the hood then bounded up to the roof, pulling one of the spare magazines from his pocket to reload. The girl was gone and he spotted her disappearing into the undergrowth at the side of the store, tote bags of groceries in her hands.

"*You're welcome,*" he grumbled to himself, then waited a few minutes for the shufflers and shamblers to make their way to him. He let them all gather around the RV and start reaching for him before he began killing them again. He checked each face, looking for a brand new one that may have been with the girl but they were all years old, lips dry and broken, exposing their snapping teeth. He attached his blade in the bayonet lug Griz had fixed for him and stabbed easily into their dead skulls. When they all lay in heaps around the camper, he double checked the bodies he'd already killed and they were all withered and dried out, too. No freshly turned zeds. The kid had been alone. She wasn't too bright, though, if she'd loosed a pack of zombies on herself. Jessie wondered if she had recently lost her guardians. No way she'd been out here on her own for very long. She'd made a bunch of rookie mistakes. She wasn't armored. She didn't have weapons or a go-bag on her back and she had just run in a blind terror to climb on top of the RV. She would have been dead in a day or so if he hadn't come along.

Now he had a choice. Go gear up or take off after her immediately. It would take a solid half hour to get to the car and back, then try to find her trail before it disappeared. He grimaced, the old, poorly healed scar on his face pulling his mouth into an unintentional snarl. Both choices were bad. The smart thing to do would be to leave her. She'd ran off and left him, she could take care of herself.

But she couldn't. That had been pretty obvious. She'd had maybe a ten-minute lead by the time he'd finished off all of the zombies, so he skipped the armor and started off at an easy jog into the undergrowth. The woods and kudzu were slowly reclaiming the town, the back of the building already covered in the vines, the dumpster shapes barely recognizable. He had seen where she went in and it was easy to pick up her trail. She was running in a panic with an armload of supplies. He followed the broken branches and the bent weeds over the edge of the hilltop and down the grassy hillside.

The little town of Cattle Creek was situated on a South Carolina knoll with only a few dozen streets and the one county road snaking through it. The area behind the Piggly

Wiggly dropped off into a valley and there was another wooded hill on the other side of the creek at the bottom. Her path through the waist high grass was easy to see and when she started following a game trail on the other side of the stream, her footprints were evident in the dirt. Small, bare feet left impressions alongside the hoof prints of deer.

Jessie was hot, sweat was rolling off of him and biting insects buzzed his head. *This is ridiculous* he kept thinking as he swatted mosquitoes and deer flies. *Why am I even bothering?* But every time he was ready to call it quits, head back to his car and get something cool to drink, he would see her bare footprints. The girl didn't even have shoes. He could only imagine she was the last survivor of some hillbilly clan that was way up a holler. There couldn't be any adults left alive, not if some ten-year-old with no training and no shoes was going into town on her own.

He trudged on.

He almost missed where she turned off the trail, he was too busy muttering curses and trying to kill a particularly annoying horse fly that kept buzzing his ears. There was a break in the underbrush that branched off up the hillside. He double checked, there were no footprints in the grass but it was still bent where she had stepped. He wasn't far behind her.

Ten minutes later, he was looking up at a cluster of houses situated in the woods on a low rise. He could see the dirt road leading into them was washed out in places, overgrown with weeds and unused for years. He didn't see the girl, so he hunkered down beside a tree in the wood line and watched, evaluating what he saw. He didn't want to get shot, just wandering up. There were five houses and a few mobile homes, run-down to the point of decrepitude. Sagging porches. Missing tin from the roofs. No cooking fire smoke. No solar panels. A couple of them looked like a strong wind would knock them over. There was a garden, a big one, set off a good distance from the houses with a couple of scarecrows stirring around in the slight breeze. He turned his gaze back to the shacks. Maybe the kid had been after medical supplies. There was a small woodpile and an ax in the chopping block. Maybe her mom or dad or whoever, had gotten hurt. He watched, looking for any indication of life. Other than the scarecrows and their ragged clothes flapping in his peripheral vision, nothing moved.

Jessie crushed a deer fly that bit his neck, smearing blood as he cursed its mother, its cousins and every relative it ever had. He made up his mind, he couldn't stay here in the oppressing summer heat, swatting flies, waiting for something to happen. He stood and walked quickly towards the houses keeping a close eye on the one that looked like it was actually in use. The closer he got, the more apparent it became that only one of the shacks was lived in. The dirt path leading to it was the only one not overgrown with uncut grass. He heard the sounds of someone eating noisily as he approached and off to his right, he heard the sudden keening of the undead.

The garden. They're coming through the garden! His mind screamed as he swung around and brought up his carbine. He heard the girl shriek behind him.

Ambush! he thought, *they saw me coming.*

She was the closest threat so he brought the gun back around to her but she burst out of the door and ran past him to the zombies in the garden, standing in front of them with her hands up, yelling at him in a foreign language. An explosion of crows came flurrying out of the nearest trees and took to the air, cawing their annoyance. The undead were almost on her, one fast and one shambling. He yelled at her to move and brought the gun up to his shoulder. Jessie could hear the closest zombie snapping at her, his teeth clacking noisily. It tried to reach for her but his arms were tied to a pole running across his shoulders, holding them straight out from his sides like he was crucified. He stopped suddenly with a jerk. Jessie watched as he screeched through shredded vocal cords and thrashed violently against the chain holding him. She stayed in front of him, protecting him, as she gabbled on in some language Jessie couldn't understand. He yelled at her to move again and motioned her away, the other one was getting close but the girl held her ground, hands up, pleading.

What the hell was going on? Jessie sighted above her mop of tangled hair at the feed sack over the head of the closest zombie; it had a smiling face painted on it.

It was the scarecrows.

He looked closer and noticed the chains around them that snaked back to large, round, fence posts driven deep into the ground. He snapped his sights over to the other one, it had obviously been dead much longer and was just now shuffling to the end of her restraints.

What was this? They both had burlap bags over their heads with happy faces painted on them.

The crows cawed and circled, the little girl babbled on and the undead cried for blood. Jessie didn't know what to do. He had ALWAYS killed them. He never hesitated. There were two right in front of him but the kid was begging for their lives. Lives? No, not lives but whatever they were, she was pleading for him not to end it.

Jessie lowered the gun in frustration.

"ENGLISH!" he yelled at her. "Do you speak English?"

She stopped babbling in whatever language she was yelling at him in and nodded her head.

"Get away from those things." He jerked a finger at the scarecrows and motioned her over.

She shook her head and started up again in her weird tongue, pointing at the zombies and then at his gun.

"Oh, for the love of Pete," he said in exasperation and slung the rifle over his shoulder, then showed her both his hands. "I won't shoot them. Just get away from there."

He motioned her over again and she came slowly, her dirty, tear streaked face showing mistrust.

She was small, brown skinned, malnourished and had numerous cuts and scrapes on her that didn't look like they were healing very well. Her hair hadn't seen a brush in months and the tangled mess hung wild. She was young, Jessie guessed maybe eleven or twelve. She still had food on her chin from where she'd been hungrily eating something from the bag she had brought back.

"You're here alone?" Jessie asked "No mom? No dad?" He was trying to remember high school Spanish classes but she didn't sound like she was Mexican. It sounded like something else. She didn't really look Mexican, either. He couldn't put a finger on it, but she just looked different. More... exotic, maybe.

She pointed behind her.

"Mamma. Poppa," she said and indicated the two scarecrows struggling at the end of their chains to get at them.

Jessie needed to sit down. He'd seen some messed up things these past five years but this had to be right there at the top of the list. He looked closer, seeing the chains that could be reeled in to keep the two zombies away from the garden so she could harvest or weed. He saw the knee-high fences along the rows that kept them out of the vegetables but close enough to scare off any crows or raccoons or deer that tried to help themselves. He looked at the two walking corpses. The mom had been long dead. She had been pulling scarecrow duty for years from the looks of it. The dad was still fresh, no more than a few months dead. Jessie could see the bite mark on his arm. He had probably gone into town to get things they needed and came back infected. Before he died, he had rigged up his chains so she could make the garden larger and keep more animals at bay.

Desperate, hard and sad times. He had tried to be a good father to her. He had tried to give her a life. Jessie stared at the painted boot black smile on the bag covering his snarling face. He knew if he removed it, he would find the remains of a Middle Eastern man. One of the Muslims in hiding. He sighed heavily and closed his eyes. He opened them to the gentle tugging of the girl, she was pulling him towards the house.

Away from the scarecrows.

Away from the people who loved her enough to become eternal guardians of the garden.

It wasn't enough, though. She was out of food; the vegetables weren't ripe and she was starving. She had made her first trip into town and had almost died. She'd never survive on her own. Her parents hadn't taught her the skills she needed in this unforgiving world. The father had been raiding surrounding houses and stores for years but he'd made a mistake. Had gotten bitten.

He sat in the small house as she insisted on setting out food for him. They'd been hiding out, fearing the zombies, fearing the Americans and trying to scratch a living from the land. Probably afraid to fire a gun because if it didn't bring the dead around, it would bring other survivors. They couldn't be found, couldn't be seen, or they would have been killed. Even the child.

Jessie sighed again. The other Retrievers would probably sell her into indentured servitude to the King of the East or maybe to Casey's Raiders. If he just walked away and left her, she'd be dead before winter. She'd never make it on her own. He *could* take her back to any of the free settlements in the Lakota territories, they would accept the children of their enemies but her life there wouldn't be easy. She'd always be a second-class citizen, always mistrusted and despised for what her people did. Tolerated, but never "one of us."

Jessie didn't know what to do. If he left her here, it would be the same as killing her. To him, every human life mattered, there were so few left in the world. He wondered if he could pass her off as Hispanic. Teach her better English and say he found her in Texas or something.

"How old are you?" he asked as he watched her finish eating from the can of corn.

"I think I am sixteen," she said with a halting and thick accent, pulling the words from a long way back in her mind.

Jessie blanched. She was so tiny, so skinny and flat chested. He thought she was maybe twelve, at the most.

He slowly rolled a cigarette as he thought. Only two options were left for him. He wouldn't condemn her to a miserable life in the settlements or sell her as a slave. He could either leave her to die or take her with him.

Not much of a choice, really. He'd been traveling alone for years, had gotten used to it. He didn't generally care for people too much. They were always trying not to stare at his face but they always did. This girl didn't bat an eye. Maybe living with your parents as zombies made little things like a scar unimportant.

Maybe she could ride with him for a while, help him go after some of those paintings in New York no one had been able to retrieve. It might be nice to have someone to talk to. He could teach her how to survive on her own. Maybe he could find a bookstore and get some of those Spanish courses on CD, teach her the language and she could pass as a Mexican or Guatemalan or something. If she did that, she could join the settlements in the heartland.

If she wanted to go, that is.

When he asked her and she finally understood, she jumped up and ran into one of the back rooms. She came out a few minutes later, draping a small silver necklace over her head and stood looking at him, expectantly.

"Guess that means yes," Jessie said, his half smile looking more like a snarl.

She smiled back, her eyes bright and dancing.

"We'll have to get you a pair of shoes," he said and stood.

They left the falling down shack, heading back for his car, and she took nothing from her old life except memories, the necklace and the clothes she was wearing. She wiped the dust from her feet as she crossed over their property line and stopped. She pointed to his gun, to her parents, then turned and walked down the hill.

She jumped a little at the two quick shots that echoed through the valley but she didn't look back. Her parents had been gone for a long time. Now the scarecrows were, too.

FLASH FICTION
THE LITTLE STORIES THAT STARTED THE BALL ROLLING

The Operating System Mythos
By Michael Peirce

I was trying to download a musical backing track using Linux. It was a jaunty piece from the black metal outfit called "Tentacle Tendencies," rocking a New Orleans cult favorite: "Lovecraft Calls the Darkness."

It didn't sound quite right somehow. The new violin player, some cat named Eric Zann, seemed to have taken them down a dark corridor that just went on and on...

Unfortunately, it was about that time that some slime came oozing out of my DVD drive. This horrific mucoid substance seemed almost sentient and somehow I could sense its murderous hatred of Microsoft.

The computer itself was starting to flash sparks, to rumble and to lose its shape, slowly melting into a substance scarcely different from the slime oozing out the drive door.

That gelatinous horror was headed for my Windows machine. What could be happening?

A mephitic stench that had not assailed human nostrils since the mad Arab Abdul Alhazred himself had finally cremated that blasphemous thing he should never have invoked…caused my gorge to rise and I shamelessly fled.

It turned out that the Great Old Ones hated Microsoft and when the stars were aligned just right at last, the chants were chanted, the sacrifices slaughtered - it began.

Soon all the Windows Machines will be subsumed. Many of the users have already been trapped and translated into the two dimensional universe where such beings can thrive, at least for a micro-second or two.

There is some bad news as well: The Great Old Ones dislike human beings just marginally less than they do Microsoft products but find our screams of terror immensely satisfying in some arcane region of the multidimensional space in their hideous forms where blasphemous appetite is located and serviced.

So take your Windows Machines up to the roof. Get your guns, your blades, your slime removal implements. Quickly, before Home Depot closes - forever!

And while you wait for some shogguth to suck the very marrow from your bones, you should ponder at last, the consequences of choosing the wrong operating system!

Leena the Zombie Killer
By T.D. Ricketts

Her dark raven like hair showed reddish-black in the sunshine. She climbed up and slid in the passenger seat. Her preferred spot. She smiled at him as she wiggled her rear end to get comfortable. Her birthday suit was dirty and needed a bath but he still loved her. They had saved each other several times in the last few days of madness. He realized she had gotten a bit skinnier since she couldn't have her favorite meal, a half pound bacon cheeseburger. But, as Raven (Corb) Shepherds go she was a big girl to start with, her parents worked a farm and were large working stock.

We were running down the road in our Kenworth minding their own business when people started walking into the road. They ran at his truck as he passed through a small town. One person he couldn't avoid and hit with his truck. Wondering what the heck was going on he stepped out of his truck turning to Leena he said "pază". He walked towards the form on the ground figuring the others were running to help. One person was just getting there and passed the still form on the ground. The man had wild eyes and blood on his face and shirt. Something was wrong. The left arm hung by the tendons and he shouldn't have been even able to move. As he rushed towards me a black blurr shot past me. Leena leaped grabbing the zombie (ok I said it Zombie) by the throat his body went out flat in the air like a football player being clothes lined. The impact between the back of his head and the black top road shattered his skull.

Thats how Alina....errr Leena saved my life and the adventure started.

Over for Dylan
By Pam Kelly Fields

Dylan awoke to a thud and the slight rocking of his Kenworth. "What the hell?!" He thought. Surely some damn rookie didn't back into me in the middle of nowhere! He pulled on his pants and stuck his head out of the sleeper. Hmm.. nothing put the huge empty parking lot of the warehouse out in the sticks where he was delivering in the morning. "Weird" he said as he grabbed his mag light and started down the truck steps. He pointed the light towards the front of the truck.. nothing. Then he heard what sounded like growling and scuffling coming from the rear. "Must be some stray dogs" he thought, as he headed back to check it out. "

"SHIT!!! Those aren't dogs!!" There were what appeared to be... PEOPLE crouched over another man and biting ("eating???") him. "Hey!" I'm callin' the cops!" Dylan thundered in a misguided attempt to save the doomed man. They turned to him, all of them, moving as one...then he saw. Horrendous wounds, ripped open stomachs, missing eyes, gashes too numerous to even take in. "OH MY GOD... But, but.. zombies aren't real!!" He uselessly bellowed as he turned to run.

His only hope was that the broken shambling creatures wouldn't be able to catch him before he reached the safety of his semi.

Then he heard it, the rapid slapping sound of many RUNNING feet! "No NO!! This can't be happening!!" screamed through his head. Just as he leaped for the truck steps and grappled for the hand rail, something hooked into the back of his shirt and pulled him up short. A hand he realized.. a filthy bloody hand. Then there were more hands, on his back, his arms, and finally his legs, dragging him shrieking from the side of the truck. He turned to see the twisted, mutilated, ravenous faces swarming towards him..

In the Louisiana backwoods, on the very outskirts of the "industrial" area, near where the land turned to swamp, no one heard his dying screams as the zombies ripped him to shreds and fought over the scraps to try and quell their ceaseless, maddening hunger. For the rest of the world it was just beginning, but for Dylan, it was over.

~

Sweetie
Pam Kelly Fields

The storm had been bad, the worst one this year. Jacob bulled Power One's big F350 down the rough muddy backroad trying to assess how many power lines had been brought down during the violent squall. All dispatch could tell him was that the line interruption was somewhere in zone 12, east of that science testing facility place. Biogen.. or some damn thing. Why the hell they wanted to put it all the way out here was a mystery to him. Right now, however, the only mystery he cared about was finding the damn downed lines, radioing dispatch the info so they could get the crew rolling, and go the hell home.

As he was bouncing along the washboard like road, aiming his spotlight up at the lines, sudden movement closer to the ground caught his eye. He quickly yanked the spotlight down. There, in the middle of the washed out muddy road, stood a little girl of maybe eight or nine. "How the fuck did she end up out here?!" he thought.

He turned the big light out so as not to blind the poor child before he climbed out of the truck. "Hey honey, are you ok? Where are your parents?" he asked as he approached the little waif who was standing slumped, with her head lolling forward as if she were hurt or simply exhausted. The closer he got, the more worried he became that she might need immediate medical attention. The mud splattered headlights didn't show much detail, but it looked as though there might be blood on her clothes, too much blood.

Before he took his next step, she slowly raised her head. "Mother of God!" Jacob gasped. The girls face looked to have been ravaged by an animal. Then he noticed her eyes, flat white, almost lifeless. "Sweettie.." he stammered out, still thinking she must be the victim of some horrible accident, but starting to get a very bad feeling as well.

Her mouth opened and an inhuman keening erupted as she suddenly began to sprint straight at him. "Screw this!" Jacob thought as he turned to run, "She might be small, but something damn weird is wrong with her, my ass is outta here!"

His foot slipped out from under him in the slick mud as he ran, and he slid down a small embankment to a shallow ditch. A quick glance over his shoulder revealed the girl springing at him like a hunting cat! He managed to get his feet under him, but the demon child, or whatever the hell she was, was now between him and his path to the truck. "The little hell spawn may be screwed up with something, but I'm a grown ass man, I can outrun her!" he thought. He darted at an angle, figuring to gain distance, then aim back for the truck. He just poured it on, not looking back, watching his footing on the treacherous ground.

Suddenly he heard that soul searing keening again, and the girl ("Beast, creature??") landed squarely on his back with enough force to cause him to go down again on the rough terrain.

He instantaneously felt hot, burning pain as small sharp teeth latched on to the back of his neck. They were biting, tearing... burrowing. "OHMYGODNO!!!" he wailed as he felt those sharp teeth CRUNCH. Then blinding unimaginable pain, then... nothing, anywhere.. "Oh Jesus, she ("IT!") bit through my spine!!!

The girl, the UNDEAD girl, was small, so ingesting even part of such large prey was slow work...

Jacob, very unfortunately, got to hear the rending, ripping sound of his flesh being stripped away, and the guttural chewing, sucking, gnawing sounds of it being consumed for far longer than any person could and remain sane. By the time shock and blood loss took him, his mind was already shattered.

The small, deadly new predator, raised it's bloody mangled face, and keened loud and long. In the distance, a chorus of wails joined in and filled the night..

MORE FLASH FICTION
COLLECTED SHORTS FROM THE DAVID SIMPSON FAN CLUB

The Allergy Snow
By Alina Ionescu

It was a bright day ...the sun had a out of this world shine that made all the cotton flakes that where filling the air look like some weird kind of spring snowfall...The girls decided to ignore the "allergy snow" and drive outside of town..." Let's go ! We have all this light working for us and a real poppy field will always look better than a photoshopped one !"...After a while they gave up on looking for a radio...there where just news...weird news of attacks connected to the cotton fluffs in the air maybe ? How can this be dangerous? I do sneeze my head off , but it can't cause anything else than a rise in sales for the pharma industry ...

The poppy field was out of a dream...Red flowers that where dancing in the wind .."Are you ready , let's do this! " Dia was anxious to get a good shoot out of the day ...Ana was a pro , she already modeled in worse conditions .. The road was empty.. there was a stillness unnatural ..as of nature would held it's breath.. " What the fuck?" A loud crash took them out of the reverie..Both of them ran into the direction of the loud sound...it was burning true the peace of the sunny day ... A truck crashed into a old willow tree on the side of the road ...that was weird...be driver was outside of the cabin already ...covered in blood. "Let's see if we can help " He just lay there...The driver was laying in the middle of the road. Pieces of broken glass where sticking out from his back and scalp...blood was everywhere...Kneeling next to him , Dia was checking for vitals..."no heartbeat ! "...Taking a step to the side she cleaned her hands on her pants before picking up the phone... She turned his back to the corpse before dialing 911. A sharp pain in her neck was one of her last memories...Arms with shards of glass sticking out of them where holding her in place ...a cold wet and sticky grip of death..

~

"Looks as if we rock at flash fiction, how about we try a new one using these words : truck, zombies, chocolate, moonshine !"
(Yes, the admin really did come up with this contest...)

Goblin wasn't sure if it was the chocolate or the moonshine that had his world spinning as he roared down the highway in his truck he had decked out for battle. All he knew for certain was that he was a zombie hunter. He would eliminate any that he encountered between El Paso and Tulsa, as he hauled his precious cargo of humans toward the last vestige of humanity, the fortification point known as Eden. **By Jason Heckler**

I was all hopped up on chocolate moonshine the night shit hit the fan. The zombies came from nowhere and over ran the town. I'm not sure why the walked past and ignored me but I believe the chocolate moonshine holds the secret. To this day I search for that trucker who appeared that night with a truckload of it and just the name on his shirt: David. **By Cassie Eisenschenk**

I drove over the zombies with my truck and celebrated with chocolate and moonshine. The end. **By Michael Benicek**

While driving my truck after drinking some moonshine, I could have sworn I saw some chocolate zombies. **By Joan Macleod**

As I was hauling a load of moonshine in my truck over to the next state, I became aware of a quiet that I had never heard before. I got out of the truck and grabbed a chocolate bar to munch on, I stood just listening....and nothing. No birds, crickets, no nothing. As I was walking back to my truck, I saw someone shuffling toward me. I waited thinking that he needed help but as he got closer, he looked like someone had been eating on him. I threw my chocolate at him and ran back to the truck hauling ass. I looked back..and saw him eating my chocolate! **By Louise Feagans**

Driving my truck down the highway, eating chocolate, drinking moonshine, and running over zombies. .... (i know you shouldn't drink & drive, but it is the ZA, so what the hell) **By Phyl Lamattina**

As the icy north wind blew I hid in my truck drinking moonshine infused with chocolate. All of a sudden I heard a thump on the door so I squinted through the glass and couldn't believe my eye's at the number of what looked like zombies out there. Before I could think about it they opened the door and grabbed me out. The last thing my mind could process before they got me was damn and that was such a good drink... **By Alison Pridie**

The trucker was hauling his load of moonshine down the highway and thought it strange that nobody else was on the road. He pulled off at the roadside service station as he was craving a chocolate bar. As he got out, he saw the zombies running toward him so he jumped in the truck and grabbed a couple of bottles, made some Molotov cocktails, lit them and threw them. While the zombies were burning he ran inside the store and grabbed a bunch of chocolate bars. As he pulled out of the station, he thought to himself, maybe I should stop listening to this audiobook and listen to the radio more! **By Amy Marler Bowles**

AFTERWORD

Thanks for checking us out. This is going to be short and sweet because I want to get this released on Veterans Day 2017 and it's already late in the afternoon. On Veterans Day 2017. We are donating ALL proceeds, every single dime, from this book to the Wounded Warriors Project and that will continue until the Army's 243rd Birthday, June 14th 2018.
Thanks again.
Have fun.
Be safe.
Don't get hit by a bus.

David A. Simpson
Saturday, November 11, 2017
Veterans Day

"It's like herding cats, getting these guys to do what they're supposed to, when they're supposed to do it."

Anonymous (but thought by every editor, compiler, manager, publicist, artist, etc., etc., etc.)

A very special thanks goes out to Tamra Crow, the editrix who worked tirelessly with this group of Scribblers, and Dean Samed, cover artist extraordinaire.

Tamra Crow

Tamra Crow is a brave new force in the world of editors, lending a brand new voice to the leading hats that make your favorite authors shine! She lives in Sacramento California with her three kids. Known for being all over the place, she divides her time between making killer compilations of music and reading from her TBR pile that stands taller then her! (She's micro) When she's not editing away at the impossible (no job too big) she does a top notch job with her kids and is always up to some sort of mischief!

You can contact her at Tcrowedits@yahoo.com

∾

Dean Samed

Dean Samed is a UK-based illustrator / cover artist, and a specialist in the horror genre. He has illustrated the works of Stephen King, Clive Barker, H.P. Lovecraft, Graham Masterton, as well as a wide range of genre authors, internationally.

Dean started freelancing at the age of 14, and throughout his young adult years, worked with promoters and record labels in urban dance music. Later, the e-publishing boom allowed him to switch focus to his first love, macabre art. As a horror specialist, he is known for his complex creature designs and sharp compositing style.

He holds a First Class degree in Digital Media, and is currently undertaking his Masters in Fine Art. Dean likes to explore horror, occult, sci-fi and cyberpunk themes in his personal and commercial work.

You can see more of his work at Deansamed.com

∼

Printed in Poland
by Amazon Fulfillment
Poland Sp. z o.o., Wrocław